Lincolnshire
COUNTY COUNCIL

Working for a better future

discover libraries
This book should be returned on or before the due date.

To renew or order library books please telephone 01522 782010
or visit https://lincolnshirespydus.co.uk
You will require a Personal Identification Number
Ask any member of staff for this.
The above does not apply to Reader's Group Collection Book.

5/19

'Intelligent, enthralling and ...   ew

D1333958

05234457

Shona (S.G.) MacLean was born in Inverness and brought up in the Scottish Highlands. She obtained an MA and PH.D. in history from Aberdeen University. She began to write fiction while bringing up her four children (and Labrador) on the Banffshire coast, and has now returned to live in the Highlands. *The Redemption of Alexander Seaton* was short-listed for both the Saltire First Book Award and the CWA Historical Dagger; *The Seeker* was winner of the 2015 CWA Historical Dagger.

By S. G. MacLean

THE ALEXANDER SEATON SERIES

The Redemption of Alexander Seaton
A Game of Sorrows
Crucible of Secrets
The Devil's Recruit

THE CAPTAIN DAMIAN SEEKER SERIES

The Seeker
The Black Friar
Destroying Angel
The Bear Pit

THE DEVIL'S RECRUIT

S. G. MACLEAN

Quercus

First published in Great Britain in 2013
This paperback edition published in 2019 by

Quercus Editions Ltd
Carmelite House
50 Victoria Embankment
London EC4Y 0DZ

An Hachette UK company

A CIP catalogue record for this book is available
from the British Library

PB ISBN 978 1 84916 319 4

10 9 8 7

Typeset by Jouve (UK), Milton Keynes

Printed and bound in Great Britain by Clays Ltd, Elcograf S.p.A.

To Patrick

Introductory Note

The Thirty Years' War (1618–48) was sparked by the acceptance of the Bohemian crown by Frederick V, the Calvinist Elector Palatine, in the face of counter-claims by the Catholic Habsburgs. The war devastated the mainly German lands of the Holy Roman Empire throughout which it was fought, and embroiled virtually all other European nations in a brutal and increasingly complex territorial and religious struggle.

The armies of both sides in this struggle depended to varying degrees on the recruitment of foreign troops. While Scots fought on both sides, they joined the anti-Habsburg forces in quite astonishing numbers. It can be estimated, for instance, that of 62,700 men raised in the British Isles by foreign powers between 1618 and 1648 to fight the Habsburg armies, 52,400 were Scots.[*]

The reasons they followed the recruiters were many: they

---

[*] From figures given in Steve Murdoch (ed.), *Scotland and the Thirty Years' War, 1618-1648*, (2001), p. 19.

went in defence of Frederick's Stuart queen, Elizabeth, daughter of James VI, or in defence of their Calvinist faith; they went because of lack of opportunity for social or economic progress at home, they went because they were running from something. They went, at times, because they were given no choice.

Some returned to Scotland to answer the call of the Covenanting Wars. Some never returned at all.

PROLOGUE

Aberdeen, 8 October, 1635

The young woman's hair lay in perfect waves on her bare shoulders. A carefully chosen pearl, a gift from her mother, adorned her neck. She wore her best dress, although one not well suited to the weather, but that was of little relevance, and she really did not feel the cold. One or two townsfolk might have seen her hurry along Schoolhill to the Blackfriars' gate by which he had told her to enter the garden, but none had seemed really to notice her. There was plenty else afoot in the town to take their interest tonight. She knew the way to the meeting place very well, although she had been puzzled as to why he had chosen it. There was little chance of course, particularly at that hour, that they would be disturbed: indeed, he must have chosen it for that very purpose for they were not disturbed, and that was a pity because, by the time – many hours later – that another came along the path to the frozen pond, it was too late to cut her down from where she hung, ice frosting her lashes and her dead lips already blue.

Aberdeen, one week earlier

The ship lay behind him, a silent hulk of black against the greying sky. Darkness would fall and he would go out into the streets, down the alleyways, enter the inns and the alehouses and find those who had something to run from. They would listen, eyes brightening, as others offered them tales of something different, a dream of something better, the adventure of being a man. They would marvel at the possibility of wealth, titles, land in places they had never seen. *He*, on the other hand, could promise them a nightmare beyond their imagining: brutality, starvation, disease, the corrosion of anything good they might once have been, the certainty of death. But they would not listen to him – they did not look at him. Often, they did not even see him.

Unlike the lieutenant, his senior officer, the recruiting sergeant rarely left the ship unless it were under cover of darkness, and it wanted a little time yet for that. And yet he was drawn, in spite of all he knew to be wise, away from the hidden places of the quayside and up the well-remembered lanes and vennels behind Ship Row and into the heart of the town.

The college roofs rose up ahead of him, behind the houses that fronted the Broadgate. The scholars who had their lodgings in the town were hastening home, showing little sign of being tempted astray to an inn or alehouse and away from their hearth and their landlady's table – however mean it might be. Gowns were pulled tight, caps held to heads and oaths against the elements uttered. Few remarked upon him. One or two children, late already for their supper, darted across the street and down narrow pends and closes, laughing in strange relief as they disappeared from sight. Women on their own quickened their step. Those in twos or threes cast him swift glances and murmured in low voices to their companions as they hurried on.

He stopped in the shadow of a forestair jutting out into the street. 'Changed days,' he thought, 'that I should stand here unnoticed.' But the observation was a reassurance to one who sought obscurity. Gradually, the bustle at the college gates faded to nothing, and the doleful ringing of the bell above St Nicholas Kirk told the porter that it was time they were closed against the darkness that had now fallen. Three nights he had waited thus; three nights he had been disappointed. He was on the point of giving the thing up as lost, a lesson from fate, a message from the God from whom he had so long ago parted company, when the billowing form of a solitary man in the gown of a regent of the Marischal College emerged on to the street. The figure called something to someone behind him, and the gates were hastily drawn to against the growing turbulence of the night.

The recruiting sergeant held his breath, scared almost to move. The voice. It was the voice, he knew it, and by a trick of the years it called to something in him that he had thought long dead. At this distance he could discern no grey in the hair, no line on the brow, and as the other crossed the Broadgate and disappeared down the side of the Guest Row, he knew it was the very walk. Even after all these years, there could be no doubt: it was Alexander Seaton.

The stranger pulled his cloak tighter round him and turned back in the direction of the quayside and the ship. It was growing colder, and it had been enough. There was time yet, and he had other business to attend to tonight.

1

Downie's Inn

Aberdeen, 1 October 1635

Downie's Inn was as full as I had seen it in a long while, and worse lit than was its wont, the poor light from cheap tallow candles doing more to mask the dirt ingrained in every bench, every corner, than the landlady's cleaning rag had ever done. A sudden, noxious warmth hit me, of steam rising from damp clothing mingled with the usual odours of long-spilt ale and burnt mutton. I shouldered my way through a knot of packmen and chandlers to the hatch from which Jessie Downie dispensed only bad ale or sour wine. Just before I reached it, there was a small commotion to my left as four of Peter Williamson's scholars bolted from a bench in the corner and out of the back door of the inn.

Jessie avoided my eye as she passed a jug of beer out through the hatch. 'There are none of yours in here tonight, Mr Seaton.'

'Are there not,' said Peter, having spotted Seoras MacKay, a Highland boy from my senior class. 'You've been told before you're not to serve them.' He jerked a thumb in the direction of the bench where Jessie's daughter was giggling and making only a half-hearted resistance to MacKay's advances. He was very drunk. Of his habitual and more generally sober companion, Hugh Gunn, there was no sign.

'Ach, you, Peter Williamson. You were never out of this place yourself not so many years past. It did you no harm,' Jessie responded.

'I would hardly say that, but I was never here when the recruiting ships were at anchor in the harbour. Have they been in here tonight?'

She pursed her mouth and nodded very briefly towards a darkened neuk in the shadow of the stairs. 'Over there. And watch yourselves with that fellow; he's a charmer, but he has a look about him I do not like.'

'His money's good, though, eh, Jessie?'

'A damned sight better than yours,' she muttered, before shouting at her daughter to see to her work or find it out on the street instead.

I had almost reached Seoras MacKay, slumped now on his bench, when he finally noticed me. I saw a look spread over his face that I had seen before and that did not bode well for our encounter. He roused himself, holding his beaker up in the air. 'The good Irishman! Bring us whisky, Jessie, that Mr Seaton and I might toast our ancestors together!'

'You'll have no more to drink tonight, Seoras.'

'Ach, Mr Seaton, come now, there are some stories I

would tell you – and I've heard it's not so long ago you liked a dram yourself.'

Peter Williamson was there before me. 'On your feet, MacKay. You'll be in front of the principal tomorrow morning and see what stories he has for you.'

Seoras MacKay stood up, stumbling slightly and righting himself on the window ledge as he did so. 'Do you speak to the heir of MacKay like that, Williamson? You who owe your allegiance to my father?'

It was not the first time that Seoras in his drink had thrown his father's chieftainship over the Williamsons in Peter's face; the dark-eyed charm of the Highlander was lost on my young colleague, and I thought I would have to hold him back as his fists clenched and his jaw twitched in real anger.

'I've never set foot in your midge-ridden boglands, MacKay, and I owe your father nothing. Now find Hugh Gunn and get back to the college before I have you thrown another night in the tolbooth.'

The student surveyed Peter Williamson with contempt, before slumping against the wall. 'I believe you'll find Uisdean over there,' he said, using Hugh's Gaelic name.

I could see nothing at first, through the fug of steam and tobacco made worse by the sooty smoke from the poorly swept chimney. 'It's a wonder this place has not gone up in flames,' I muttered as we pushed through protesting bodies in the direction Seoras MacKay had indicated. The dregs of the town were here. I noticed as we passed that the bench vacated by Peter's students had been taken by a large, genial-looking man and his smaller, less friendly-seeming companion. I caught some words I thought to be French between them. If I had known the tongue better I would have told them of places in the town where a stranger might find better entertainment than this.

And then I saw Hugh Gunn. He was in earnest conversation with someone out of my vision across the table, and was sitting with his back to us. He had a quill pen in his hand and appeared to be preparing to sign the paper in front of him. The man opposite him leaned towards him a little as if in encouragement, and in doing so moved into the light. I caught his features just a moment before he registered mine. He was slim, and appeared to be of good height. His hair reached below his shoulders in long ebony rings that glinted when caught in the candlelight. He wore no beard or moustache, and a fine silver scar travelled across his lip to the edge of his left cheek. When his grey eyes met mine I instantly understood Jessie Cameron's apprehension. They took only a moment to form themselves into a smile and he rose and offered me a gauntleted hand.

'Mr Alexander Seaton, if I am not mistaken? I had hoped we might meet before now.'

I did not take his hand. 'You have the advantage of me.'

Letting his hand drop, he inclined his head very slightly, his eyes still set on me.

'Lieutenant William Ormiston of the Scots Brigade in the service of Her Royal Majesty, Queen Christina of Sweden.'

'Recruiting for the wars,' I said coldly.

He raised an eyebrow. 'I hold a licence from the Privy Council, sanctioned by the king himself. I do nothing illegal here.'

'The boys who signed up with you from the colleges of Edinburgh and St Andrews were not free to do so – they were matriculated students in those places. The parents of the students of Marischal College have placed them in our care. You can have no legitimate business here.' I plucked the quill pen out of Hugh Gunn's hand and scored a line through the contract in front of him.

'Get back to the college, Hugh, and take Seoras MacKay with you – I doubt if he is fit to find his way anywhere by himself tonight. You will present yourselves to the principal in the morning, and if there is any repeat of this incident you'll scarcely have time to pack your bag before he sends you back up to Strathnaver with nothing more than a flea in your ear and a report of your disgrace to take back to Seoras's father.'

The boy stood to face me, sullen, his eyes level with my own. 'Seoras's father will have me in the wars soon enough anyway, cleaning his son's boots and paying off his whores. I'll sign with the lieutenant here and make my own way. You don't need Latin to wield a pike or raise a musket.' He bent to put his name to the spoilt paper, but to my surprise, Ormiston stayed his hand.

'And yet, from the classical authors there is much to be learned about the commanding of armies and the leading of men,' he said. 'Perhaps you should wait a year or two after all – the wars will still be there, I can assure you.'

The boy stared at him a moment in almost furious disbelief, then uttered an oath in Gaelic as he pushed past me. I was tempted to return the compliment. He strode across the room in impotent fury to take his friend roughly by the arm that was not occupied by the serving girl, whom Seoras had accosted again as she was setting bowls of a rancid-looking stew down before the two Frenchmen. 'Come on, before you take a dose of the pox.'

'Ach, Uisdean.'

Being appealed to by his Gaelic name had no effect on the more sober of the two Highlanders, and, taller and more strongly built, he had the other up on his feet with another determined haul. 'Never mind "Uisdean". Get up that road, and if you vomit this time I'll leave you where you lie.'

As he was pulled out of the door, Seoras MacKay turned to throw one more jibe at Peter Williamson. 'You see, *Mister* Williamson, the Gunns know their place. There is much you could learn from your scholars.' Another threat from Hugh and he was hauled beyond the doorway and into the night.

Peter, now white with rage, said, 'If I find Seoras MacKay in a place like this again I will sign him up for the Swede myself. There is little wrong with him that a bullet from a Spaniard's musket would not put right.'

The soldiers at Ormiston's back moved slightly towards us. This was not the place for that kind of talk. I put a hand on my young colleague's arm.

'That's us finished for tonight, Peter. Get away to your own bed now and get some rest, and for the goodness' sake, dry yourself off.' I reached in my pouch and handed him a few pennies. 'Here, give that to the porter and he'll bring you something for your fire – I cannot spend another day listening to those squelching boots.'

Peter took a moment to regain his control, managing a 'thank you' below his breath. He nodded towards the recruiting officer and his men, and asked me, 'Will you be all right?'

I looked at Ormiston as I spoke. 'I doubt I have anything to fear from a law-abiding subject of the king,' I said.

'Nothing at all,' said the lieutenant. 'I can assure you.'

Peter was unconvinced. 'Well, mind you don't sign yourself up – I'm not taking that class of yours as well.'

After he had gone, Ormiston signalled to the two men who lurked about the table, clearly not officers, and they took themselves to the serving hatch where Jessie had tankards and a jug of ale waiting for them. They recommenced their trawl of the inn.

'So this is your method?' I said. 'You get the men so drunk they don't know what they're putting their mark to until it's too late?'

He motioned for me to sit down. 'A drunk is of no use to me. I need men of discipline, not a soak who will dance after the last man to set a jug of beer in front of him.'

I laughed. 'Then I have to tell you, your intelligence has failed you tonight. This is the lowest drinking hole in

Aberdeen. You will not find men here whose greatest wish is to defend their distressed brethren overseas against the Papist Habsburgs. There are no men here who dream of dying for the Queen of Bohemia.' I declined the glass of wine he had pushed towards me. He shrugged and put it to the side.

'I have those men a-plenty. Younger sons of younger sons, bred as gentlemen, bred to adventure, but scarcely a penny or a scrap of land to their name. They serve foreign kings for their standing and their dignity, and to make their name and their fortune. Their faith, their loyalty to the House of Stuart, have been bred into them since their first breath. Those men, and I am one of them, Mr Seaton, are the finest officers in all of Sweden's armies.'

'You will not find them in places like this.'

'No, but I have come here for something else.' He pointed to a bench to the left of us, where one of his men was in earnest and, it seemed, sympathetic conversation with a gloomy-looking cooper. 'I need foot soldiers as well as officers. You see that cooper there? He has been twice before the kirk session over a promise to marry his master's daughter. The girl is no great enticement, it would seem, and her father and the kirk are running out of humour with his delaying. But the session will allow him out of his promise if he will sign with me to fight the Papists.'

'I see.' I knew what he said to be true.

'And you see that one there?'

'The man who scratches at his arm?'

14

'Scabs, left by manacles,' said Ormiston. 'He has been out of the tolbooth three days – a minor offence, but he has lost his employment and the roof over his head. What should he do? Throw himself, able-bodied as he is, upon the charity of the good burgesses of this town? You know how that would end. They will both be aboard my ship by the end of the week.' He refilled his own glass. 'I offer a life to those who would run from what they have, or who have nothing at all.'

'Hugh Gunn is only seventeen years old; his life is hardly behind him.'

'That is the student we both so offended?'

'Yes.'

'You are right, I had not expected to find one like him in here. He is in the other category, a younger son of a younger son, beholden to the good graces of his chieftain. That's why I wanted him rather than his drink-sodden, whore-mongering friend. He will make a fine soldier, a good officer, one day.'

I suspected he would be proved right, if the boy could learn to master his temper better. 'And yet you let him go.'

He sat back and smiled and I realised this was what he had been waiting for. 'I did it as a favour to you, Mr Seaton.'

'You don't even know me.'

He watched me a long moment. 'Do not be so certain about what I know.' Some movement at the top of the stair seemed to catch his eye. I looked up but could see nothing in the gloom. The lieutenant shifted slightly in his seat.

'My past is old news in this burgh, lieutenant,' I told him. 'You'll find there is little capital to be made of it now.'

'Oh, I very much doubt that, Mr Seaton, but it is late already and I daresay you and I will meet again, and so further our acquaintance. For the meantime, I hope you will rest easy on the matter of Hugh Gunn – I will not be enticing him aboard my ship.'

If he expected my thanks, he was disappointed. I gave him no answer at all, and was glad to get out of the place whose foul air was filling up my throat. The Frenchmen, I noticed, had already abandoned their bowls of inedible stew, and left the place before me.

The inn was on the edges of town, beyond Blackfriars where it met the Woolmanhill. It was a fitting night-time haunt for vagrants, criminals, those who did not want to be seen or found. My shortest route home would take me past the back of the fleshers' yard, and I knew that the gutters there would be overflowing after the torrents of recent days. I had no wish to bring the smell of the charnel house with me to where my family slept, so I elected to take a longer route, one that would bring me past the near end of the loch and up by the old public garden that backed on to George Jamesone's house.

George had fulminated often against the dilapidation of the walls that allowed all sorts of the burgh's displaced humanity to live out their debauches there in the night within hearing, and sometimes sight, of the back windows of his own fine residence. The garden where once plays profane and godly, music and dancing, trysts of love and childhood games had had their moments was now abandoned to tangles of thorns, feral creatures, and those who could find their pleasures in no lawful place. It was not somewhere any God-fearing person would wish to find themselves alone under cover of darkness. A happy Eden once, turned by the fears and prohibition of our Calvinist kirk into a den of ungovernable vice and iniquity.

I had just passed the rusted gate that led from the overgrown gardens out on to the long vennel to Schoolhill when the sounds of a disturbance came to my ears. It was evidently coming from somewhere in the gardens – there were muffled shouts and cries, the sound of blows being exchanged. My first thought was of Hugh Gunn and Seoras MacKay – the place was a favoured short cut for scholars making their way back to the college in the hope of not being seen. I doubted that Peter Williamson, even in his haste to get to the warmth of his bed, would have taken the chance of cutting through here alone. Nevertheless, unsheathing my knife, I doubled back and entered the garden.

I could have wished for a light for the moon was clouded over, and I had to trust to my senses and my memory. Rather than go right out to the middle of the gardens, I judged it safer to keep to the walls surrounding it until I came upon the old middle path that led to what had once been a stage. Formerly used by mummers and actors in the Mystery plays, the amphitheatre was now the favoured haunt of the sturdy beggars and masterless men who roamed this place by night. I strained to listen for noises that would give me better direction, but the sounds of the scuffle were becoming less frequent, and after two long, low cries they ceased completely. I should have turned for home then, but I was already regretting allowing Hugh to take Seoras back to the college alone – the boy in the state he had been in would be handful enough for two men, let alone one. And so I pressed on. The further into the garden I went, the deeper the darkness became, to the point that I knew to continue would be folly. I began to turn, thinking somehow to retrace my steps, when my foot struck the unseen root of a tree and I found myself tilting headlong towards the ground. I put out a hand to stop myself and felt my flesh tear on a low branch of hawthorn. Before I could wrestle my way out of it, a figure had launched itself at me from above and pressed me to the ground. I attempted to raise my head as surprisingly strong hands bound my wrists behind my back. My head was instantly thrust back towards the ground and I tasted dirt, then blood, from my own lower lip. My assailant told me in no uncertain terms that another such attempt would cost me an ear. For all the shock and discomfort of the moment, my overriding sensation was of incomprehension, for the voice was one I knew very well.

2

Tales of the Missing

The principal regarded me with utter disbelief. 'George Jamesone? George Jamesone did this to you?' he said, circling me closely to inspect the swollen eye and cut lip to which my artist friend had treated me late the previous night. My head ached already, not much helped by a sleepless night occasioned by the discomfort of my injuries and the outraged amusement of my wife. Her words had prefigured Dr Dun's almost exactly.

'George Jamesone did this to you? I do not believe it. Why would George ever do this to you?'

'Because,' I had said, wincing as she helped me remove my torn and filthy coat, 'he thought I was one of the ruffians who has been running rampage in his gardens recently, and the constables' response being unsatisfactory he had decided to take the defence of his property into his own hands.'

Even in her sleep, I could have sworn Sarah's mouth twitched occasionally in amusement. This morning, however, I was anxious to get beyond the matter of my own misadventures because what I had to report to the principal made me very ill-at-ease.

It was not the first time I had had to tell him that a student had failed to turn up for the morning lecture, or that on further enquiry it had been found that he had not been seen in the breakfasting hall, nor his bed slept in either. That on this occasion it should be two students rather than one made me less alarmed for their well-being, and yet Dr Dun took the news very badly.

'You are certain of this, Alexander?'

'The porter confirms that no one came in by the gate after Peter Williamson returned.'

'And why, in God's name, did Peter not check that they were back in their chamber before he retired to his own for the night?'

There was little I could say to defend my colleague, only the truth. 'Because I do not think he trusted himself to deal with Seoras MacKay as a regent should with a scholar. Peter wears his heart on his sleeve and that has made it too easy for Seoras to bait him. He mocks him for his lack of means – for Peter let slip one day that he would be away to study medicine if only the money could be got to support him. Seoras makes great play of the Williamsons' supposed subservience to the MacKays.'

'I did not know of this. Peter Williamson should not have to put up with such treatment from a student.'

'No,' I agreed. 'Seoras shows his contempt for him at the best of times, but in drink he is thoroughly obnoxious, and he was last night. Had it not been for Hugh Gunn there would have been trouble in that inn, real trouble. I had planned to have them both up in front of you this morning.' Though I knew I could speak freely with the principal, I hesitated. 'To be honest, Patrick, I will not be sorry to see the back of Seoras; the deeper the trouble the better he likes it, and somehow, when all is laid bare, nothing redounds to him.'

Dr Dun sighed. 'Well, it is about to redound to us.' He pushed towards me an opened letter which had been lying at his elbow when I first came in. The red wax of the seal attached showed a short sword clenched in a right hand, the words *manu forti* just legible beneath. It was not a crest I recognized. 'What is this?' I asked, picking it up, but unwilling to unfold so impressive-looking a document.

'A communication that arrived yesterday afternoon, from Sir Donald MacKay of Strathnaver, Lord Reay.'

'Seoras's father?'

'The same. He is good enough to inform me that he'll be passing this way – his very words – with forty of his best Highlanders, en route for Dundee, at the end of this week. Not only will the town be obliged to entertain his Lordship and his men, but I strongly suspect he will be expecting us to produce his younger son.'

Lord Reay's name was known not only from here to his clan's Highland heartland in Sutherland, but throughout the battlefields of Europe, where the regiment he had raised in defence of Protestantism against the depredations of the Papist Habsburgs had fought first for the Crown of Denmark, and then of Sweden. Thousands had followed his call to the defence of Elizabeth Stuart of Bohemia, sister of our own king, and all that she stood for. He was not a man who would take kindly to the mislaying of a son.

'Not just a son, but a foster son also,' the principal reminded me. I had forgotten that Hugh Gunn was more than just a servant to Seoras MacKay. 'I have heard it from more than one quarter that MacKay has more affection for his foster son than for his own. If those boys haven't turned up by the time he gets here, all Hell will be unleashed on the streets of this town.'

Hell seemed a place far distant when, little over half an hour later, I pushed open the rusting gate in the east wall of the old burgh gardens behind George Jamesone's house. It was a cold, bright October day that showed the town at its best. In the garden, fallen leaves formed a soft carpet under my feet as I picked my way over old pathways between overgrown bushes, where much of the light was obscured by the dark branches of beech and chestnut overhead. Blackbirds and sparrows squabbled over treasures in the rowans and among the last of the brambles.

I stifled an oath as I caught the sleeve of my coat on the thorny outcrop of an old rose. George had told me last night of his plans for the garden. The council, a few months since, alarmed by the outrages reported to have been committed in this place around the forbidden Midsummer bonfires, had allowed George's petition that the gardens be granted to him for his personal use during his lifetime, to be gifted back to the burgh on his death. In the meantime, he would remake its walls, secure its gates and put right the drainage that saw the spa well of Woolmanhill turn the bottom corner of the field into a bog. He would also, though this formed no part of the magistrates' stipulation, restore it to its former beauty. In the wake of many apologies on his part, I had promised him last night, after we had dusted ourselves down and parted, still laughing, at his street door, that I would call on him soon to see his plans. The disappearance of Seoras MacKay and Hugh Gunn had led me back to the garden earlier than I had intended, to search for signs of them there.

In the cold brightness of the late morning it was a place quite different to the black tangle of thicket and broken wall that I had stumbled through last night. And yet, it retained the sense of a place not quite at peace with itself, a place that was not quite safe. After a few minutes and not a few more scratches, I was glad to come to a clearing in a hollow which I thought must be the arena of last night's scuffle. And it was an arena: the grassy slope that descended from the Woolmanhill came to rest in a row of moss-covered stone benches that fringed what had once been a stage. I sat down for a moment, and tried to imagine the scenes that had been played out here, decades before I was born.

Staring at the past would not help me find Seoras MacKay or Hugh Gunn. I got up from my stony seat and began to examine the ground of the stage area. It had been raining hard for two hours by the time Peter Williamson and I had made the final check of our rounds last night, at Downie's Inn. By the time I had left, the rain had stopped, and as the night wore on, a hard frost gradually set in. It had never lifted, and sculpted into the mud were what looked to me to be the signs of a recent struggle: footprints at crazed angles to one another, an indentation where perhaps someone had fallen, a furrow in the hardened ground, as broad as a man's back.

As I bent down to examine the marks more closely, voices reached me from the path off to my left. I straightened myself and a moment later was greeted by Louis Rolland, the young master of the town's French school, and two men it took me a moment to recognize as the Frenchmen who had been in Downie's Inn the night before.

As ever, Rolland was dressed in a blue coat of good quality, though worn now in places and starting to fray, and a frilled shirt which, while clean, was of similar vintage and a worsening state of repair. Like all the town's schoolmasters, it was expected that he should maintain the appearance of a certain standard of living without having any adequate means of sustaining it. Unlike most of his fellow schoolmasters, Louis seldom grumbled at his lot, although I knew he had harboured hopes of something better. He had been a student of mine not so long ago, before leaving with his young sister to spend a year in his Huguenot mother's home-land. The sight of me in the clearing surprised him.

'Mr Seaton, do not tell me George Jamesone has you working in here too?'

'No doubt he would have, had Sarah not made plain to him my ineptitude with a hoe.'

'Ah,' he smiled. 'I see.'

I glanced at the two men behind him, and Louis apologized. 'Oh, yes – I should introduce to you George's new gardeners: Guillaume Charpentier and Jean St Clair.' Charpentier, a well-built, handsome man with fair hair and warm hazel eyes, smiled and nodded towards me. St Clair, small, dark, restless-looking, did not. 'Guillaume here has a little English and a very little Scots; Jean none at all. For which you may be thankful,' Louis added, under his breath.

I raised an enquiring eyebrow, but he did not elaborate.

'You are here to put right the garden, then?' I asked the more genial of the two.

He pushed out a bottom lip, considered my question. 'We begin, only. But we begin.'

'It will be no small task,' said Louis. He waved an arm around us. 'You can see the state of the place, but Jamesone would have it an arcadia by next spring, or summer at the very latest. How they will even break the ground with a shovel today is beyond me.'

'We cut. Today we cut,' said Charpentier, golden eyes crinkling in the sunshine as he brandished a lethal-looking axe.

'Then I will not keep you any longer,' I said.

He dipped his head to me and to Rolland, before following after St Clair who, evidently bored by our encounter, was already striding away, axe twitching in his hand, towards an impenetrable-looking thicket by the north wall.

'You study their conversation?' I said to Rolland once the two men had disappeared from view.

'Not quite that. George Jamesone's own French is passable enough, but does not extend to matters horticultural, and so I, and sometimes Christiane, am called upon to translate. To tell the truth, I suspect much of our work will involve explaining to George, as diplomatically as we can, why much of what he wants done cannot be done. Why other ideas would be better.'

I laughed. 'I do not envy you the task. I hope he is paying you, Louis.'

'Very well. And we have Guillaume and Jean lodged with us too. It is more comfortable for them, I think, and Guillaume's conversation has enlivened our evenings. I suspect, in fact, that Christiane may be a little smitten with him.'

'A strong arm, a ready smile and a twinkling eye – it would be a wonder if a young girl like your sister was not. And I doubt he finds his companion any great rival for her affections.'

'Nor mine, either. I have seldom come across such a taciturn, sullen fellow. There's scarcely a word to be had out of him. But Guillaume says he is a worker, and knows his plants, so if George Jamesone is prepared to pay for him I must be prepared to put up with him.'

A thought struck me. 'Have you been all round the garden with them today?'

Louis sighed and indicated his muddied shoes and spattered stockings. 'A great deal more of it than I could have wished. Guillaume has been making notes of what will need to be cut down, or back, and what can be kept. Why do you ask?'

'Because I am here in search of two students of mine who have not been seen since they left Downie's Inn last night. I think they might have cut through here on their way back to the college and fallen to fighting among themselves, or been set upon. I had been half-hoping they would be discovered, insensible, in the bushes.'

Rolland shook his head apologetically. 'I have seen no one, I am afraid. Who are they?'

When I told him it was Seoras MacKay and Hugh Gunn who were missing his expression changed from interest to real concern. 'Seoras and Hugh? No.'

'You know them?'

'They are both private pupils of mine, have been these past months. It was only yesterday afternoon that I had a lesson . . .' The bell of St Nicholas began to toll the hour and Louis muttered something in French. 'I am sorry, Mr Seaton, I have some pupils due at twelve and it looks like I am already late. But we must talk of this further. Will you send word when they are found?'

I assured him that I would and he went quickly up the

slope towards the Blackfriars' gate, as the bell of St Nicholas finished striking the hour.

It was evident that there was little point in me continuing my search of the garden, and so I decided to call on George to see whether he had recovered from our midnight encounter.

As George's wife, Isobel, pointed the way up the turnpike towards his studio, her words were harsh but her eyes danced in amusement. 'You should have your hides tanned, the pair of you, rolling in the mud like two schoolboys at that time of night. And you to be a minister of the kirk? We are in the Last Days, surely.' She went down the corridor, laughing quietly to herself.

I blessed God that had sent me last night to that foolish scuffle with George, just for being able to hear her laugh again. It had been almost a year – ten months – since my friend and his wife had been plunged into almost unsupportable grief by the death of their third child, a beautiful boy carried off by the smallpox that had pillaged the cradles and schoolrooms of this town. Somehow, as if by some Passover blessing, my own home had escaped, the plague had swept past without extending its tentacles beneath our door to where our children slept. But George and Isobel's baby son now lay with his two older brothers in the cold earth of St Nicholas' kirkyard. For weeks, I could hardly face her, and the pain I had often seen in those eyes that today danced still tore my heart.

George, bent over a large table in the middle of his studio, was delighted to see me. 'I thought Isobel would have banned you from the house. She tells me she doesn't know how Sarah puts up with you. I was constrained to agree with her, for the sake of a night's sleep.'

'I am glad you managed it,' I said, 'for I am black and blue and did not get a wink.' I glanced at the work he had laid out before him. 'A landscape?' I said, surprised, for George was a painter of portraits, and had garnered great wealth and fame, far beyond our town, for his skill.

'No, come, see here,' he said, waving his Dutch clay pipe as he spoke.

He had four large folio sheets, side by side on to which he had sketched what I now saw was a detailed plan of a garden. Only by one or two names and landmarks did I recognize it as the place of last night's combat and of my recent visit.

'What do you think, then?' he asked, gesturing again with the unlit pipe.

I bent closer to look. It was magnificent, a magnificent folly, and regardless of any objection of gardener, kirk or council, I knew George would bring it into being. From the north window of his studio, which looked out over his own present back garden to that burgh wilderness and finally the loch, George would in future years see a knot garden, intricate box-framing beds of roses, the central path between them leading the eye to a summerhouse, and an avenue of fruit trees at the northern end of which, in its hollow, was the theatre.

'And we shall have some plays there again, Alexander, I am determined upon it.' George had often reminisced on the time in his childhood when a troupe of players favoured by King James had come to Aberdeen, and for their royal favour been royally entertained. Five nights of plays there had been – comedies and tragedies and histories of gore. The kirk session had been in near apoplexy, but could do little in the face of the council's letter from the king. George's eyes still glowed when he talked of it. My heart sank within me, for I knew that by the time his playfield was ready, I would be a minister before my session, and could not sanction any return to such public profanities.

To one side of the auditorium, there was to be a maze of privet and holly. I could not make out what was on the other side, where the garden wall met the spa well of the Woolmanhill.

'That is an old pond. A rancid bog in the summer months and a danger to public health. In the winter it fills with water from the loch source and freezes; it is treacherous to any who come upon it unawares. I have a fancy to put a fountain in it, in the Italian manner. The Italians have many ideas that we might happily adopt. Look here.' He heaved open a large book – Francesco Colonna, *Hypnerotomachia Poliphili* – at a marked page and indicated one of the woodcuts there. He looked at me expectantly, but I was at a loss.

'It's a temple,' I said.

I could see my answer disappointed him.

'It is not. It's a pavilion.'

'My apologies. But what is the difference?'

He had been waiting for this question, and triumphantly opened the other tome at his left hand. *De Re Aedificatoria*. 'Alberti says here, you see, "Let there be porticoes where the old men may chat together in the kindly warmth of the sun in winter, and where the family may divert themselves in the shade in summer."'

He was evidently waiting for a response that I was ill-equipped to give. Unperturbed, he continued. 'What I plan, you see, is a *diaeta* such as Raphael planned for Cardinal Medici,' – here I thought I might choke – 'a pleasant place in winter for civilised discussions.'

I did not wish to dent his enthusiasms, but I felt someone should open his eyes to the reality of the thing.

'But George,' I said, 'these gentlemen are, or were, Italians.'

'Indeed,' he agreed.

'Had they been Scotsmen, they would certainly not have spoken so blithely about sitting out in winter. Look around you, man, for pity's sake.'

George did, and gradually the incomprehension on his face was replaced by a broad grin, then outright laughter.

'Alexander, my friend, I was trying to explain the purpose of these structures, not suggesting that we should sit out there in the wind and snow. But all the same, the sun even shines occasionally on this benighted corner of

God's creation, and would it not be pleasant if you and I and other friends could sit out of a summer's evening and discuss the wonders of philosophy and the beauty God has laid at our door? What think you?'

I smiled at my friend. 'I think you are the wisest fool in Christendom, and the kindest.'

He looked a little abashed, then slapped me on the shoulder. 'And come tell me what you think to this, and what your kirk session might say to it.'

He led me to a workbench where there was laid out a diagram describing a machine of some complexity.

'What is it?' I asked.

'It is an idea I have adapted from the French. I had thought to put a fountain in the middle of the pond, near the spring, have a statue in the middle, perhaps Diana, the Huntress.'

'Not bathing,' I interrupted.

'No, no, of course not, but perhaps pulling back her bow, and releasing jets of water as she does so.'

'It would certainly be a . . . curiosity,' I said.

'But not objected to?'

'Oh, you may be sure it would be objected to, but if you were able to show that the movement was the result of means mechanical and not diabolical, it would be allowed.'

He nodded, and I saw that this was only half the story. Emboldened, he added casually, 'And around the pond I thought, perhaps, a nymphaeum.'

I looked at him. 'George, you are in jest.'

'No, I am not. It would be perfectly respectable, a series of modestly clad nymphs in . . .'

I could not help but laugh. 'Modestly clad nymphs? Carvings of young women scarcely covered by a film of gauze, you mean. No, that would not be permitted in this burgh. All your time in the homes of the great has loosened your morals, and your memory, I think. There are to be no nymphs, George. Perhaps something such as is to be found at Edzell would be permitted.' The gardens of Lord Lindsay's castle in the Mearns, laid out in the last century, were a horticultural and astrological wonder, marrying a vision of planting with panelled stone walls depicting the Virtues, the Muses, and the mythology of the heavens.

'I am already ahead of you there. I have poached two of Lindsay's gardeners, you know.'

'I met your gardeners today,' I said.

He seemed surprised. 'I cannot think they were in the college. Or do not tell me Dr Dun has a mind to ape my schemes?'

I laughed. 'Would that the college could afford it.'

'Ach, it will not be as expensive as it looks. The main thing is to get the well fixed, and then the walls built up, and then I will not perhaps be beset with marauding college regents in the dead of night.'

'Nor their students,' I said, and told him of the disappearance of Seoras MacKay and Hugh Gunn.

He was thoughtful, looking out over the dark mass where his dream of a garden lay. 'If they are lying there injured, which I doubt from the silence that descended on the place after our own little scrap, Charpentier and St Clair will find them: they are determined on knowing every inch of the place.'

'Well,' I said, straightening myself and stretching my arms, 'I would not like to wake up to the sight of the little wiry one brandishing an axe over me.'

'No, nor I,' agreed Jamesone. 'He is a sullen devil. Yet Charpentier says he is the best plantsman he has ever worked with, and knows the Netherlandish bulb fields as no other. They met at the palace gardens in Brussels, and moved northwards together, until they happily chanced at Edzell, where I found them. Lady Lindsay is not best pleased that I have purloined them, as she puts it, and I doubt I shall have my commission from her now.'

'You are a rogue, George, and will lose half your patrons if you steal from them their most prized workmen.'

'Ach. So be it,' he said dismissively. 'Edzell is a wonder indeed, but it was designed long ago and its labour is one of maintenance, not creation as here. Guillaume found my proposal a challenge he could not refuse.'

'And St Clair?'

Jamesone made a gesture of indifference. 'Who can tell? His face is as sour here as it was at Edzell. But I am not constrained to spend my time with him, and if Louis and Christiane Rolland can thole him, then so will I.'

I peered at George's sketch of a herb garden, and wondered how Louis Rolland would manage to explain to him, on Charpentier's behalf, that the designing of a garden cannot be carried out on the same principles as the planning of a painting. Even I knew that no gardener would set delicate herbs against a north-east facing wall, not half a mile from the North Sea.

Just then, voices that were Aberdonian to their core burst in on Jamesone's Elysian fantasy. He strode over to pull close the shutters which he had opened for better light and air. 'God in Heaven! Have I to buy the street too, to find some peace in my own home?'

I went with him to the window and what I saw drove all thoughts of gardens from my mind. I ran down the turnpike stairs more quickly than was safe to do, and was out on the street in less than half a minute. Being hauled down Schoolhill from the direction of Back Wynd, was Hugh Gunn, on either side of him one of the burgh's burliest constables. The boy looked to be utterly drenched, though it had not rained since he had left the inn, and almost unable to walk by himself. He was shivering in the sharp October air, his face and hands were bruised and cut, and his long fair hair darkened and matted by water and weeds.

I ran after the trio, who were attracting loud and uncomplimentary attention from those townsfolk out on the streets. At the foot of the Upperkirkgate I caught one of the constables by the shoulder. The fellow was about to swing a fist around at me, but saw at the last minute who I was.

'We've found one of the devils at least, Mr Seaton. We'll

have to march the wretch to the magistrate before we can turn him over to you.' He snapped round to the scholar on his arm, whose knees were buckling beneath him as if they could hold him no longer. 'Stand straight, you devil, or by God, you'll never see the Broadgate, never mind the college gates.'

I could scarcely believe the boy I was looking at was the same young man who had been determined to sign up for a soldier only the previous night.

'Hugh, what happened to you?'

No answer but a half-swallowed mumble and another buckling of the knees. I turned again to the constable. 'Where was he found?'

'Passed out in a cooper's yard near the Green.'

'Like this? Soaked?'

'That is the way I came upon him. They had maybe thrown water over him, to rouse him.'

'It must have been a bucket straight from the Putachie Burn by the look of him. Was there anyone with him?'

'Not a soul. Whoever he was with is no doubt dead to this world in someone else's yard or midden. Now, I'll have to get this fellow up to the Castlegate; as if the town hadn't delinquents enough to deal with.'

I held up my hand. 'Wait a moment. Hugh? Where is Seoras?'

The boy looked at me stupidly, as if he could not understand me. I tried again, in his own tongue. '*Uisdean? Cait a bheil Seoras?*'

This time, he understood. He seemed to have great difficulty in moving his tongue, and the words that he eventually produced were difficult to make out: '*Chan eil fios agam. Chan eil fios agam.*' Tears were in his eyes as he looked desperately at me over the shoulder of the man dragging him away. *I do not know.*

3

The Drummer Boy

It was nearly eight o'clock that evening before I finally arrived home, by which time Hugh Gunn had been safely returned to the college and placed under the care of Peter Williamson, whose remorse at what he saw as his dereliction of duty towards Hugh and Seoras was very great. He insisted on caring for the rambling boy himself.

I had been unable to learn anything further of Hugh's experience, or Seoras's fate, occupied as I was with my class all afternoon. Before supper, I had accompanied Dr Barron, Professor of Divinity in the college, to a meeting of the ministers of all the kirks in Aberdeen, and had dined with them afterwards. It seemed hardly possible even now when I thought about it, but ten years on from the greatest disappointment of my life, from my public disgrace at a meeting of the presbytery of Fordyce, I was on the point of being called to the charge of the East Kirk of St Nicholas in Aberdeen. At the age of thirty-five, I was finally to attain to that thing I had wished for my whole life – by Christmas, I would be preaching the Word to the people of Aberdeen as a minster of the Kirk of Scotland. Dr Dun had preparations well in hand for my replacement as regent of the highest class at Marischal College, and was gradually releasing me to other duties in the town, more commensurate with my new status.

Also more in keeping with the standing of a minister of the kirk, my family was to move to a new home, on the Gallowgate, a larger and grander house than the little cottage on Flourmill Lane that my friend William had leased to me at a derisory rent for the last seven years, since my marriage to Sarah. There were six weeks yet until we were to shift, but Sarah was already busy making preparations for the move. I expected to find her engaged in some spinning or needlework when I arrived home. Instead, what I found was a house with an atmosphere more chill than that I had just stepped in from, the two younger children lying awake but silent in their bed, my wife staring defiantly at a neglected fire, and our older son, Zander, nowhere to be seen. On the floor at Sarah's feet were two wooden drumsticks, snapped in half.

Nobody spoke as I walked over to pick up the broken toys. I looked from them to my wife, but she studiously avoided my eye. 'What has happened here?' I asked. 'Where is Zander?'

'He is upstairs, where I sent him. Had you asked that question two hours ago, you would have had a different answer.' She was determined I would drag it out of her. There was nothing to do but oblige.

'Why?'

At last she looked at me. 'Because he was not here. He did not come home until well after seven, when William Cargill brought him and James from the harbour.'

I put a hand on her shoulder to reassure her. 'I'm sorry he missed his supper, and I'm sure he will be sorrier, but you know, it is a natural thing for boys of nine to forget to go straight home after school. I did it often enough myself, and even a boxed ear and an empty stomach failed to remind me the next time there was something more interesting to do. I suspect they had gone down to look at the troop ship.'

She shook my hand from her shoulder and I saw fire in her eyes as her head swung round towards me. 'That is exactly where they went. Down to look at the troop ship. That boy has nothing in his head but the war and going to be a soldier. He has no talk but of marching and sieges and guns and colours. And all your talk of Matthew Lumsden and Archie Hay has not helped – Matthew is forever at the long end of the law, and look what became of Archie's dreams of glory!'

I sat down, hurt and perplexed. 'Granted, Matthew is no good example, but I talk to Zander of Archie because it pains me more than anything else in life that he will never know him. And I doubt if there is a boy in Aberdeen who does not dream of being a soldier, who has not been down to look at the troop ship, seen Ormiston and his officers in their fine coats with their swords at their belts and their scars of honour, and wanted one day to be like them. What else should they want? A life of drudgery and toil such as they see about them here every day? Let him have his childhood dreams; when he comes to manhood he will better see the truth of it, and if he does not, it will be because God has called him to be a soldier and it will not be ours to question it.'

Her face crumpled, all the defiance, all the rage, gone, and her eyes filled with tears. 'But what if they take him, Alexander? What if they take him on to their ship, and we never see him again?'

'Sarah . . .' I leant towards her and took her two hands in mine. 'They will not take him. What Ormiston wants is good officers, men who can be relied upon and who can lead, and soldiers strong enough to carry a musket, wield a pike. He has no interest in boys of nine.'

She sniffed and nodded, but I was not sure yet that she was convinced. She released her hands and picked up the drumsticks that I had set back down on the floor. 'I broke them,' she said. 'After William had left with James. Zander knew he would get no supper. He did not seem to care. He said a soldier had to learn to march on an empty belly, and he went and got his old drum out of the chest there. He beat it up and down the room, up and down the stair, until I could take it no more. I took the sticks from him and I snapped them in two.'

I closed her hand over them and kissed her on the forehead. 'I'll make him some more.' I went over to the recess in the wall where Deirdre, clutching her doll, was pretending to sleep. I kissed her too, and leaned across her, a finger to my lips, to rub the sleepy head of our three-year-old, Davy. The mischief in the smile he gave me told me that he would tax his mother's heart more often even than did his brother.

Upstairs, Zander was waiting, his bottom lip protruding a little, and his eyes fixed on the stairhead in a determination not to cry. He moved sideways a little to make space for me as I sat down beside him. 'Your mother is very sorry about the drumsticks. I will make you some new ones.'

He nodded, the tears threatening to brim over. 'It is because she is worried. She is scared you will go away with Lieutenant Ormiston, and that she will never see you again.'

'We did not want to go away, yet. We only wanted to look at the ship.'

'And did you get a look at it?'

'Yes.' Sullen still.

'Tell me about it.'

'It is a Dutch merchantman, a hundred feet and five hundred tons.' His face was brightening and his voice becoming more animated as he went on. 'And we saw the soldiers, the recruits, at their exercises. And they say they took on boxes of pistols and muskets at Dundee, and gunpowder, and that they are bound for Gluckstadt.'

'I hope they will have taken on plenty of hides and barrels of dry biscuit.'

'I did not see any of that.'

'Oh,' I looked at him ruefully. 'Then the soldiers will be very cold, and very hungry, for they will sleep out in the open fields, and find very little to eat as the winter takes hold.'

He thought about this a while. 'Will I get any supper tonight?'

I shook my head. 'Perhaps the next time you will think of your mother at home and waiting for you. Now you go down and say you are sorry, and get off to your bed.'

He turned towards me as he set his foot on the third step from the top. 'Do you think we should tell the sergeant? About the biscuits and the hides?'

Something, some indiscernible fear crept into my chest and stomach. 'The sergeant?'

'Yes. He is always there, watching. He keeps to the dark corners. The boys are all afraid of him. He has a bad leg, but he can limp as fast as others run, they say. His face is covered in scars, but no one sees it – he keeps his hood up. And he has a patch over his eye. James said the right, but I knew it was the left. I was right and now he owes me a penny.'

The fear tightened. 'How do you know you were right?'

He looked surprised at my question. 'Because I saw it. All the other boys ran away when he came towards us. James wanted to too, but I called him a coward, so he stayed. Some of the boys had said the man was a Spaniard, because of his skin. But he speaks Scots, and we could understand him.'

'He spoke to you? What did he say?'

'He asked us our names, and when we told him, he asked us who our fathers were, and then he smiled and went away. His face did not frighten us so much when he smiled.'

I lowered my voice. 'Zander, did you tell your mother of this?'

He shook his head, the sullen look returning. 'No. She did not let me speak.'

'Don't tell her. You promise me?'

'I promise,' he said, in the manner of a little boy well-used to the giving of such promises. 'Can I go down to the ship again? If I tell you first?'

I looked at the child who had filled my heart for nine years, the bastard son of another man, and I felt my nails press into my own palms. 'No,' I said. 'You cannot.'

4

At Baillie Lumsden's House

William shook his head as he mopped the last of the stew from his bowl with a hunk of the bread we had shared. 'I do not think it is anything to be concerned about. The poor fellow must be so used to children running at the sight of him, he would have been intrigued by two who did not, and probably said the first thing that came into his head.'

As ever at this time of day, the cookshop was filled with advocates, notaries and clerks. I usually took my mid-day meal in the college, but the principal had given me business to do out in the town this afternoon, so I had taken the chance to spend a half-hour with my lawyer friend William Cargill here instead. I had drawn William aside from his favoured table by the fire, to a bench where we might talk more privately.

'Have you seen him?'

'The recruiting sergeant?'

I nodded.

'I don't think so. I have seen Lieutenant Ormiston and

the other officers, but the sergeant has never taken my notice. I think that is the way he prefers it. I have heard he has been greatly disfigured by his injuries, and rarely shows himself ashore.'

'He comes out at night,' I said, 'when they make their tour of the inns and alehouses. He's Ormiston's watchdog. The innkeepers and brewsters are always glad when he has gone from their place. He has not his master's power to charm, it seems, and does not encourage conversation, but I suspect they are two halves of the one coin.'

William signalled for the cook's boy to bring us more ale. 'You are not much taken with the lieutenant, are you, Alexander?'

I did not see any need to deny it. 'It takes more than a studied manner and a fine cut of clothing to endear a man to me,' I said. 'And I do not like his pretending to know more of me than he does.'

William looked at me pointedly. 'How many of your own scholars have taken ship for the wars when their college days were done?'

'Too many,' I said. 'Many more than will come back.'

'Aye,' said William sombrely. 'But those who have gone will speak of old teachers, fondly remembered. There is nothing sinister in Ormiston knowing your name, or in his sergeant taking a moment to speak kindly to the only two boys in the town not to run away from him.'

I conceded that William might be right, and our conversation moved on to other things – the unwelcome interest of English archbishops in the affairs of our kirk and the king's ill-judged meddling in the business of our burgh council. William kept his voice low. 'Can Charles truly believe we will allow interference from Whitehall that we would not take from his father in Holyrood? This will not end well.'

'Hmmn, I fear not,' I said. 'And I am to go to Baillie Lumsden's house later today.' Despite his wealth and influence, the baillie was strongly suspected of sailing too close to the wind in matters of religion and politics. He was also the cousin and namesake of Matthew Lumsden, the old student friend of William's and mine whom Sarah had decried the night before, and who was openly and defiantly Papist.

'Oh?' William was interested. 'What is the college's business there?' We had finished our meal and were stepping out on to the street.

'I don't know yet. Dr Dun said Lumsden would explain it to me, but I am not altogether at ease about it. I noticed a power of armed men at the baillie's door as I passed by his house this morning.'

William raised his eyebrows in surprise. 'Yes, but those are there for . . .'

'For what?'

A mischievous smile had come upon his face. 'Truly? You do not know? Well, I daresay you will soon find out.' He slapped me hard on the back. 'Courage, my friend. Courage!' And he was still laughing as he disappeared from view into the depths of Huxter Row.

It was with some trepidation, then, that I approached Lumsden's residence on the Guest Row. With five storeys of towers and turrets, it was better proportioned than many castles I had seen, and one of the grandest houses in the burgh.

The armed men I had seen in the morning were still there, and I had to have one of Lumsden's servants vouch for me before I was allowed in. I was directed up the west turnpike to wait upon the master in the small parlour there. As I reached the head of the stair, a maid went past, carrying a tray of wine and cake in to the great hall, leaving the door slightly ajar behind her. I had my hand on the handle to close it when a voice from inside rose above the soft female murmur that had been coming from the room.

'Isabella, shut the door for the girl before we all freeze to death! I never knew a house of such draughts.'

I placed the voice at the same moment as my eyes fixed on the young – perhaps not so young now – woman who had risen to close the door. I had not seen her in nine years, but I knew her instantly. Isabella Irvine, niece to Sir Robert Gordon of Straloch, friend to Katharine Hay whom I had loved and abandoned before I properly knew what love was. Isabella Irvine who, on our one and only meeting all that time ago, at the house of her uncle, had made it clear to me that she despised me more than anyone else on earth.

The shock on her face matched my own, and a small, surprised 'Oh!' escaped her throat before she recovered herself sufficiently to continue the process of shutting the door in my face. But she had not moved quickly enough, for again came the commanding voice, a little more forceful this time.

'Wait! Mercy, girl, is that not Alexander Seaton you are about to disfigure? Mr Seaton? Are these the manners the town of Aberdeen has taught you? Show yourself, man!'

And so I stepped into the room and found myself in the presence of Katharine Forbes, Lady Rothiemay, fifty years old, five years a widow of the murdered William Gordon of Rothiemay, mother to his sons, one of whom had been burned to death in a tower, the other, a child of nine, who had been forcibly taken from her care by a kinsman seeking to control her lands. In her grief and fury, beyond the power or inclination of the law to assuage, Katharine Forbes was at feud with more interests than I had friends. No longer the sylph-like sacrificial bride she had been thirty years ago, she was nonetheless slim and striking still. There was scarcely a grey hair among the chestnut folds on her head, and a little faded though they now were, her startling blue eyes could put the fear of God and the love of woman into any man in the North.

'Your Ladyship,' I made my long-disused bow, 'I had not realised . . .'

'No doubt you had not. Your head was rarely out of a book. But you must be the only man in Aberdeen who didn't know I was in residence here with Lumsden.'

'The guard . . .'

'Indeed. Would that others had as little interest in my

movements as yourself, Mr Seaton. But enough of that. Tell me, when were you last at Banff?'

'Three months ago, in the summer.'

'And all is well with the good doctor?'

I knew my friend Dr Jaffray had several times tended to Lady Rothiemay and her children when their own physician from Huntly could not be got. 'All well.'

She nodded, satisfied. 'Good. Tell him he must visit me the next time he is in Edinburgh. Tell him to bring with him a deck of cards. He relieved me of twenty Dutch florins the last time I saw him, and I would win them back.'

I glanced briefly at Isabella Irvine. 'You are going to Edinburgh?'

It was Lady Rothiemay who replied. 'Aye, that cesspit of ministers and politicking. My enemies are busy, defaming me daily before the Privy Council, and it will not be long, I'd wager, until they have me on the back of a cart headed down to one of the castle jails.'

This was enough to rouse Isabella at last. 'No, my Lady, your friends . . .'

'My friends can only do so much without they set a noose around their own necks.' Her voice softened and she smiled at the younger woman. 'You have surely seen enough of the world by now to know that. Anyhow, I doubt Mr Seaton takes any great interest in our affairs.' Living as I was in a town constantly agog at the depredations said to have been visited upon her foes by men loyal to Lady Rothiemay, I did not demur. She turned slightly to address me once more. 'I hear you are still regent at the Marischal College. Can no place be found for you at King's?'

The lady was suspected of strong sympathies with Rome, and I judged it best not to mention to her my forthcoming call to the ministry. 'I am content at Marischal, your Ladyship.'

'I am sorry to hear it. I will get Dr Forbes to work upon you.'

I took this opportunity to turn the conversation away from myself. 'Dr Forbes tells me your son does well in the schools.'

She softened further. 'Aye, he does. And he is to bring him here to me tonight. Only God knows when he might see his mother again.'

'I will pray that it might be soon.'

She inclined her head a little. 'Thank you, Mr Seaton, but I begin to wonder if God listens to prayers when the name of Katharine Forbes is mentioned. And your own boy does well with Mr Wedderburn here?'

Jaffray had told me before that this woman forgot nothing about the lives of those in whom she took an interest. 'He makes progress, but at the moment he dreams of nothing but being a soldier.'

'That is as it should be. And your daughter, what age is she now?'

I told her that Deirdre was almost seven.

'Then she might make a pupil for you, my dear.'

In my anxiety to avoid the undiminished odium that

radiated from the eyes of Isabella Irvine, I had not noticed Christiane Rolland, the young sister of the French master, Louis, seated rigidly on a stool a little to the left of her, quietly sipping at her wine. She seemed a small thing, a delicate article of fine china, in this room of power and substance.

'Christiane, I am sorry, I had not noticed you there.'

She nodded back, attempting a smile. 'Mister Seaton.'

Lady Rothiemay was pleased. 'You know my young friend then.'

'Very well,' I said. 'Her brother is a former scholar of mine, and a friend.'

'I'm glad to hear it. That is something in her favour.'

I dared not glance in Isabella Irvine's direction to gauge her reaction to this remark, but I was certain Lady Rothiemay had, and I began to suspect that her companion's hostility to me had not gone unnoticed. Her Ladyship waited a moment, then continued, 'Your business here today is not with Baillie Lumsden, but with me. You may have heard that I have it in mind to found a school for girls here in the burgh of Aberdeen. I had my own schooling here, and whatever my troubles in the world have been since then, they would have been a lot worse without it. I intend to provide for a schoolmistress who will teach the girls to write and sew, and do anything else whereof they might be capable.'

'Which is often much,' I said.

'Indeed it is, and has to be. A woman without husband

or father to protect her must live on her wits, and without lawful employment is a person at once vulnerable and suspect everywhere she goes. If it is in my power to prevent even one young girl from falling prey to the evils that the world holds ready for her, then my money will be well spent. The town council will only accept my gift on the understanding that they have a voice in the appointment of my schoolmistress. I made it known that I wished you to be that person.'

'Me?' I was somewhat surprised. 'I am . . . honoured, but why me?'

She looked at me a long moment. 'Because you are a Banffshire lad, and will not be caught up in the interminable politics of this town. And also, I know something of your wife, and I am of the view you are not a bad judge of women.'

There was nothing I could say, and she seemed pleased with this state of affairs. 'Christiane here is one of the candidates for the post, and I have had several others. I wish you to be present at their trials in two days' time, to give me the view of the college on the candidates that I might make my decision.'

My heart sank at the very thought of it, but I knew I was unlikely to find a way out of the task.

'Now,' said the lady, addressing the other two, 'I have some other business to discuss with Mr Seaton, and it is not for the ears of young women. Isabella, you might profitably spend an hour with Christiane here – see what George

Jamesone plans to do with that garden of his. You would do well to remind Jamesone that it was myself that recommended those fellows to him in the first place, and Lady Lindsay is now in very high dudgeon with me after his poaching them.' As Isabella was following Christiane Rolland out of the room, Lady Rothiemay added, 'And Isabella, I will detain Mr Seaton here no longer than a half-hour, then you may safely return without fear of encountering him again.'

Her young companion curtseyed and made her exit, partly confused and partly infuriated.

The light outside was fading and the room becoming cooler, despite the fire that already burned in the vast sandstone hearth of the hall. 'Pull over those drapes, would you, Mr Seaton? Little enough light gets in at those windows anyway. I would be happier in the small parlour, but Lumsden thinks he must keep me here in state. We could light another candle, though – I can hardly see your face.'

I did as I was bid, then took a seat in the velvet armchair across from her.

'You must give Isabella a little time. She has nursed her wrath against you many years, and I had not warned her to expect you here today. Perhaps I should have done.'

'She has grounds for her dislike of me. She has been a constant friend to one I badly wronged.'

Lady Rothiemay shook her head impatiently. 'It is nonsense, and I have told Isabella that. Katharine Hay would have had no life with you, disgraced and penniless as you were. You knew that nine years ago, do not pretend other-wise.'

'I . . . I was angry at what I had lost myself. I did not think of her, at first, I . . .'

It was so many years since I had spoken of this, and to so few people, that I could not believe I was talking of it so openly to the woman before me.

'Well, whatever your reasoning, the outcome has been the right one, and Isabella understands less of the affairs of men and women than she thinks she does. I fear she may have made a bad choice of her own.' She pondered a moment then put the thought aside. 'No matter. That is a subject for other ears. What I want to talk to you about is Seoras MacKay.'

I sighed heavily. 'There is little I can tell you, your Lady-ship. You know the events of the last two days?'

She nodded briskly. 'That he was sent from Downies' Inn in the company of his foster brother, and has not been seen since.'

I could not see the direction of her interest. 'I had not realised that Seoras was . . . known to your Ladyship.'

She sniffed. 'Hmf. You are scarcely a man of the world Mr Seaton, if you do not know that I am related to half the country round. There is a degree of cousinage between the MacKays and my own family, and Seoras's father and I are friends of old: the Forbeses have long been allies of the MacKays in the north. I hear you yourself saw Seoras in Downies' Inn the night the recruiting officers were there.'

I acknowledged that I had done.

'Then I fear there will be no happy outcome to this tale.'

I did not know how to tell this woman who had suffered so much unjust loss that not every misadventure must end in tragedy. I chose my words carefully. 'The boy will be coming to in the back room of some drinking place, or lying low until he thinks the furore over his absence has passed. It has happened often enough like this before, and they always come back.'

'Not this time. His companion has already been found, has he not? In what condition was the boy?'

So I told her of Hugh's cuts and bruises, his sodden clothes and the weeds in his hair.

She stared away from me, into the fire. 'Tell me exactly what happened, what was said in Downie's Inn the night before last.'

And so I did, although I could not see what purpose it would serve. When I had finished, she was silent a few moments before saying,

'Then Seoras MacKay is dead, Mr Seaton. He is dead.'

Her words startled me, and before I could respond, we were interrupted by the arrival of Matthew Lumsden's wife, and all chance of asking Lady Rothiemay how she could pronounce with such certainty upon the thing was lost, but I reflected on it that night, and on several after.

5

Rumours at the Session

Sarah had had little to say when I told her that evening of Lady Rothiemay's good regard of her. In fact, she had looked almost displeased by it.

'She meant well by it, you know.'

'I have no doubt she did, but it would please me better to know that no one in Banffshire remembered my name.'

'Sarah,' I sighed, 'it was a long time ago, and of those who remember it at all, none will blame you.'

I knew the minute I said it that I had done wrong. I wanted to bite back the words, but it was too late. When her response came, it was slow, and deliberate.

'Will they not? That is very good of them.'

She had never forgotten, could never forget, the jeers and the stones hurled at her as she had been driven, pregnant by her brutish master, from the burgh of Banff nine years ago, and while we had made, over time, this life for ourselves here in Aberdeen, I had never once been able to persuade her to return to that town with me. It was a matter we rarely spoke of, and I was glad to leave it now.

'Do you think I am a fit person to judge who will make a good schoolmistress?'

Her face softened, and a mischievous look came in to her eyes. 'You are a terrible person to judge such a thing. I do not know what her Ladyship was thinking of. You think a stocking well-turned if your heel does not go through it at the first wearing, and letters well learned if the Catechism can be recited back to you.' She glanced at Deirdre, who was busied in plaiting a strand of my hair with one of her own ribbons. 'Look at you. You appear beyond comprehending that little girls might ever need the slightest discipline. If left to you, the schoolmistress's post will be awarded to the one who can best look up at you with the eyes of a lost doe.'

I pulled her towards me. 'And when did you ever look up at me in such a manner? A she-wolf more like, indignant that I should even speak to you.'

She laughed and teased herself away from me. 'You had not yet learned to pay a proper compliment.'

I had glanced at her casually when I'd mentioned Isabella Irvine, but seen little reaction, voluntary or otherwise, in her eyes. I had told her, years ago, of everything that had passed between myself and Katharine Hay. She had known most of it anyway, through rumour and gossip, and we had rarely spoken of it since, but I had never mentioned to her Isabella's friendship with Katharine or consequent dislike of me. To talk of it now would be to threaten something in her that I knew was still fragile, and perhaps always would be.

Neither had I told her of Lady Rothiemay's pronouncements upon Seoras MacKay. On hearing of the young man's disappearance, Sarah's first response had been that the recruiters had taken him, and no reasoning on my part could shake this conviction from her. I had called on the master of the grammar school on my way home from Lumsden's house. David Wedderburn had told me that the boys in the school still had nothing in their minds but the recruiting ship, to the extent that he had abandoned normal lessons and taken them instead through the Spaniard Cervantes' account of the Battle of Lepanto. No sighting of the recruiting sergeant had been made anywhere near the school yard that day, and Wedderburn was vigilant on the matter, on account of the fears of the mothers of the burgh. I did not tell Sarah of my visit to the schoolhouse. It would do her little good to know that the matter that so exercised her fears did mine also.

It was a little before seven when William arrived to accompany me to the weekly diet of the kirk session. He had been called to the eldership of the kirk several years before I had, and had never known, as I had, the shame of being forced to sit in sackcloth on the stool of repentance before the whole congregation. Whether that made me a better judge of my fellow man, I could not tell.

It was a short walk down the Netherkirkgate to Correction Wynd and the Kirkyard of St Nicholas, and given the cold and the hour, few were out on the streets. I took the chance to castigate William for not having forewarned me of Lady Rothiemay's presence in town, and he laughed heartily. The dullness of his own day had only been enlivened by a fight between two cottars from Woolmanhill over accusations of a stolen horse. 'I nearly took a dunt on the head myself, helping Baillie Lawson to separate them.'

'And it would have been well deserved, I am sure.'

We arranged our faces and lowered our voices as we went in by the door of the East Kirk. William smiled as he saw me glance up at the pulpit that would soon be mine. 'Have you your sermon written yet?'

'Nine years since,' I said, under my breath.

Steps took us down to the small chapel of St Mary's below the kirk, where the session was to meet. The others were already gathered there, under the groined stone vaulting of the roof. A fire had been lit in a brazier, but could do little to dissipate the cold echoing from the very stones of the place. My breath was in front of my face when I spoke. There was a great deal of stamping of feet and rubbing of hands, and I heard the hope expressed more than once that we would not have over much business to attend to tonight.

Dr Barron, the Moderator, opened with a prayer that the Lord might grace our assembly and grant us wisdom in our judgments. Mr Andrew Melville, reader in the kirk, read from the book of Deuteronomy, chapter twenty-four, and the clerk followed by reading to us the order of business. An apprentice tailor and his master's housemaid were brought before us for the third time to answer to an accusation of fornication made against them; they had denied the charge three times and it had not yet been found proven. The tailor's wife having accompanied them gave assurance that the girl, to her absolute knowledge, was not with child, and the pair were admonished to see in future that their carriage did not draw suspicion of loose living down upon themselves. Several more townsfolk came before us and were similarly dealt with. Last to be summoned was a cooper, Gilbert Wilson, made to appear at the instance of Archibald Wallace. The cooper had promised to marry Wallace's daughter, but had delayed time and again in setting the banns before the kirk. When questioned, the young man, whom I recognised from the night in Downie's Inn, produced a testimonial from Lieutenant Ormiston showing that he had signed for the Scots Brigade. The session accordingly loosed him of his obligations to Wallace's daughter, much to that man's displeasure, and prayed God's blessing on the holy enterprise against the forces of the anti-Christ. The reluctant bridegroom made his escape with profuse thanks and evident relief.

The subject of the recruiting ships seemed to exercise one of my fellow members, Deacon Gammie, particularly, for he twitched and worked at his gums continuously through the examination of Gilbert Wilson, as if there were matters of mighty import to be discussed instead. The sound of Wilson's feet on the flagstone stair had not yet faded when Gammie came half-way out of his seat to pull at the sleeve of the Moderator.

'Yes, Deacon,' said Dr Barron, in a manner which suggested that he had no great faith that what the Deacon was about to say would be of any relevance to our proceedings at all.

Gammie got to his feet like an excited child kept waiting too long for his turn to speak.

'While we are on the matter of the soldiers, it has come to my ear that Matthew Lumsden has been sighted in the burgh.' He pursed his lips and nodded curtly in the direction of where William and I were sitting. Matthew was an old friend from our student days and the nephew of his namesake, Baillie Lumsden, whose house I had been in that day. Unlike his uncle, Matthew had never settled to a respectable trade or business, and was known to be a willing sword in any cause of his master, the Marquis of Huntly, the most powerful nobleman in the North of Scotland and one whose family had ever about them the whiff of Rome. Gammie clearly felt that the mention of Matthew's name should be enough to put the session on the alert.

This point had escaped the Moderator. 'And what would you propose we do with this information, Deacon?' he asked.

Gammie was taken aback. 'Be vigilant! The man is a Papist, out and out, and may draw others in his snare.' Again he looked pointedly at William and me.

William smiled. 'I can assure you, Deacon, that I am ever alert, in my lawyer's mode, to such snares, and in twenty years of friendship with Matthew have side-stepped them with ease. And as for Alexander, given his calling, I think you may rest easy.'

'Besides,' I said, 'I was at Baillie Lumsden's house today – there was no sign of Matthew there, nor indeed the Marquis of Huntly either.'

There was a great deal of suppressed laughter at this, but Gammie was none abashed. 'You may mock, Mr Seaton, but these are dangerous times, and the poison of the war on the continent may seep into our own body soon enough if we do not look to our own imperfections.' I regretted mocking the man now, for he was right – much though I loved him, Matthew was a blemish, a wound on the body of our kirk and commonwealth which, if not kept in check, might thoroughly infect the whole body.

'Quite so,' said the Moderator, 'and we should study to avoid such a calamity.' There was much shuffling of feet and murmured agreement from the embarrassed elders.

Matters of discipline and rumour thus dealt with, and all who were not members of the session being gone, the clerk became grave and warned us that what we were about to discuss was not to be noised abroad in the burgh, for fear of encouragement of superstition and unrest. A report had come from the kirk session of St Fittick's Church in the parish of Nigg, across the mouth of the Dee, of a demonic Sabbath thought to have been held at the kirk only two nights since. Lights had been seen, for which there could be no lawful cause, and a great howling heard. Dancing amongst the gravestones and flight through the trees above the kirkyard had been witnessed by the minister himself, who was now in a state of terror and constant calling for succour upon the Lord. The session of St Fittick's begged our prayers for the restoration of their minister's senses, and urged vigilance upon us lest the coven take mind so to pollute the kirk of St Nicholas. Fervent prayers were duly said on behalf of Mr John Leslie, minister there, and resolve was taken to keep a nightly watch on our own kirkyard.

'Have you seen anything of Matthew in the town?' I asked William, after we had bid goodnight to Dr Barron and the others at the kirkyard gates.

He shook his head dismissively. 'No. Old Gammie sees Papists under every bush, and besides, when do you think Matthew ever learned discretion? If he was come home from whatever the Marquis has him at abroad, you and I would both be nursing sorry heads and empty purses. I was so drunk the last time he was here it was only by the quick thinking of one of my clerk's boys that I escaped the notice of our good deacon myself.'

'What, after you had refused to come home with me?'

'Aye. Young Willie Dodds noticed Gammie creep in to Madge Ronald's inn on his rounds, and threw a sack over the top of me before I could be spied. He and Matthew then sat on me until Gammie was safely gone.'

'No chance of such times now,' I murmured, after our laughter had drawn the attention of passers-by. 'Between my tours of the inns in search of students who might be tempted to sign up with Ormiston, and taking my turn at the kirkyard watch, I will be lucky if I can get home to my own house one night in three.'

'Ach, it will not be for long,' said William. 'Ormiston will be gone in little over a week, I'll wager, once he has toured the lairds in the country round and conscripted a few of their sons. Besides, he cannot tarry here much longer if he is to reach safe to the Elbe and have his recruits securely quartered with their regiment before winter sets in.'

'That will be a relief to the whole town.'

Although we had gone our separate ways from the minister and other elders, he leaned towards me and lowered his voice further. 'And as for the minister of St Fittick's, you're as like to find *him* in an alehouse as you are one of your students, and that is the cause of his demonic visions.'

'John Leslie? No.'

'But aye, John Leslie. Surely you know the man is seldom sober?'

'I did not know,' I said.

'Well, my friend,' he said, raising an eyebrow at me, more than half serious, 'if we are to make a minister of you, you will have to learn to listen to gossip, for some of it will be true. For instance, Elizabeth told me six weeks ago that Gilbert Wilson only agreed to marry Jeannie Wallace because he'd lost a drunken wager and was desperate to extricate himself from his promise from the moment he woke up sober. The arrival of Ormiston's troop ship has been as a blessing from God to him.'

'I know it; I saw him sign up myself.' My mind went back to the image of the young cooper eagerly putting his name to the paper the lieutenant's men had set in front of him. And then a thought struck me. 'William, the night in Downie's Inn, when Gilbert Wilson signed for the regiment, Hugh Gunn was planning to also. I had the strong sense that it was to take himself out of the shadow of Seoras MacKay. Did you ever hear of bad blood between them?'

'I never heard their names until yesterday, but I have heard tell of more than bad blood between them today.'

I stopped, conscious of a vague stirring of hope. I hadn't been back to the college since the morning. 'Has Seoras returned?'

'Not by the time I met Baillie Lawson when I was leaving my chambers tonight. It seems Hugh Gunn is accused of having had a hand in his foster brother's disappearance. Hugh claims to remember nothing of what happened after he and Seoras left the inn, until he was found in the cooper's yard yesterday morning. But that he was in a fight is clear, and the state he was found in has led to rumours that he drowned his foster brother. The baillies have agreed that the boy might remain under the custody of Dr Dun in the college, although how he is to shield him from the wrath of Strathnaver, I do not know.'

Nothing cheered by what William had told me, I bade him goodnight him on Correction Wynd, where he had business to attend to. Lady Rothiemay's words, asserting that Seoras was dead, returned to me. But what had I told her to convince her of it? That I had stopped Hugh Gunn from signing up with the lieutenant? Surely she could not believe the boy would murder his foster brother over that? And yet I could not think, on a night like this, that Seoras would be hiding away of his own accord, although of course out in the town, there were places where a man might secrete himself, briefly, if he so wished it.

A half-hour's walk to clear my head before I went home would do me no harm, and I found myself going deeper in to the town, in the hope that I might come upon some hint of him. My feet took me along lanes and wynds, where gates and doorways set into high walls might lead to secret places, narrow pends giving off on to dark courtyards, forgotten gardens, places where the hopeless poor slept amongst the derelict dwellings of men long dead, but I doubted that Seoras MacKay would have been able to evade discovery in any of them for two days and nights. Even in the darkness, a man could not hide from his thoughts, and those that dogged me could not be shaken off, evaded, by a sudden turn into an unexpected close. Images came, unbidden, unwanted, to my mind's eye. Lady Rothiemay's words echoed again in my head; the look on Hugh Gunn's face as he had pushed past me in Downie's Inn, the bitterness in his voice as he'd addressed his companion would only leave my mind to be replaced by the memory of the state he had been in the previous morning, and the weeds which had hung from his sodden clothes. A terrible thought came to me and I tried to push it away, but it kept coming back like the body of a drowned man, brought inevitably to the surface.

At some point in my wanderings, a strange notion that I was not alone attached itself to me, but no matter how often I turned, I saw no one. Nevertheless, I was glad to finally emerge back on to the Schoolhill, where the moon in the clear sky reflected blue light off the frost that covered the ground. I could see my way before me now as clearly as if I had a lamp in my hand. Again though, after a moment, I almost believed I heard footsteps shadow mine, stop less than a heartbeat after mine had stopped, but I realised my foolishness when I saw a well-known figure hurry past a doorway only a few yards ahead of me. Louis Rolland.

'Louis,' I called softly, for fear of waking those already in their beds. He did not hear me. 'Louis,' I called again, and this time the French master visibly jumped before he turned, startled, to face me.

Relief flooded his face. 'Mr Seaton!'

'I'm sorry, Louis, I didn't mean to frighten you.'

'I, no, it is all right . . .' It took him a minute for his breathing to return to normal.

'You are late abroad.'

'Yes,' he said, still breathing heavily. 'I was in the old town, where I have some pupils. I had hoped to be back home before now.'

As I took a step towards him, I could see he was trembling, and not with the cold.

'Louis, what's the matter?'

'It's nothing, just foolishness.' He looked around him, then lowered his voice. 'I have been listening too much to Christiane. She's convinced someone has been watching the house. For the last two days she has been on at me about it, and I didn't take her seriously. When you appeared so silently from that close, I thought for a moment . . .' Then he laughed. 'Dear Lord, I have let her nonsense turn my head. The council will have my licence from me if they suspect me of such foolishness.'

'And who would teach their merchants and young gentlemen the intricacies of the French tongue then? I suspect you and your licence are safe enough. But let me walk as far as your house with you – I had wanted to hear more of what you know of Hugh and Seoras anyway.'

Louis Rolland kept his school in a small house at the far end of the Schoolhill. His grandparents had fled Paris with their daughter, Louis' mother, in the wake of the massacres of St Bartholemew's Day, and he and his younger sister had been brought up in the tongue and manners of its people as much as they had the Scots. His lessons were in growing demand among the merchants trading in French goods, and students who aimed at higher studies in France or the Swiss cantons. I had tried to persuade him before that he should address me now as 'Alexander', and see me as a friend rather than the Mr Seaton who had taught him for the only year he had been able to attend the college. I tried again now, and he acceded, if a little uncomfortably.

'I'm not sure there is anything I can tell you of the pair

that will be of any use. As I say, they have been coming to me for lessons since the summer. Seoras's father had a mind, it seems, that it would do his son no harm to serve a term in the *Garde Eccosaise*, and Hugh, of course, would go with him.'

It seemed likely enough. Since our country was presently at peace with France, the Marquis of Huntly was free to assume his hereditary position of captain of the personal bodyguard of the king of France, and many young men of good birth seeking favour and preferment followed him. 'And so they came to you, to learn the French tongue?'

He nodded.

'And do they progress?'

He stuck out a bottom lip in a manner I had observed in other Frenchmen. 'Well, Seoras in particular seems to have a natural gift. Hugh has to work harder, but to good purpose. By the time of their graduation next summer, I think they will both be ready to make their way in Paris unhampered by difficulties in language at least.'

I sensed we were coming to the grain of the matter. 'But there are other difficulties?'

Louis seemed unsure as to how he should continue. 'I know what's being said about Hugh around the town and I have no wish to give credence to such talk . . .'

'You may speak to me in confidence.'

He nodded. 'Very well. I do not dislike Seoras. In fact, there are times when he is very good company, but he is . . .'

'What?'

'Difficult. Volatile. He's not a person with whom I would ever truly feel at ease. Hugh can manage him – seems to understand his moods before they become dangerous – but of late he's had less and less patience with him. It has made Seoras goad him all the more. These last few weeks there's been a hardness between them that I did not see before.'

'You have no idea what's at the root of it?'

He shook his head. 'None. Seoras has always been hard work for Hugh, but there had been an affection there. Of late, I do not see that affection. I think Hugh's tolerance with his foster brother is almost at an end, and I don't see how they will travel happily together to France if the matter is not resolved. The atmosphere between them has become so unpleasant of late that I have stopped Christiane from joining in our classes – she used to come in to help me accustom them to conversation in French. I don't think she's sorry to have been relieved of that duty.'

'She has much on hand in any case, it seems, with the schoolmistress trials and her help to George.'

Louis smiled. 'That has been a blessing. Although I fear it too might lead to problems. She has conceived a great liking for Guillaume.'

'Charpentier? The gardener?'

'Yes. He's a very fine fellow, and I could not wish for a better husband for her, but I don't think he sees her in that light at all, and then I will have a broken heart to attend to.'

I patted him on the shoulder. 'The troubles of a school-master are legion,' I said. 'I don't envy you. But tell me, how were things between Seoras and Hugh when you last saw them?'

'Bad. It was late last Wednesday afternoon. We hadn't got through the first part of our lesson, a conversation, before Seoras began to taunt Hugh. What about, I do not know, for when he is in the greatest devilment he will talk to Hugh only in the Gaelic tongue. Hugh was becoming visibly livid. I had to give the lesson up in the end, for fear of violence between them. Seoras never appeared for the Monday lesson, and I've seen neither of them since.'

'Do you have any idea where Seoras might be?'

He shook his head. 'None. I was his French master, nothing more, and he certainly did not confide in me.'

'And Hugh?'

'Hugh? I think Hugh has spent his whole life knowing he cannot confide in anybody.'

We had almost reached Louis' house by now, the painted sign that hung from his porch illuminated by the blue light of the moon. He thanked me for walking with him, and as I was turning away he said, 'If you should come upon my gardening friends, let them know the house will be locked soon. My sister and I must get to our beds.'

'But they cannot be gardening in the dark?'

'You would think not, wouldn't you? But there are dug-up bulbs to be dried apparently, long-buried roots, corms and tubers to be divided, sorted and noted for replanting.

George, as you know, is a man of determination as well as genius: he has made sound an old gardener's workshop where such activities might be carried out at almost any hour. He will have his Arcadia, come what may. He has cleared a yard too, for the wood that will be hewn. I have been promised enough firewood to take me through this winter and the next.' He rubbed cold hands together in a fruitless effort to keep warm. 'There are many benefits to be had in housing George's workmen.'

'But there's a price to be paid too, I think. I cannot imagine the small one, St Clair, adds a great deal of cheer to your table.'

Louis laughed. 'Little cheer and even less conversation. But Guillaume more than makes up for it.' He reached out his hand and I shook it.

'We should talk like this more often, although perhaps in a warmer place,' I said.

After the door had shut behind him and I found myself alone in the street, the slight sense of foreboding I had felt earlier gradually returned. In the full moon, every star that I knew was visible to my eye. Every turret, every corbel, every rooftop was sketched sharply against the deep midnight-blue of a sky that on other nights was black. Frost glistened off the stones, sparkling almost at the reverberation of my footsteps. With Louis gone, I felt like the last living soul in a place abandoned. And yet, I knew I was not alone. It had only been a glimpse, as I'd turned from saying goodnight to Louis, but a glimpse had been enough to show me the figure, three-quarters hidden in the shadow of St Nicholas Kirkyard gate, that watched me. The figure I had seen fleetingly at the top of the stairs in Downie's Inn as I had spoken with Ormiston. Hood well down on his head, leaning awkwardly to one side as if the other could not properly support him, a hand hiding his face, it was the man who had approached my son at the harbour only yesterday, but this time I knew that the recruiting sergeant was watching me.

I should have made for home then, quickly, but there was something I had to satisfy myself of first. I made my way once more down the vennel by way of the old place of the Blackfriars, through the rusted gates into the garden.

The hut in which Charpentier and St Clair worked must have been somewhere on the other side of the garden, for no light or sounds reached me here from there. I walked along the moonlit pathways towards the place I sought. The grass was white and crisp beneath my boots, and I saw that I left a trail of light prints in the frost as I went. I tried to recall the sketches the artist had shown to me earlier in the day, and the one that came most clearly to my mind was that of the garden as he planned it; I had to search further back, to one that had been of less interest to us both, that of the long-neglected garden as it was now.

My progress slowed as I had to pass beneath overhanging branches of beech and ash that blocked out much of the moonlight. The darting of a fox across my path startled me, but after a few minutes I had found it, beyond a screen of willows and knotted brambles – the pond. I approached it tentatively, grateful that the cold had turned the mud at the edges as hard as iron. I stooped down and saw that bootprints from before the freeze had now been sculpted into the earth. It was difficult to tell in the darkness, but it did not seem to me that the markings showed signs of a struggle of any sort. I put out a foot and carefully tested the edge of the water – it had already begun to ice over and by the morning would be frozen through. I picked up a long, broken branch and started slowly pushing it through the iced water to probe whatever was beneath. I worked it through tangles of weeds, fallen branches and other debris until it reached the sludge below. I made my way around the edges of the pond in this manner for some time, until my fingers were in an agony of cold. At last, I came to where I had started and, in all, there was a relief of sorts, for I had not found the dead body of Seoras MacKay.

I was almost back at the gateway when a sound, some-where behind and to the left of me, took my attention. I turned around quickly, but not quickly enough, for all I saw of the man was the edge of his cloak and the back of his boot as it disappeared into an opening in the thicket towards the eastern gateway of the garden.

Left standing with her back to me, at the entrance to what I recalled from Jamesone's map as 'the bower', was Isabella Irvine. Her hood was down and her hair loosed. She seemed to watch the man long after he was gone. I stepped quickly behind an old rose as I saw her lift the hood to cover her head. Then she turned around and walked past me and out of the garden. I waited a moment and followed her, keeping as far back as I could without losing sight of her. I watched her until she was safely admitted to Baillie Lumsden's house, then I turned at last towards Flourmill Lane and the cottage that would be my family's home for only a few weeks more. I glanced in every doorway that I passed, turned at every movement, but I saw no more of the recruiting sergeant that night.

6

Lord Reay

If I had hoped for a night's sleep after my late wanderings I was to be sorely disappointed. At some point in the early morning, a little before five, the whole household was woken by a commotion out on the streets. Doors were being banged upon and all able-bodied men being called from their beds by night watchmen bearing torches.

'The Wappinschaw!' I said, struggling into my clothing as Sarah went to calm the frightened children.

Outside, I joined my neighbours as they ran to the appointed station where Baillie Lumsden was directing the men of our quarter to our positions. Each month, though at a more godly and fore-ordained hour, we practised our muster for defence of the burgh from attack by sea. We had been well drilled, and I soon found my way through the smoke, the shouting and the running to my position by William on the Castle Hill.

'What is it? Do they know yet?' I scanned the horizon to the south-east but William pointed northwards, and I saw then the warning beacons, lighting the night all the way down the coast from Slains and Newburgh and Blackdog, and no doubt places further to the north that I could not see. And powering down that coast, torches burning and pennants flying, was a long barge, driven by two dozen oarsmen.

'I cannot make the flags out – but they're not Spaniards, nor even Dutchmen,' said William, screwing up his eyes the better to see the advancing vessel.

'No, they are not,' I said dully, adrenalin giving way to a hollow dread, for, better-sighted than William, I could make out the flags, and with them the emblem flying at the head of the craft – I had seen it on the seal of a letter shown to me by Principal Dun only two days earlier. Sir Donald MacKay of Strathnaver, Lord Reay.

'We are about to be visited by a kinsman of Lady Rothie-may,' I said.

I left it to William to explain to the provost; the Wappin-schaw would by no means be stood down. I ran to the college and demanded entrance from the startled porter.

Exempted from the Wappinschaw, the principal was patrolling the college corridors with the regents, making sure that all was well among the excitable scholars.

'Where is Hugh Gunn?' I asked breathlessly, as I at last found Dr Dun in the back-house where the poorer students' dormitories were.

'In the regents' quarters, next to Peter Williamson's chamber. Your own old room, I think. Why?'

'Seoras's father has arrived.'

★

It was in little over an hour that we finally heard the sounds of music, a march of pipe and relentless drum, coming up the Broadgate from the direction of the Shiprow. Two of the college's burliest servants were left guarding the room where Hugh Gunn lay under the care of Peter Williamson and a nurse from the town, and all the other students were sent to an early breakfast, the regent in charge of them being warned to have the door to the dining hall bolted.

From a high window overlooking the roofs of the houses fronting the college, we had seen the snake of almost forty men, their coloured plaids illuminated by the torches that flanked them, follow the pipe and drum towards our gates. At their head was a tall, richly dressed man, who even at this distance bore the habit of command like a second skin.

'Well,' said the principal, already making his way to the top of the stone stairway that came out in to the court-yard, 'we are to be honoured with a visit sooner than I had hoped. Let us welcome our guest.'

What honour he would do to us when he found his son missing and his foster son insensible I did not wish to think. I followed after Dr Dun.

I had never seen Seoras's father before, but as he marched through our gates I would have known him anywhere. He had the same restless energy as his son, the same lightening look in his eye, the same handsome cut of features that even the wounds of war could not disguise. Unlike his son, though, every inch of him proclaimed him to be a leader of men. He was perhaps forty-five years old, and stood a head taller than almost every man around him. Highland chieftain he might be, but he wore a finer cut of clothes than even Lieutenant Ormiston. The sword that hung at his side was the finest-wrought work I had seen, and the scars on the hands from which he had removed his gauntlets told that it had earned its place beside him. Out in the street, few had returned to their beds and all attention was on the great soldier and his retinue of savages. Many wore nothing on their legs or feet; those that did had trews with leather strappings crossed around their calves. They were all swathed in the coloured plaid that served as cloak, gown and blanket to them, over shirts of saffron. I felt for a moment a wrenching in the pit of my stomach for those of their like I had known in Ireland, seven years ago now, when I had answered, for a time, the call of my mother's family there. But this was the matter of a lost boy, not a people, and I prayed God it might end better.

The principal's bow was deep and careful, MacKay's response slow and gracious, and the college held its breath. Lord Reay's voice held the easy lilt of one for whom Scots was not the mother tongue. He surveyed the gathering of academics ranged behind Dr Dun. 'I see you have had intelligence of our arrival.'

Patrick Dun was measured. 'The beacon watch along the coast can be a little over-cautious, perhaps. There have been skirmishes to the north between Spaniards and the Dutch. We had not expected your Lordship for two days yet, or there would have been a more appropriate welcome for

you, and' – he looked warily past Strathnaver to the ranks
of soldiers behind him – 'your men.'

'Ach, never heed my men. Not to be met by gunfire and
cannon shot is courtesy enough for them, and they will
find their welcome hot enough in a few weeks when they
advance on German towns.' His eyes were still scanning
the gathering of teachers and college servants and he was
losing interest in the conventional civilities. 'But I do not
see my son here to greet me, nor yet his foster brother.
Seoras was ever a sluggard to rise from his bed, but I'm
surprised not to find Hugh here.'

There was a silence for a moment, and then Dr Dun
cleared his throat. 'Perhaps, if your Lordship would come
inside . . .'

Something in the principal's tone did not please MacKay,
and I wondered whether, on his march up from the quayside, some rumour about the disappearance of his son had
already reached him. He glanced at his men gathered behind
him. 'I take it the students are at their breakfast, or in private
study just now. Perhaps you would be good enough to have
my sons sent to me.'

Patrick Dun spoke again. 'Will you come in to the
college, your Lordship? Your men will be given food and
drink in the Great Hall, and we could talk at our ease in
the principal's rooms. There is something you need to
know.'

MacKay was utterly unmoving. His men were silent. 'My
men can go days without food and drink, or a roof over

their heads. They will stand here, as will I, until Seoras and Uisdean are brought before us.'

Dr Dun did not flinch under the Highlander's gaze. 'I cannot. Your son has been missing since Monday night, when he left an inn in the town.'

The soldier's jaw moved slightly. 'I see. And Uisdean?'

'Hugh was with him. He wasn't found until the next day. He has no memory of what happened and has been ill with a fever ever since.'

MacKay swallowed. 'Take me to him.'

'Your men . . .' began Peter Williamson.

MacKay scarcely glanced at him. 'My men will stand there until they are told to do otherwise. Now take me to my foster son.'

There was nothing more to be said. Dr Dun, intimating that MacKay should follow him, turned away towards the regents' tower. Not confident of what Lord Reay's reaction to the sight of Hugh would be, I went after him.

As we climbed the stairs, Dr Dun explained some of the details relating to Seoras's disappearance to his father, and tried to prepare him for the condition in which he would find Hugh. 'He was next to insensible when he was brought back to us. He seems to have lost all facility for the Scots tongue. One of the third-year students, a boy from Strathnairn, has been trying to talk to him, but can get very little of any use from him. He can recall nothing after he left the inn with Seoras, does not know where they went, how he came by his own injuries, or why he was found in the place or condition that he was. His clothes were sodden, and by the time we could get him out of them he already had the makings of a fever. I fear you'll find him ill-suited for visitors.' I could tell from his tone that Dr Dun was almost as concerned for Hugh Gunn as he was for Seoras.

It was indeed in my own old room, next to Peter Williamson's, that Hugh had been placed. An old woman from the town had been hired to watch over him through the night. A fire burned in the hearth and the shutters were tight shut against the icy air. The one candle that flickered as we entered the room did not cast its light far. On the cot that had been set near the fire, a man I would not have recognised as Hugh Gunn shifted and groaned slightly, his mouth moving in words incomprehensible to me. There was bruising around his jaw and on his neck, and cuts, bandaged now, on his hands. His cheeks were flushed and his lips cracked and dry. His face was distorted by some image that seemed to torment him from behind closed eyes.

The small room was made smaller by the entry of Dr Dun, Lord Reay, and myself. The principal had murmured to me as we entered the room, 'Stay close to his Lordship, Alexander: I want to know what is said between them.'

And indeed, Lord Reay did address Hugh Gunn in the Gaelic language. If any of us had harboured fears that the man would blame his foster son for the disappearance of his son, we were wrong. So soft did he speak at first that I could hardly catch the words, words in a savage tongue from a man at home in the company of kings, repeated over and over.

'Uisdean, my boy, my son. What have they done to you?'

Forgetting where he was a moment, he turned and said something to the old woman who had been sitting with Hugh. Panic flickered on her face because she did not know what he was saying.

'She does not understand, your Lordship,' I said, 'but I believe the fever only came full on him in the night.'

'And why is there no doctor here?'

The principal intervened. 'I am a physician . . . the woman has been instructed . . .'

Lord Reay looked at him with undisguised fury. 'The woman be damned. You,' he said, addressing me once more in Gaelic. 'Go out and call for my own doctor. Lose no time.'

I went without question and was back within three minutes with a man who looked like he could wrestle a black bull single-handedly and have the better of the encounter. He was dressed as one of the common soldiers, not like MacKay and his officers. He exchanged a few words with his chief before bending close and beginning to examine the boy.

'This is your physician?' Dr Dun did not attempt to mask his incredulity.

'Ossian's family has served the MacKays as doctors for as many generations as there have been generations. His son will serve my son. There is no man with whom I would more readily trust my life.'

I remembered it from Ireland, the hereditary septs of doctors, lawyers, genealogists that served the leader of a clan. Lord Reay's Lowland dress and manner, his reputation across Europe, had deceived me into forgetting for a moment what he really was – a Highland chief.

The principal was evidently not persuaded by what he saw before him. 'Yes, but does this man – the folk ways have their uses, but . . .'

The man named Ossian turned around and fixed Dr Dun with a long gaze before saying, in Latin that would not have been out of place on the steps of the Senate of Rome, 'My father and grandfather and their fathers and grandfathers before them were as learned as any doctors in Europe. I learned from them on the Braes of Ben More and in the valley of Strathnaver, but if it will put your mind at ease on the matter, I also studied in the schools of Montpellier and Padua. I have attended to cattlemen and fishermen, princes and kings. I have known Hugh Gunn since the day he was born.' And then he called to the old nurse and began to give her instructions, in Scots, as to what she was to bring to him.

As the doctor attended to Hugh my ear became accustomed once more to the words of their Gaelic tongue. Ossian would murmur phrases in Latin, the names of medicines and authorities, committing things to his mind, but these phrases would be interspersed with more deliberate utterances to Hugh himself, reminding him of incidents from his and Seoras's common boyhood, ploys they had been involved in, scrapes they had got in to, and I realised he was trying to find some connection, some common ground, that might spark off in Hugh's mind a recollection of what had happened on the night of Seoras's disappearance. But there was nothing, save a repeated jumble of words which I could not understand.

'Loose the horse?' said Ossian. 'What horse, Uisdean? Whose horse?'

But Hugh just kept repeating the same words again and again.

Lord Reay shook his head impatiently. 'Horse theft. Seoras has too much of his grandmother's Gordon blood in him. Be it horses, cattle or land, they cannot keep their hands from what is not theirs. If I find this is the tail end of a thieving escapade, I'll tan that boy's hide for a saddle when I lay hands on him.'

'You think Seoras is – responsible – for all of this?'

MacKay turned impatient eyes on me. 'Of course he is responsible. It would not be the first time he has laid himself low for a few days until trouble has passed. What else would it be?'

I looked to Principal Dun and he asked the old woman to leave us. When she had gone he said, 'Your Lordship, forgive me for what I must tell you, but there can be no point in dissembling. It has come to be believed that your son must be dead, murdered, and that Hugh Gunn, by some means or another had a hand in it.'

The colour that drained from Lord Reay's face seemed

to take with it every particle of warmth that was in the room. There was no movement save the occasional shifting of the sick boy in the bed. In the foster father's eyes I saw the cold wrath of a northern storm.

'Who has spoken of murder?'

Dr Dun replied. 'It is all the talk of the streets, but the magistrates too have begun to consider the possibility – likelihood, in fact. Hugh has clearly been in a fight, and he was the last person to be seen with your son – he was sober whilst Seoras was not. Mr Seaton here was witness to their last exchanges in the inn. I think it likely that you must prepare yourself for grief. Even if he is not dead, should Seoras have been lying somewhere since Monday night, in the cold we have had . . .'

Lord Reay spoke slowly. 'If my son is dead, it will be none of Hugh's doing.'

Dr Dun was hesitant. 'They were known to have fought.' Then he looked directly at Lord Reay. 'They did little else.'

Here I thought the soldier would explode. 'Fight? They were foster brothers. What else should they do? Write sonnets? Play the lute? We have women in Strathnaver to do our embroidery!'

The physician got up without speaking and left. Lord Reay seemed barely to notice. He turned his attention once more to me. 'Tell me what happened in the inn.'

And so I told him almost all that had passed in Downie's Inn. But it was not all that I had told Dr Dun, and Dr Dun said nothing to correct me, for I suspect he understood the thought behind my deceit. I did not tell him that I had come upon Hugh in the act of signing up for Ormiston's regiment. I feared he would take it as a betrayal. The next few moments proved me right.

Dr Dun, who had remained by the doorway for much of the time, said, 'It may be, you know, that no harm whatsoever has come to Seoras, and I pray God it is so.'

Lord Reay looked away from the boy on the bed to the principal. 'You think he has gone of his own accord?' Some of the anger was out of him now, and he seemed almost ready to consider the possibility of something better.

'He may have signed up with the lieutenant . . .'

Those words were enough. Lord Reay dropped Hugh's hand and stood up, all trace of benignity gone. 'My son,' he said, a rolling anger in his voice, 'the son of Donald MacKay of Strathnaver, will serve in the *Garde Eccosaise* and then go to the German lands and fight in his father's old regiment, as will Uisdean here, God willing. I was Colonel of the Scots Brigade in the service of Gustav Adolph of Sweden. Wherever else Seoras might be, he is not on the recruiting ship of a minor officer of my regiment.'

At that moment, the physician re-entered the room with four of MacKay's soldiers behind him. Without reference to Patrick Dun or myself, two took up their position outside of the door, the other two inside. The principal cleared his throat.

'You cannot post armed men here in the college. We are

under the jurisdiction of the burgh council, and I cannot authorise the presence here of these men.'

Lord Reay looked him full in the eye. 'Authorise what you will, but there are almost forty of my men in your courtyard, who will only be leaving on condition that these men stay. I can assure you, and any other power in this land, that neither your council nor anyone else will put manacles on this boy's hands.'

With some final words of reassurance to an unhearing Hugh, and instructions to his physician, MacKay left, a living reminder that the law of Scotland, even now, was only as strong as a nobleman's arm.

I should have been angry, insulted for the privileges of my college, the claims of my town, but instead I felt a strange surge of admiration for this man who valued loyalty and faith above the dry ink scrawled by long-dead clerks on rolls of parchment. More than that though, I too could not believe that the death of Seoras MacKay – for dead I was certain he was – was the doing of the boy who lay, hurt and fevered, on the bed in front of me.

7

The Recruiting Sergeant

The departure of Lord Reay left the college in a heightened state of tension, worse than the days of waiting for his arrival. An emergency session of the burgh council was held, and by midday it was made known to us that the provost and magistrates had agreed to allow Lord Reay's men to search every property in the burgh in the hope of finding Seoras. The principal, anxious that all our boys should be safely accounted for, decreed that those who lodged out in the town were to be brought within the safety of the college walls until the Highlanders and the recruiters had left.

The principal and all the other teachers would remain in the college, but it was understood that I was reluctant to leave my wife and family alone for even a night. Four years ago, one of my fellow regents, driven mad by spite and malice, had assaulted her in our home and left her near for dead. If ever I had to be away now, she and the children moved into the home of William Cargill. She, who had been so independent before, never argued now that there was no need. But the day had been so busy I had not fore-warned them, and so they were at home alone. It was well after ten at night that the porter unlocked the gates for me, and that I stepped out into the silent town.

Again, just as I had been on the previous night, I was taken by a desire to be alone a while. Between my day at the college and my nights at home, there seemed to be no time at which I could give proper thought to the changes that were being wrought in my life. I knew that once I had my manse there would be more space for our family, and even a room to myself where I might study and pray in peace. I looked back to the roofs of the Marischal College as they rose above the houses on the Broadgate. For nine years now, that place, that rabble of buildings surviving from the days of the Grayfriars who had first inhabited them, patched and added to over the years as the college expanded, had been a foster parent to my adult self. And yet, for all that my longest-held dream was about to be realised, I felt a knot of apprehension in my stomach as to how I should manage, cut adrift from it, when in a few weeks' time I walked out of those gates a regent of Marischal College no more.

The town I walked through had its own concerns. It was a place waiting, but for what I did not know – for soldiers in the night, for what tomorrow might bring. Candles burned in windows where usually there would be none at this hour – a single light in each home, godly citizens of a godly burgh, warding off the darkness. On the Guest

Row – *the Ghaist Row*, or Way of the Spirits, as our fore-bears had called it – lights at upper windows sent flickering shadows on half-hidden courtyards and narrow closes. I did not look up at Baillie Lumsden's house, afraid of the ghosts of my own life residing there, the memories that had been stirred in me by the face of Isabella Irvine. Perhaps it was a good thing that I had so little time to give thought to my own life, for things I had thought buried were coming back to haunt me, and I knew they could bring little that was good to the life I lived now.

My way became darker as I left the Guest Row and turned on to Flourmill Lane. The blades of the mill, caught white in the moonlight, creaked, not quite still at the other end of the lane, like a ship waiting in an unnatural harbour. I could see no one out in the lane, but again I felt that I was being watched. I slowed my pace and walked more carefully, taking the time to glance in each doorway, each pend, that I passed. No one. By the time I reached the entrance to our court, I was chiding myself for my fool-ishness and more concerned with getting out of the cold than with whoever else might be out on the streets tonight. Just as I turned under the archway, a sound stopped me, some movement at the mouth of the close across the lane. I turned around but saw nothing – an animal, a trick of the mind.

The door was locked, as it always was now after dark, and I found the fire almost dead and the two younger chil-dren fast asleep in their bed. A candle had been left for me in the middle of the table, and I lifted it to guide me up the wooden stairs. Zander murmured something to himself and turned over as I held the light above his cot on the upper landing, but he did not wake. The door to our bedchamber was open, and the blue light of the moon streamed across the rush matting of the floor, but the bed was empty. I pushed the door open wider and found Sarah standing silently with her back to me, by the gable window that looked on to Flourmill Lane. Her voice was dull. 'He is there.'

'Who? Who is there?' I went to the window beside her.

'In the close mouth across the street. He's been there, watching, for the last two hours.'

I was looking at her face, a study in terror, and not out at the window. 'Who, Sarah?'

'There,' she said, pointing, 'there. The recruiting sergeant.'

I went closer to the window to look, and as I did so, a figure stepped from the close mouth in to the open lane. He wore no cloak but a thick leather buff-coat. His hat was low on his head, but for a short moment he lifted his face, half-covered by the patch over his left eye, to the full light of the moon and slowly raised his arm in salute. He held my eye for a moment after he lowered his arm and then he moved away into the night.

I had not yet removed my boots and was at the top of the stairs before Sarah caught me.

'Alexander. Stop. Where do you think you're going?'

'I'm going after him,' I said quietly.

'After him? You cannot! Have you gone mad?'

I lifted her restraining hand from my chest and went past her.

'Alexander!' she cried.

'He has come for me, Sarah. He has come for me.'

A cat from the forestairs next to our house squalled angrily as I disturbed her in pursuit of some prey and I heard my Davy stir in his bed, calling out for his mother as I closed the door behind me, but I did not wait or turn back. I turned right at the top of the pend, in the direction I had seen the sergeant head. At first, coming to the fork of the Netherkirkgate, I could not tell where to go, whether up towards Grayfriars or down to St Nicholas Kirkyard. And then I saw him: he had paused a moment by the wall of Lumsden's house on the Guest Row, and after making sure that I saw him, he moved off again. A curious, fast, limping gate. The gait of a wounded man who had learned to overcome his wounds, and in that gait I could almost recognise the walk. I quickened my pace and he did his, so that thirty yards of distance remained resolutely between us. He paused again, momentarily, looking over his shoulder at me before crossing the Broadgate and making off in the direction of the Castlegate. I followed as fast as I could, but still I did not gain on him. By the time he had passed in front of the vast edifices fronting the Castlegate – the Earl Marischal's town house, the tolbooth, the courthouse – and crossed towards Futty Wynd and the gate to St Ninian's Chapel I no longer wondered where he was going: I knew. And he knew that I knew it. He was making for the Heading Hill.

I lengthened my stride, and each step took me backwards in time. I thought not, as I had done when a young man, of the gruesome deaths, deserved and undeserved that had been meted out to the burgh forefathers in that place, but of the possibilities, the dream of a future that I no longer had. As the frosted moss gave way beneath my boots, I felt the spring of it in the warm sunshine under my bare heel and sole. The fresh salt smell of a winter sea gave way to the summer scents of clover and thyme. I turned only once to look at the burgh below me, the spire of St Nicholas standing clear in the night sky as it had done then, the new roof of the Marischal College library, restored at last after the fire that had ravaged it.

I crested the hill so that I could no longer see the burgh behind me, only the land to the south and the sea to the north and east. The North Sea, that had called too loud and too often. It was there still, the bank in the hollow that made for a natural hide, and he was there, waiting. I stopped about ten yards from him. He stood up slowly, carefully, and turned to me, the hat laid aside, the needless bandage removed from his eye. He extended his hand a little and opened his mouth as if he would speak. I did not hear him, I could not hear him. The world before me blurred and I could not see him. I fell to my knees and cried.

He was down beside me in a moment and I felt the strong arms around me, the beat of his familiar heart. My whole body was wracked with shaking, cut off in itself from the cold of the cold night. It seemed the breaths I took would not go to my lungs. I heard the smile in the golden voice. 'It was always you who looked after me,' he said. 'How are we to manage if that has changed?'

The laugh that lurched from my throat helped me to master my own breathing, and I managed to look up into his face at last. A ravaged face. Disease had been there, and shot, the blade of a sword or knife. But a beautiful face still, alive in the eyes that were whole and undamaged, and in the ungovernable curve of the mouth. The face I had last seen fourteen years ago, and which I had thought I would never see again. One word was all I could manage. 'Archie.'

He smiled again and hoisted me to my feet. 'Aye Alexander, Archie. It has been a long road home.'

8

The Devil's Recruit

Fourteen years it was since I had last seen Archie Hay. Fourteen years, since that damp, dark morning when we embraced on the quayside of Aberdeen as he was about to embark on the ship that would carry him to Denmark, and sworn, as we had done so often in our young lives, our everlasting brotherhood. It had been three years later that the messenger I had every day dreaded had banged on my door demanding I should make haste to Archie's home at Delgatie, and his parents and sister, for Archie, he told me, was dead.

For almost two years we had heard nothing, save that he was wounded at Stadtlohn, where Christian of Brunswick's army, in which he served, had been decimated by the Catholic Imperial forces under old General Tilly. Christian's army had suffered six thousand dead and four thousand taken prisoner that day, and for long we had persuaded ourselves that Archie had been among the latter. Lord Hay would happily have sold every last stone of Delgatie and the souls of everyone in it to ransom his son, but no such ransom was ever asked, and then had come the news that it never would be.

News of his death had torn the heart out of his family, and what had come to pass afterwards meant that the woman I loved and the calling I had worked my whole life to attain were lost to me. For I had loved Archie's sister Katharine, and she me, and we had fondly believed we might marry when Archie returned to take his place as his father's heir. But on news of his death, my Katharine went from being indulged daughter to the hope and future of her family and their name, and the penniless divinity student who had been welcome as their son's friend was not welcome as her husband. When her father learned that she had anyway come to my bed, he had banished her to a marriage, far to the south, with a much older kinsman, and denounced me before those who held the keys to my ministry in their hands. Bitterness and despair had been my companions for long afterwards, until the love of good friends, and of Sarah, who was now my wife, had lifted them from me.

And yet, here he sat now, by my side, and even through our clothing I felt the warmth of the blood that pumped in his veins. Archie Hay. A living, breathing man. No ghost, no spirit: I knew the very scent of him. He waited, almost scared to speak, it seemed, as my eyes took in the truth of the sight of him.

'It cannot be.' My words were barely audible. 'They told us you were dead.'

He looked away to the sea before he answered.

'I was dead. Not as you thought, perhaps. But I was dead to all I had ever been before I went to the wars.'

I did not understand him. 'But how? We waited . . . surely you knew that we waited, we would never have given up . . .'

He shook his head. 'I know that, Alexander, but the man who was carried insensible from the field of Stadtlohn twelve years ago was dead before he ever saw it.' He opened a flask of brandy and offered me some, before drinking himself. 'In a battle, some men desert, others are taken prisoner, or wounded and never found by their comrades. There are those in the field who will not hear the drummer beat the retreat, or will not see their comrades through the smoke and dust: they will be left behind. At Stadtlohn, I was one such. The last thing I saw was the cannon ball that had taken half my knee take the heads off six of my men. After that, I remember nothing until I woke to find myself in the barn of a kindly German peasant who had found me close to death after the rest of my regiment was long escaped into Holland. His old wife nursed me several weeks, in memory of their own son who was lost to them in some other war many years before, and when I was recovered, they urged me to go home.' He smiled. 'I told them I would, for their sake, for their son's. I knew that I never could. I found my way to Mansfeld's army, and heard news of my own death from an English officer there who did not know who I was. And so, one freezing winter's night with little food and less pay, Captain Archibald Hay of

Delgatie died and Sergeant John Nimmo, whose family were of no account and who was not given to seeking promotion, was born.'

'Nimmo?'

He shrugged, the old grin on his face. 'It was the nearest I could get to Nemo. I did listen to old Gilbert Grant in that schoolroom in Banff sometimes, you know.'

Nimmo. Nemo. No one.

Still I did not understand. 'But why? Because you were rumoured dead you thought you could not come back alive? Good God, Archie, your parents . . .'

'My parents would not have known the man who returned to them, and neither would you.'

'But however bad your wounds . . .'

'Will you *listen*, Alexander? The wounds you see are but the outward show of something worse, something that does not heal. What I had seen even in those two years before Stadtlohn rendered me something else. I had thought I was ready for the bloodshed, the brutality, all in the name of honour. But I knew nothing; I was ready for nothing.' He took another drink from the flask. 'Do you know what happens in a siege?'

'Of course I know what happens in a siege.'

He shook his head. 'No you don't. You don't know what happens to the people of a town that is held as a stronghold by one army in the face of assault by another.'

'I know that eventually, when there is no food or water left, and no sign of relief, the commander of the town will surrender, or the opposing forces will undermine or storm the walls.' He was listening to me with almost dead eyes that registered only disappointment. 'Archie. I'm not a fool. I know you will have lost comrades, seen men maimed . . .'

'Oh, I have,' he said. 'I have. But it is not that that I am talking about, for you expect that in war. What I had not expected was the sight of the inhabitants of a town we had just stormed or relieved. The first time, you know, I expected gratitude, a joyful welcome from the people we had liberated. I found instead creatures who could hardly stand up, near-skeletal mothers guarding the graves of their dead babies for fear they would be removed from the earth by others near starvation.' His voice was relentless, as if he had forgotten he was talking to me. 'I have, with my comrades, dug mass graves into which we threw a hundred bodies because there was no one else to bury them, and we had not the time to give them any more honourable a service.' Then he came to himself and looked up at me. 'Do you know, after the Swedish forces took Frankfurt an der Oder, it took six days to bury the dead? Six days.' His voice dropped. 'The worst were the times when the defending commander would not agree to terms.'

I did not want to know, but I knew I had to ask the question. 'And if he did not?'

'Then Hell was made real on earth. No quarter. For garrison or citizenry alike. Men, women, children slaughtered. Homes ransacked for every last thing of any worth that could be carried away. I have seen commanders powerless to stop it as their men turned to beasts before their eyes, young girls violated alongside their mothers, houses and churches burned.'

I could say nothing, and he continued. 'I have march'ed in armies from Prague to the Netherlands, from Sweden to Bavaria, Poland, to the very doors of the Habsburgs. I have looked on at the councils of kings. Nowhere is the soldier wanted, not by the townspeople they have come to protect or relieve, not by the peasants on whom they are quartered or whose lands are stripped bare that one army might have food and deny it to another. And I *am* a soldier. How could I have come back here? "With wolves we learn to howl and cry." That is what my commander said as he ordered one of our regiment shot for the rape of a Saxon farmer's daughter. He was right: every day we must guard ourselves against descending to the brutality of the beast. Every day. And the man who every day has to remind himself of that is no fit person to return to the society of friends and the love of the family into which he was born.'

I forced him to look at me. 'I do not believe that of you.'

'I think you must.'

'But Archie, you do not need to continue on that path. I know. *I know* that with God's help and the love of friends a man can put behind him the worst of himself.'

He said nothing, and I heard my voice rise in frustration. 'And so you just continue in that life? And you go with Ormiston to entice others in the same way?'

He sighed. 'No, Alexander, I do not. Not as you think it, anyway. I am as good a soldier as the next man, better than many. But the John Nimmo that I have become does not seek promotion. There are times when an anonymous man is of greater use to an army than a platoon of pikemen. I am a spy for my masters. The greater the intelligence I can bring them, the more I can misinform the enemy, the sooner this conflict will be brought to a close. I fight with my mind and my tongue now, not with my sword. Unless I have to,' he added in a way that gave me to understand this was not a rare occurrence.

'So why are you here with Ormiston?'

He shrugged. 'Chance. I have met in with him from time to time, in the course of my travels. However you might dislike him personally, he is a good soldier – driven.'

'How do you know I do not like him?' I asked, with an uneasy laugh.

'Hah! Because I know you, and I know the more the likes of Ormiston seek to please those around him, the less they will please you. And' – he cleared his throat – 'I was in Downie's Inn the other night and was able to witness your civility in making the acquaintance of the dashing lieutenant. It was all I could do not to cheer you on, so pleased was I to see how little you have altered. You are still the Alexander of old, and it is a long time since anything has warmed my heart so much as that.'

'You . . . ?'

He sported a huge grin now. 'Aye, at the top of the stair, in the shadows.'

I laughed, in spite of myself. 'I knew it, I knew it.'

'Did you, Alexander?'

I remembered now the movement that had caught my eye, the sense I had had ever since of being watched. And then I remembered what had been happening in the inn. 'But you recruit for Ormiston all the same, chance or no?'

He shook his head again. 'I rarely go among the recruits. This is only the second time I have returned to Scotland in fourteen years, the first that I have come here. I am with Ormiston only because I knew he was coming here, and I wanted a passage home. My mother died last year, as you know . . .'

'I was sorry for it.'

'I too, and every day has made me sorrier for the grief I gave her. I cannot do that to my father also, and have determined to see him one more time before he too passes.'

'But why like this – in secret? No one would expect the Archie Hay who returned from the wars to be the same as he who left for them.'

He raised a sad eyebrow. 'Wouldn't they? But you and I would know, just how greatly he was altered, and we would mourn a second time the Archie that was gone. I do not think I could live day to day with that grief and the knowledge of it in your eyes. He will only live, as he was, in our minds if we let him lie in peace in the mud of Stadtlohn.' He shivered against the cold, and passed me the brandy bottle. 'Besides, I will have enemies, enemies to my cause. I'll be of little use to the world of espionage should my identity be revealed here.'

I could not argue with him about that. The north still crawled with Papists who took heart from the reverses of the Protestant forces in Europe since the death of the great Swedish king, Gustav Adolph, and would not scruple to tell their contacts on the continent of the resurrection of Archie Hay.

'So what will you do?'

'I will ride out to Delgatie in a few nights' time, when the full moon has passed and I can do so in greater darkness. I will spend one night there with the old man, tell him whatever lies it comforts him to hear, and then I will be away with Ormiston when he has finished his recruiting, on the first favourable tide.'

I nodded, not really listening, trying to take in the fact that the friend I had thought lost was not returned for good, but would soon be gone again.

I think he guessed my thoughts, for I felt his arm around me as he continued. 'But before then, I thought God might grant me a few hours, a few evenings, with the friend I have loved more than any other, and who knew me when I was a better man.'

The brandy flask was long empty by the time I made my way back down in to the town, more than two hours later. If there were rumours at the session of St Fittick's about demonic goings-on in the kirkyard at Nigg, worse might have been imagined by any unwary passer-by on the Heading Hill that night. The worst said and left in its proper place, we had moved on to Archie's eager enquiries for news of old friends, and then, as such things must, to reminiscence of events past. Voices that had been low and measured became louder and more careless, smiles turned to laughter, memories of long-gone nights brought snatches of song. And then we had come to happy silence, and I realised that for all he had asked me about William Cargill and Elizabeth, about John Innes, Dr Jaffray and other old friends from Banff, he had asked not one question about me.

'Archie,' I began.

'Yes?'

'Two days ago, at the quayside, when the lads from the school were down looking at the ship . . .'

His eyes softened. 'I met your son.'

'He is . . . his mother, my wife . . .' I did not know how to say it.

He put a hand on mine. 'I know about Katharine. I know what happened to you both. May God forgive me, and I have often prayed that you, and she, might, but I knew, when I decided never to go back to Delgatie, that what we three had dreamed of could not be. You lost my sister, and much else besides, and I knew it would be so, and I sit before you now and tell you that I am sorrier for that than almost anything else I have done.'

He did not ask, directly, my forgiveness. On this hill,

sheltered a little from the wind but not the night's raw cold, I remembered things, feelings, faces, her face, that I had schooled myself, forced myself, over the years not to think on, to the point where they really had become just memories, nothing else. But tonight, for the first time in years, I felt the cold shock of them once more.

Archie watched me uneasily, waiting for something from me. At length I found what I thought might be the right words. 'What happened, or did not happen, was God's will, and what was not His will was my doing, not yours. I – I cannot speak for Katharine . . .' I looked at him, but his expression remained the same and he offered me nothing, 'but in my own life there have been . . .'

'Compensations?' he suggested.

'No, not compensations.' The word suggested something inferior, something that might be a palliative, go some way towards making up for what had been lost. 'New, unforeseen directions. Blessings I could never have looked for.'

Archie nodded. 'She is a beauty, Alexander, a rare beauty. Do not take offence, now, but if I had been here, I'll wager I would have given you a run for her affections.'

I laughed. 'You would have run, all right; Sarah would have seen through your wiles in moments, and what she did not see, Elizabeth Cargill would have lost no time in telling her. What she sees in me, I still do not understand.'

'Ach, you are not the worst, I suppose.' He hesitated. 'And the boy?'

'He is not mine. Sarah was a servant in the house of Gilbert Burnett in Banff.'

'The stonemason?'

'Yes.'

I did not need to explain further. Archie spat. 'It is a wonder no one has murdered him by now.'

I remembered a night when a friend of ours almost had, but I would tell him of that some other time.

'He is a fine boy though, and named for you. He will do you credit – I could see that. But your fiery dame – and I think she was near enough coming out at me with a poker tonight, for I know she saw me – has another two that clamour about her skirts, and they have the look of Seatons if ever I saw them.'

I had trouble finding my voice. 'Will you come to the house, Archie?'

He was up on his feet before the words were fully out of my mouth. 'Tonight?'

I laughed. 'Not tonight, they are all abed; all except Sarah, I suspect, and she will need a deal of bringing round and explaining to first – she's not always wont to listen at a first telling.'

'In my experience, too many of them listen too much, and hear more than has been said. But yes, another night. I forget, you see, that others do not live as I do, and that night and day are not simply degrees of concealment.'

It was settled between us that he should come to our house at eight o'clock the following night, and then we went our separate ways, I to my home and my watchful wife, he to his ship.

She was waiting, of course she was waiting. When I saw the light glow from our window as I turned in to the close, I could have cursed my stupidity. I should have taken a moment to tell her there was nothing to fear, that I knew who it was. For all I could tell, she might have sent William, or even the watch, after me. At best, she would be in that little house, frightened for my life.

She was there, at the table, and her face slumped in to her hands when she saw me.

'Thank God.'

I went quietly to her and took her hands. The fire had been long dead in the hearth and she was chilled to the bone. 'Sarah, I am so sorry. I should have told you.'

'Told me what?' she said.

'That there was no danger. That I knew who he was and that he meant me no harm.'

She straightened herself, fully awake now. 'The recruiting sergeant? You know him? But how can you know him?'

I took a deep breath. There was no easy way to say it, no lead-up that could prepare her. 'Sarah, do not be frightened by what I'm about to tell you: it's Archie.'

Her face blanched and her lips moved, but no words came out. I tightened my grip on her hand but she pulled it away. 'It cannot be,' she said at last, her face contorted in incomprehension, 'It cannot.'

'He didn't die, Sarah. It is him, flesh and blood. No impostor. He has been so altered by the war – he chose not to come back.'

She stood up, nearly knocking over the chair on which she had been sitting. 'No, it cannot be,' she repeated. 'Because then you . . .' She shook her head at me, horrified almost. 'You, and I . . . the children. No. You are lying. It cannot be so.'

I reached out for her but she stepped back from me as if it was I who was the spectre. 'None of this would be.'

'Sarah.' I reached for her, but I did not even know if she was listening to me. 'What would or would not have been is of no matter. None. It was God's will and God's purpose that I did not know. Only what *is*, now, matters.'

She stared at me, and it was a moment before I understood what I had said wrong. 'To you, perhaps,' she said quietly, before taking the candle and walking up the stairs.

As I sat in the darkness, in the cold stillness of the house, staring uselessly into the ashes of the dead hearth, it came to me at last what I had done: I had not told her that even had I known, in time, that Archie lived, I would have chosen her anyway. For years now, when I thought of it at all, I had believed that myself. But that was when I had believed Archie dead. Now that I knew he had lived all these years, I knew in my mind and my heart that I could not, in God's truth, have told her that I would have chosen her.

9

The Schoolmistress Trials

I had held Sarah through the night, and while she had slept, eventually, I had not. In the morning, we moved uneasily around one another, our conversation stilted until I had, almost out of the blue, told her that Archie was to come to our house that night. After her initial shock and disbelief, she had asked me more questions, and by the time I left for the college she had accepted that there could be no danger in it and was, I thought, almost looking forward to meeting the man of whom I had so often spoken.

After the disruptions and revelations of the night, the last thing I wanted was to be forced to listen, five times over, to the listing of the virtuous living of five young women, to hear proofs of their competency in letters, their frugality – this a particular concern of the burgh fathers – and to examine minutely their dexterity with a needle. Dr Dun, however, would not listen to my pleas that another might be sent in my place to represent the college at the trials for Lady Rothiemay's schoolmistress.

'Katharine Forbes specifically requested you, Alexander.

She seems to have conceived a liking for you, and it is not an accolade she bestows lightly, I can assure you. And I, for one, am not the man to cross her.' He cleared his throat and looked up from the papers he had been arranging on his desk. '*If* it was essential that you spent an evening carousing, you would have done better, I think, not to do it on the night before these trials.'

I was astounded, and could not see how he had guessed at my activities of the previous night. Then a thought struck me that chilled me. 'Were you on the Heading Hill?'

He grimaced before replying. 'If you think I have been amongst scholars my entire life without being able to tell when a man has spent an evening in drink, you know me very ill. But the Heading Hill?'

I opened my mouth to answer him but he held up a hand. 'Tell me no more. What I do not know I will not be constrained to lie to the session about, but for God's sake, Alexander,' he put down the papers in frustration, 'you are to be inducted as a minister of the kirk in a few weeks' time: this is not the time to revert to the behaviour of an undergraduate.'

I bowed my head in embarrassment in the manner of just such a creature. 'No, Sir.'

He nodded. 'Good. Now get yourself to Baillie Lumsden's house. Her Ladyship is not a person who likes to wait upon events – or tardy schoolmen.'

The guards at Lumsden's door had been warned of my coming and let me pass without any great degree of examination. The place was a warren of stairs, corridors, and inter-connecting rooms, and I had to descend by one turnpike from a floor I had reached by another before I found a servant who could tell me where to go.

When I was shown in to the Great Hall, I felt my shoulders relax and a great sense of relief spread through me to see that while the master of the house, in this instance representing the council, was already there, neither Lady Rothiemay nor her young companion, Isabella Irvine, were in sight.

Lumsden got to his feet and greeted me cheerfully. 'So, Mr Seaton, the short straw has fallen to you. And are you an expert on spinning, the sewing of a sampler, the making of a poultice, perhaps?'

'Her Ladyship appears to be under the impression that I am,' I said quietly, not sure how far away the two women might be. Indeed, I had an irrational fear that she might be positioned secretly by the 'laird's lug' – the hidden listening place which all the houses of the powerful had, that the master might hear what was said of him by those who paraded themselves as friends.

Lumsden smiled. 'Never fear – you can speak freely for the minute. Lady Katharine and Isabella have gone to view George Jamesone's garden plans. Her Ladyship has a notion for improvements at Rothiemay, and was bent on quizzing the gardener. No doubt George has held up proceedings, as he is wont to do.'

Lumsden motioned that I should take the chair opposite

his, by the huge hearth that dominated the room. The tiles were Dutch Delft, and indeed, I would have guessed that much of the furnishing in the room was of the best Dutch, or occasionally, English, craftsmanship. It was a room in which men might be comfortable – solid oak rather than the delicate yews and walnuts of his wife's parlour across the landing; simple woodsmoke rather than the spiced pomanders that would catch in my throat after not many minutes' exposure. The east-facing windows, looking down on to all that passed on the Guest Row, afforded very little light, and only two candles in the long room were as yet lit. It was still morning but might have been a late winter's afternoon. I had been in this room several times before my recent encounter with Lady Rothiemay and Isabella, more often in my student days than recently, when the bailie had summoned his troublesome nephew, my good friend Matthew, and I had been persuaded along to give moral support. Matthew had been wilder, in some ways, even than Archie, although his wildness tended more to matters of religion and politics than to women and wine. There had been times, none the less, when all had come together in a dangerous mix that inevitably resulted in hot words, black eyes and burst lips. Only last night, Archie and I had laughed again at the memory of one of his fights with Matthew in which the senior student who had tried to break them up had come off worst of the three. Neither of us could remember the name of the lady whose questionable virtue had been the occasion for the fight.

Now, however, Matthew seemed to move in ever-deepening shadows. Archie hinted he had heard of him sometimes, but seemed reluctant to tell me any more, and I had not pressed him. As Deacon Gammie's insinuations at the session two nights earlier had reminded me, Matthew's attachment to the household of the Marquis of Huntly had never been a secret, and his crypto-Catholicism not nearly hidden enough. Only his contumacious absence in the face of repeated summonses from kirk session and presbytery, and the protection of his all-powerful patron kept him from punishments that lesser men would be forced to undergo. I asked his elder kinsman for his news.

Lumsden sucked at his lip and teeth a moment before answering me. 'Matthew is . . . much busied on the Marquis's affairs, which, thank the Lord, are not as dangerous now as once they were. Fortunately, the Marquis pays attention to his French associations, and is not so inclined, it would seem, to revive his family's – ah – *interests* in Spain. Spain being not entirely in vogue at the moment,' he added.

I did not need to remind Lumsden that Spain had very seldom been in vogue as far as our church or government might be concerned, regardless of the intriguing the Marquis's Gordon forebears had so enthusiastically indulged in. That we were now at war with Spain and ostensibly the allies of France could be seen as an unusual piece of political fortune for Huntly, hereditary Colonel of the *Garde Eccossaise*, the personal bodyguard of the kings of France.

'Matthew is in France, then,' I said.

Lumsden inclined his head slightly. 'I believe so. But you will understand it would not be wise for me in the current climate to show too great an interest in the politics outside our burgh.' He appeared to hesitate before continuing. 'I know I can speak in confidence to you, Alexander . . .'

I assured him that he could.

'Then I will tell you that the time is coming when we all may have to make the type of choices Matthew has not hesitated to make. I fear we have a king in London now who understands very little of this nation and its people, listening to men such as Laud who understands nothing of us at all, and does not see why he should try to. Charles Stuart should have a great care not to impose more on his Scottish birthplace than his people are prepared to accept, or it will not just be hotheads like my young cousin who will give him pause for thought.'

'He does not pay heed to the Privy Council?'

'On some matters, but in others he shows little interest, and it gives lesser men their heads to play their own interests in the face of natural justice.'

'As with Lady Rothiemay, you mean?'

He nodded. 'I have heard it rumoured that a letter is on its way to the sheriff of Banff charging him with apprehending Katharine Forbes and bringing her before the council, over her . . . activities.'

'She seeks only justice for her murdered son.'

He sighed. 'She will not get it. I know that, and so does she. But she will bow to no one.'

Through his frustration, his admiration for the woman was evident, and I suspected that even her enemies at times were caught up in the force of her charm.

'In you at least she has a friend and I pray God will reward you for your steadfastness, even if our present society does not,' I said.

He looked at me strangely. 'If we are not steadfast to our friends, Alexander, we render our pasts false and our futures empty.' He looked as if he would say more, but the sound of female voices drifting up from the stairway at the far end of the room took our attention. I do not know whether I or the master of the house was the quicker to sit straight in his chair. In a moment Lady Rothiemay appeared, closely followed by Isabella Irvine.

'Baillie, Mr Seaton, we have kept you waiting. Well, no matter, no doubt you have not been lost for conversation together.'

'We have been gossiping over old acquaintance, as men will do,' said Lumsden, standing to offer her his seat by the fire.

'Thank you. Jamesone had me standing nigh on half an hour with enquiries after my many relatives – there is no one with whom the man is not acquainted. And as for his garden schemes, it is a wonder he ever has the time to pick up a brush.' She removed her calfskin gloves and stretched still elegant hands towards the flames. 'And yet I should not grumble, for half an hour of his conversation is of greater interest than three hours' worth from many another man.'

Lumsden raised his eyebrows at me in such a manner that I was hard put to keep a straight face. 'And did you manage to meet with his gardener?' he asked her.

'What? Oh yes. An admirable fellow, Monsieur Charpentier. We shall have him out to Banffshire. He will find many commissions there amongst my friends.'

Isabella, slowly removing her outer garments, cast an eye at the walnut-panelled long clock in the corner. 'I think, if the women are here, we should begin.'

The candidates had been waiting in Lumsden's wife's parlour, and were now brought before us, one at a time. There were five women, whose ages ranged from about seventeen to forty, each dressed in what could only have been her best Sabbath attire. I recognised at least three of them – two widowed acquaintances of Sarah's and Elizabeth's, and Christiane Rolland, the French master's sister. Each interview followed a similar pattern to the first. Lumsden, on behalf of the council, having already scrutinized their letters of recommendation, quizzed them further on their families, the length and nature of their attachment to the burgh, and their present circumstances. He then examined their understanding of basic accounts and the clarity with which they could present them. It fell to me, less as a college regent than as a soon-to-be-inducted minister, to enquire after their morals and their knowledge of the catechisms, before setting them to some small task that would give proof of their proficiency in letters. Isabella then questioned them closely on their facility in various tasks of household economy and practice, from the preparing of simples to the darning of a sock. Lady Rothiemay, to my surprise, said nothing at all. It was only when I caught the look in her eye as the third candidate, a narrow, joyless spinster well advanced in years, was undergoing her trial that I realised what her Ladyship's role in proceedings was: she was deciding if she liked them.

Christiane Rolland was the last of the candidates to come before us, by which time I was thoroughly regretting the amount of Archie's brandy I had drunk and the sleep I had not had. I had known Christiane since she had been a child of eight, and so paid little heed to her answers to Lumsden's questions on her eligibility for the post and her connections in the burgh. I already knew of her proficiency in letters and set her only a very small task, which she completed with less competence than I would have expected – the quill in her hand shaking a little, and the handwriting being consequently less legible than I knew it to be. Her answers on the catechisms were perfect, as had been those of all the women, and had it not been for the rigid form of proceeding that had been set down in advance, I would not have troubled to ask after her morals at all. And yet I had to, for form, and it must have been as plain to the three others in the room as it was to myself that these were the questions that gave Christiane Rolland the greatest discomfort of all. When I asked her, at the last, if she knew of any cause for which her good name and propriety of living might be called into question, she seemed for a moment at a loss for what to say. She looked down at the hands she was wringing in her lap, not, as the other women had done, directly at me. I posed the question again, as gently as I could. This time, she replied, haltingly and in a voice that was scarcely audible, 'I trust not, Mr Seaton. I . . . I trust not.'

There was nothing to do then but release her, before the tears that I thought I could glimpse beginning in her lowered eyes became evident to all.

There was silence for a moment after she closed the door. It was Isabella Irvine who broke it. 'I do not think she is well. Will I go after her?'

'Aye, Isabella. Do that.' Once Isabella had gone, Lady Rothiemay got up and stretched her back. 'Not well, she may be, but it is no sickness of the body that is troubling that girl. I know Isabella has conceived a liking for her, as I have myself, and I see from your manner of questioning that you share it, Mr Seaton, but she will not do: she will not do at all.'

I could not argue with her, and Lumsden, whose stomach had been rumbling alarmingly for the last quarter of an hour, was in no humour to. 'We'll have our dinner brought in and once we have some sustenance in us, we'll discuss your Ladyship's pleasure, though I must say, the matter seems plain enough to me.'

It was. Before dishes of pickled herring, bread, mutton with beans and a mint jelly had been set before us, or our goblets half-filled, it had been agreed that there could only be one choice: Ruth Grahame, a childless widow of about thirty-five whose husband had fallen, over a year ago, with the Swedish forces at Nordlingen. Of the other candidates, Lady Rothiemay pronounced one to be too young, one to be iniquitously connected to a family with whom her Ladyship had had dealings, and the third – the older spinster – to have 'the sourest face I ever saw this side of the Forth'. I knew Sarah would be pleased: Ruth Grahame was a friend of hers, and a woman who faced destitution if decent employment or a new husband could not be found.

Isabella rejoined us after about ten minutes. 'The other women are down in the kitchen, but I have settled Christiane in Mistress Lumsden's parlour.' She looked to Lumsden. 'I thought some rest and food might help her, and then I will take her home to her brother's house.'

'Of course, of course,' said Lumsden. 'Ring that bell there and get one of the maids to take her up something, but for goodness' sake have something yourself – you must be half-famished after this morning's proceedings. I would a hundred times rather sit through the Treasurer's report in Council than hear another word on the making of butter.'

An hour or so later, after the disappointed candidates had been dismissed and Ruth Grahame told her good fortune, I asked that I might have a few words in private with Christiane.

'It would hardly be decent, I think, that such a man . . .'

Lady Rothiemay silenced her. 'Such a man? Dear God, Isabella, his crime is nigh on ten years old, and a thing to be got over. He is a regent in the college, long married, and' – here she fixed me with a shrewd stare – 'I am *very* lately informed, soon to be inducted a minister of the kirk of this burgh. If the girl is not safe with him then there can be little hope for her.'

And so I was shown in to the warm and well-lit parlour in which Christiane had been left. The room was furnished for a woman: there were intricate crewel-work drapes at the window and an oriental rug on the floor that I was at a loss to avoid stepping upon. That Lumsden's wife was content to have this item underfoot rather than on a wall, or at the very least, draped over a table, spoke as much for his wealth as an examination of his accounts would have done. Christiane was seated on a light walnut chair by the fireplace, a dish of sowens untouched on the small side table at her elbow. She looked only a little better than she had done an hour before, and little further from the tears that had threatened her earlier.

She was startled out of some reverie by my arrival and made a flustered attempt to stand.

'Please, Christiane, sit back down a minute. I would like to talk to you, and then I will take you home to your brother's.'

She swallowed. 'There is no need, Mr Seaton . . . please do not trouble yourself.'

'There is no trouble in it, although there would be from your brother, I think, if I were to allow you to make your own way home when you are plainly ill.'

I knew she was not ill, but could not think how better to begin drawing out of her whatever it was that so troubled her.

'I . . . it is not that.'

'Then what, Christiane? I have known you many years now, and your brother. Whatever you have to tell me, you will be telling to a friend, not a college regent, nor minister, or anything else I might be to the rest of the town.'

She lowered her head, disconsolate.

'Christiane, whatever is wrong will not be mended by your misery.'

She looked at me now, with eyes that were red and tears that threatened to spill out here in the parlour. 'Then maybe it cannot be mended.'

'Christiane,' I said gently, 'I saw Louis the other night. He spoke of – problems – with two of his scholars. I may be wrong, for I am certain Louis has no idea of this, but does your distress have anything to do with Seoras MacKay?'

She nodded and dissolved into breathless sobs. When she had regained some of her composure she said, 'I think he is following me.'

'What?' I had been ready for many revelations, but not this one. 'But you know, surely, that Seoras has been missing for three days?'

'And I think he has been watching me for three days.'

I remembered her brother's nervousness on the night I had met him after the meeting of the kirk session, his vague suspicion that someone was watching his house. I had thought then that it might have been the recruiting sergeant; now I could not imagine what cause Archie would have had for a vigil over the French master and his sister – I could not think that he would even have known them, for Louis would have been barely nine when Archie had last set foot in Aberdeen. The idea that the unseen watcher might be Seoras MacKay had never entered my head.

'Why do you think it's Seoras?'

The colour rose in her cheeks and I thought I knew. 'Seoras made advances to you?'

She gave the merest nod, never lifting her eyes from the hands that twisted in her lap.

'You rejected him.'

'He could not believe it. I do not think it had ever happened to him before.'

'Did he give up?'

'For a time. It seemed to amuse him, and then . . .'

'Go on.'

'Then I think Hugh must have said something, must have told him how – how he felt.' She looked up, pleading. 'I am not that sort of woman, Mr Seaton. I do not look for the attention of men.'

I put a hand over hers. 'I know you do not, Christiane. Did Hugh also tell you of his feelings?'

She nodded miserably. 'It was horrible. He is so good,

so kind. He has spent his whole life in Seoras's shadow, and if I could have returned his affections, I would have done.'

'But you could not?'

She shook her head. 'It would have been to do him a disservice, and I told him that. He deserves better than me.'

'How did he take this?'

She lifted her head and looked me in the eye. 'With dignity, and as a gentleman.'

I could believe this, and I could have wished for Hugh that Christiane felt differently.

'But then,' she continued, 'Seoras began to allude to it, comments here and there, little mockeries. I did not rise to them and neither did Hugh. I think this annoyed Seoras more than anything else.'

I felt we were coming to the point. 'What did he do?'

She looked at me directly. 'He came after me all the more. He started to court me. He thought I would be flattered.' I saw in her face how wrong Seoras MacKay had been. 'I have never been so insulted in my life.'

'He did not try to force you?'

She said nothing.

'Christiane?'

'The last time. Before the lesson on Monday afternoon. Seoras arrived early when I was alone in the house. He was telling me how – practised – he was, how much he might teach me.' She closed her eyes as if she could still see him before her. 'He pulled me to him and began to kiss my neck. I struggled to get away but only managed to scratch his cheek, which made him laugh and hold me all the tighter. If Guillaume had not arrived back unexpectedly, I do not know what he would have done.'

'What happened when Guillaume came back?'

'Seoras let me go. He whispered to me that I might have the spirit to interest him yet. He said I should look for him, for I had begun to intrigue him, and little enlivened him more than the chase. Then he left, tossing a coin on the table as if I was . . . as if I was . . .'

'It is all right.' I knew it pained her greatly to talk of this, but there were other things I had to ask. 'What did Charpentier do?'

'Once he had assured himself that I was not harmed, he went out in to the street after Seoras, but he could not find him. He wanted to find Louis and tell him.'

'And did he?'

'I begged him not to. Louis has few enough pupils. He cannot afford to turn away those that might give offence to me, but he would have done.'

'And Hugh?'

She did not answer me, but chewed at her bottom lip.

'When did you tell Hugh, Christiane?'

'On Monday afternoon.'

'And how did he react?'

'He went into a fury. He swore he would kill him.' She looked up at me, pleading. 'He did not mean it, Mr Seaton – they were words said in heat. I think Seoras has done this – effected this disappearance – to draw trouble down on

Hugh. I have seen movement in too many shadows, at times when I have gone out on the street, when I have been in George Jamesone's garden with Guillaume and Jean, even today, in this house: movements, creeping about, whispers.'

She had her head in her hands and I could see her worries had brought her to the brink of exhaustion, and perhaps were threatening her senses. I had known Seoras for a wild boy, and thoughtless, sometimes, but I could never have imagined him so cruel. After what she had confided in me, I could not with any certainty tell her that he would not torment her, or Hugh Gunn, in the way she now imagined he was doing. All I could say was that I believed he would be found soon, dead or not.

Despite all she had just told me, her answer still shocked me. 'I wish I could care which it was.'

I was glad that Isabella Irvine chose that moment to appear in the doorway. 'Your brother is here to take you home, Christiane.'

I followed the two women back in to the Great Hall where Louis was waiting for his sister, and then I stopped dead as through the door at the other end of the room stepped Lieutenant William Ormiston, evidently having come in to the house by the east tower.

It took him a moment to arrange his face in an appearance of pleasure.

'Mr Seaton, I had not expected to meet you here.'

'Aberdeen is a small town, Lieutenant. I am to be found

in most places, at some time or another. I am on the point of leaving.' I put on my hat, but Lady Rothiemay spoke and I could not make my exit. 'It is Lieutenant Ormiston, is it not?'

'At your Ladyship's service.'

'Ah,' she smiled, a little dangerously. 'You know me then.'

It gave me some pleasure to see Ormiston deprived of his easy charm a moment as he struggled for some means of telling the most notorious woman in the north that there were few who did not know her. 'Your Ladyship is . . .'

'Infamous, I do not doubt. But you will not know my young companion. Isabella Irvine. This is Lieutenant William Ormiston, Isabella, who recruits our young men for service under Field Marshal Leslie in Sweden, if I am not mistaken, for the defence of our brethren abroad.'

Isabella dipped her head slightly at Ormiston's bow. He had not noticed the French master and his sister, and they had been forgotten by everyone else in the introductions, but Christiane had noticed him. She stared at him, then looked at Isabella, and her face was a picture of confusion. When she saw me watching her she quickly turned away, pulling on her brother's sleeve. Louis, not judging himself of interest in this gathering, quietly led her out of the room and down the west stairs.

I would have slipped out after them but Lady Rothiemay spoke again and I was trapped. 'I had not realised you already knew Mr Seaton here.'

'We have met,' said Ormiston.

Isabella lighted me with a glance. 'I do not imagine Mr Seaton was signing up for the wars.'

I was spared the difficulty of defending myself by Lady Rothiemay. 'Mr Seaton has his own battles to fight here, no doubt, and it will do Scotland no good to be denuded of all her young men. Nevertheless,' she turned her attention again to Ormiston, 'I hear volunteers for foreign service are not as forthcoming as they were in former years.'

'It is true,' the lieutenant conceded. 'The wars have gone on so long, and with such reverses for the Elector Palatine's cause, that most who were impassioned to fight for that cause are dead along with Frederick himself. The Protestant hopes that were raised by the triumphs of the King of Sweden fell with him at Lutzen, and it is no easy thing to revive them in the name of a little girl, or indeed a beautiful woman.' He spoke of the Swedish king's young successor, his daughter Christina, and of Frederick of the Palatinate's widow, Elizabeth Stuart, sister of our own king and a refugee in the Hague.

'Elizabeth Stuart has more mettle, I think, than did her husband,' said Lady Rothiemay. 'And now she must look to her son's interests, as I must to mine. My older son was cut off in the prime of his life, and my younger is only now entering upon his college studies, but I can promise you that he will one day serve your cause. In the meantime, I would advise you to look to the countryside around for what is not to be found here in the town. There are many shiftless bodies amongst the tenantry of my neighbours that are prone to turn to mischief if not suitably employed. A turn in your ranks would relieve this land of an unwanted burden. I am sure Donald MacKay would lend you some of his men to assist you.'

Ormiston looked now to Lumsden. 'Donald MacKay? Lord Reay?'

Lumsden nodded. 'He landed from Sutherland yesterday with forty men, on their way to join the recruit bound for Hepburn's regiment in France. He thought to have paid a visit to his son at the Marischal College, but the boy is missing. Lord Reay has sworn to search the town from top to bottom until he is found.'

Ormiston took a moment to digest this information. 'I should pay my respects to my colonel then, offer my assistance in the search for his son.'

'You served under his Lordship?' Lumsden enquired.

The lieutenant nodded. 'I went up the Great Glen, my brother and I, from Lochaber, to join his brigade at the first call, in '26. We sailed from Cromarty with many other Highlanders. Two thousand men, in all, he raised then. Within a year we were reduced to eight hundred, but we were not dismayed. I fought under him for Denmark and then Sweden; I fought under his command at Stettin, Damm, Colberg. My brother fell at Stralsund. I myself saw Lord Reay hold Oldenburg against Tilly's forces.' He was reflective. 'I owe him much. I will send to him, to offer whatever is at my disposal.'

'There will be no need for that,' said her Ladyship. 'We expect him within the half hour.'

'Here?' I interjected. 'He is searching the house?'

Lumsden laughed. 'You have a low enough opinion of me, I think, Alexander, if you think me a candidate for hiding renegade students from their fathers.'

'I am sorry,' I said, cursing again my foolish tongue. 'But I know that Lord Reay is bent on little else but finding his son.'

'As well he might be,' said Lady Rothiemay, 'but Donald has had as many enemies as I myself, and will come tonight to tell me what entertainment I am to expect at the king's pleasure.'

She had lost me, and I looked to Lumsden for some explanation. He glanced at Ormiston and made the decision to proceed. 'Five years ago, when Lord Reay was in London raising forces, at the Marquis of Hamilton's request, to go and fight for Gustav Adolph, a rumour was brought to him suggesting that Hamilton planned to use the forces in rebellion against the king himself. Lord Reay passed on this intelligence and instead of being rewarded for his loyalty found himself thrown in to the Tower of London for nigh on two years, by which time the Swedish king was dead and he himself was near ruined.'

Isabella Irvine placed a hand on Lady Rothiemay's shoulder. 'It shall not happen to you.'

Her Ladyship smiled grimly. 'You are young yet, Isabella, and I fear, in spite of all, too innocent. Listen tonight to what Donald MacKay has to say, and see if you do not then understand the iniquity of enemies who have the ear of power. You should realise by now that some in this world have to make their own justice.'

I had heard too much, and was eager not to be here when MacKay arrived. I hastily repeated my intention of leaving. I think that Lumsden was glad, for my sake, to see me go. He accompanied me as far as the stairs and murmured quietly to me as he did so. 'It would be better, perhaps, not to noise abroad all that you have heard in here today. Lady Katharine is not as prudent with her words as might be politic.' It was a warning that was scarcely necessary, and I assured him that no one would know from me that anything other than the selection of a schoolmistress had been discussed in his house that afternoon.

Lumsden bade me farewell, and as he turned back into the room neither he nor Lady Rothiemay can have seen what I saw, in the oval glass that hung on the wall across from the door. It was William Ormiston, feigning interest in the Dutch still life that hung above the sideboard on the west wall, delicately running the tip of his finger across the base of Isabella Irvine's exposed neck.

10

Night Visitor

He had charmed her, as I had known he would, and she delighted him, to the point where he could not take his eyes from her as she moved around the room, dishing out our supper, pouring ale into the beakers and refilling them time and time again, ushering Zander to his bed.

He alone of the three children had been still awake when the mysterious stranger had, as arranged, walked quietly, without knocking, into our home at eight o'clock that night. It had been on pain of every punishment, every deprivation of freedom and favour he had ever known, should he breathe a word of the night-time visitor to anyone – even to James Cargill – that Zander had been permitted to remain downstairs to meet Sergeant Nimmo. His excitement, when I had told him two hours earlier on his return from school who was to visit our house that night, had been such that he could not at first speak. He certainly could not eat. And then he could not stop speaking until the arrival, at last, of the sergeant had all but struck him dumb.

The time Zander had been permitted had gone by in a blur, for all of us, I think. For Archie, after initial, nervous civilities to Sarah, had given all his attention to the boy. By the time Zander had finally climbed the stair to his bed, any doubts his mother or I could ever have had as to what he would be had been quite thoroughly dispelled: he would be a soldier, and nothing else. There can scarcely have been a detail of the war craft of Gustav Adolph, mighty King of Sweden, Lion of the North, that the nine-year-old Zander Seaton did not know, a siege he could not describe, an enemy commander he was not ready to denounce.

Most of all, and what almost broke my heart to see, Zander was utterly transfixed by the beauty of Archie's sword. After his mother's initial protests, he was allowed to hold it, to feel its weight – surprisingly light – to be shown how a cavalry officer might thrust or cut with equal efficacy. After the boy had reluctantly trudged up the stairs, to dream more spectacular dreams than he had ever before imagined, I ran my finger over the flat side of the blade where Archie had left it resting on the table. With my finger I traced the finely engraved initials of my friend, and the words *sub jugum*, 'under the yoke', the motto of his family. The silver plate of the pommel was inlaid with three escutcheons in brass, the Hay coat of arms. I fitted my hand around the pommel, marvelling how it did not quite fit my grip, but did Archie's exactly.

'Has no one ever questioned how a simple sergeant came to possess such a weapon as this?' I said, turning it over so that the gleaming blade caught the light of the candle on the sideboard.

He smiled. 'Many times. I tell them it was gifted me by a grateful lieutenant on his death-bed. And it is true enough, for it is the only thing apart from my own body that was Archie Hay's and is now mine.'

I remembered my father's humility as Lord Hay, Archie's father, had had him present his parting gift to the heir who was going off to the wars. My father had protested that it was not his place, that he was a mere craftsman, but old Lord Hay had insisted all the same, saying he could not take the credit for the gift of such a master. And it was a masterpiece, surpassing any work my hammerman father had made before or after.

'It was the finest piece he ever made,' I said, 'and there was love for you in every beat of the hammer, every mark of the graver.'

'I know it,' he said. 'And they will have to kill me more than once to take it from me. But I'll tell you this,' he said, jerking his head in the direction of the stairs, 'blood or no, your father would have loved that boy.'

I knew this myself; I had thought it often. Zander was everything my father would have had me be. He had a spirit and a will to work and a zeal for adventure that I had never managed to muster. He would have served Archie as my father thought I should have served him: to the death. I knew also that if we had allowed it, Zander would have gone into the night and whatever might come with that man whose very name, but an hour before, had been unknown to him.

Sarah knew it too, but all apprehension on that score had gone from her – I looked at her face: Archie had won her also, utterly and absolutely. In another time, I was not sure I could be certain that she too would not have left me, without a backwards glance, for my best friend.

Sarah, I knew, had always thought of Archie as first the brother of Katharine Hay, and only second, a distant second, my friend. Within a few minutes, the utter lack of arrogance, the genuine warmth in his voice, his eyes, had changed that completely. Within less than an hour, they were easily familiar, as if they had known each other their whole lives.

'And how did such a length of misery as Alexander Seaton ever persuade one such as you to marry him?' he had asked her after Zander was gone to his bed.

'He promised me a fine manse and a seat at the front of the kirk,' she said, sweeping away bowls that were empty.

'Hah!' he laughed. 'He promised me a seat at the front of the kirk, too, but mine was to be a stool with three legs on it and a coat of sackcloth to go with it. Little wonder I fled to the wars.'

They had bantered a while about me and my many shortcomings, about Archie's trials in attempting to make a gentleman of me, and his eventual, evident failure. As Sarah was making ready to leave us for the night, he took her hand. 'He is the best man I know, and I could never have seen him happier, with anyone. You understand?'

'I understand,' she said at last, and his manner lightened again.

'But while he offered you a manse, I would have offered you kingdoms.'

She smiled at him. 'Too much has been lost already, I think, by women in search of kingdoms. Good night, Sir Archie.'

'Goodnight, Sarah.'

We watched her go up the stairs, the unconscious sway of her hips, the final, light touch of her hand on the banister. 'And to think she was only a few miles from Delgatie, on her uncle's croft. A woman like that might have kept me from the wars.'

I went to the sideboard to fetch the flask of brandy. 'Nothing could have kept you from the wars.'

'Do you think not?'

'I know it.' I poured him out a measure, and one for myself. 'You were always too restless. The best adventure was always the one yet to come. And you would never have settled with one woman – the minute you had won her you would begin to lose interest in her.'

'But perhaps the right woman . . . a life like this.' He looked around the room that served us as kitchen and parlour, with my two youngest children sleeping, warm and oblivious, in their box bed in the wall.

'This would have been too small a life for you, Archie,' I said, remembering his restless energy in the finest of castles, his lust to go ever further, ever faster on the hunt, his determination at the end of a night on one more song.

'Do you think so?' He was silent a moment, thinking, or remembering, it seemed, and for a while the room was filled only by the crackling of the logs in the hearth and the breathing of the children. 'And yet it is not too small a life for you.'

I was about to say that no, it was not. To tell him again of the kirk that was to be mine, the house on the Gallowgate, where there would be many rooms, and my children would not have to eat, sleep, live in the one. But he knew all that, and that was not the life of which he spoke. He was asking me about the life I had never lived.

'It . . . sometimes I wonder how it might have been, had I heeded Jaffray.'

He was surprised. 'What, turned away from your calling? Gone to further studies overseas?'

I played with the half-empty tumbler before me. 'I would have seen the world that I will not now see. The seas the merchants sail to, the towns and peoples other scholars come back so full of, felt the heat of the sun on my face.'

'And the frost that would take the toes from your feet. I have been as far to the south as Naples, as far east as Muscovy. I have seen men poisoned by snakes and mauled by bears. I have set light to libraries filled with more knowledge than a thousand years could garner, and I can tell you, at the end there is only what you always tried so hard to tell me.'

'What is that?' I said.

'Man. Fallen man. The world over. You might travel a thousand miles and never again find what you have here, Alexander. Think of it no more.'

We drank more of the brandy and then I changed the subject. 'When did you meet Ormiston?' I asked.

He smiled. 'Now that is a story.' He put down his glass. 'I told you how after Stadtlohn I had travelled eastwards, deeper into Germany, until I met in with Mansfeld's forces? I fought under Mansfeld for over two years, as he trailed around the battlefields and towns of Europe, always too little and too late. I was with him when he attempted the relief of Breda, and there to see that city fall. I was with him at Dessau, when Wallenstein defeated us. Half our number went over to the Scots and Irish Catholic forces under Daniel Hepburn. I stayed, like the fool I was. I had done better to go with them. Then I would never have seen Weisskirchen. Dessau was in April of '26. In June of that year, I was at Weisskirchen.'

He did not need to tell me of Weisskirchen; all Europe knew of it: Imperial musketeers had garrisoned the town, refused to give entry to Mansfeld and his Protestant troops, who had, after being once repulsed, forced entry on the second attempt. For two hours, they had slaughtered every man, woman and child they could find, and then they had pillaged for two days.

Archie's hand, gripped around his glass, was shaking. 'I cannot describe it. People, human beings, utterly butchered.

Age, nor sex, nor creed mattered. I can smell the blood yet.' He pulled back the cuff of his left arm to reveal a thick purple gash. 'It was one of our own soldiers gave me that. With an axe. He was holding it over the head of a young woman, and I tried to take it from him.'

It was a wonder he had not lost his hand.

'And the woman?' I asked eventually.

He shook his head. And so, disgusted, he had walked out of Weisskirchen and sought better comrades and a better master. By the time Lord Reay's troops had landed on the Elbe, and then found service with the King of Denmark, Archie had already taken on his new identity: John Nimmo, the Scottish spy. There were Scots in the armies of both sides of the great struggle for the mastery of the German lands, the broken Holy Roman Empire, that raged to the very boundaries of Europe, and Archie had found no great difficulty in flitting from one place to another without drawing too much attention on himself.

'But did you not fear detection? John Gordon and Walter Leslie would have known you in a moment.'

Archie laughed at the mention of two old acquaintances of ours who had found their way in to the armies of the Catholic Imperialists. That they would not have recognised him was inconceivable. 'They are risen so high in the Emperor's service he has rewarded them with lands, titles, and money. Such men do not notice a humble pikeman who keeps his head down and does not draw attention to himself. But Alexander, you should know . . .' His voice was low now, but the burst of his laughter had woken Deirdre, and she cried out, frightened to see the stranger in her home in the night.

I soothed her until she at last went back to sleep. Archie said nothing all this time, but only watched us. There was a sadness in his eyes I had never seen before in all my long years of knowing him.

Fearing our evening was almost at an end, I added more coals to the fire, hoping the warmth and comfort of my home might persuade him to stay a little longer. Finally, after a long silence, he spoke. 'I had a daughter, once.'

I stopped on my way back to the table, not sure that I had heard him right.

'It is true,' he said. 'My Magdalena.' A half-smile came to his lips. 'You should have seen her, Alexander. There never was such a child. Eyes as blue as the brightest sapphire and hair in locks of ebony. Three years old, but she could sit a horse as well as I could myself. She pattered away in German, of course, but she would have done as well in the streets of Banff, for I taught her Scots and she was so quick and clever – cleverer than you, even. She would have been Queen of Delgatie.'

'What became of her?' I asked quietly.

'Dead,' he said. 'Dead.'

I hesitated. 'Her mother?'

'She too. All dead.' He swallowed some more of the brandy and, staring past me into the fire, told me. 'Her mother was a beauty, a Bohemian beauty. A burgher's daughter from Pilsen, wild as they come. I was quartered on her father's house, and well,' he grinned, 'as I said she was a beauty, and wild. I was never sorrier to leave a *dorp* than I was that one.'

'You took her with you?'

He shook his head. 'It was time for my regiment to move on, and I to move with them. I left Anna with an idea that I might return some day if God so willed it – for I still thought God took an interest in my affairs in those days – but that if He did not, then so be it. I marched with my comrades northwards, to Hesse and then to Brandenburg. After a while, I gave little thought to Anna, and lived for the concerns of the day, the hour.' He looked at me directly. 'You see, Alexander, a soldier never knows when he lays down his head at night, whether he will wake in the morning, or when he awakes, whether he is seeing his last dawn. There can be little time for regrets. But it seemed I had left Anna with more than a smile and a half-meant promise. I had left her with child.'

'She found you?' I said, astonished.

'Oh, she found me. Hundreds of miles from her home, beleagured in a field in Brandenburg, my Anna with her six-month belly found me. Her father – an old Hussite – had put her from the house, and I could hardly send her back to him, so she stayed. She joined with the other soldiers' wives, and when the time came for me to move, I found her a place in the service of my captain's wife, a German lady of means. Magdalena was born while I was at Breda, and already three months old by the time I first saw her. But I knew the moment I clapped eyes on her that she was mine, and that I would never love another as much in my life as I loved her. Nothing has ever had such a hold on my heart, Alexander, nothing, as that little girl.' He rubbed his fingers over his right palm and then clenched it tight. 'I can almost feel her hand in mine still.'

'What happened?'

His brow furrowed, as if he could not yet believe it himself. 'I returned to Brandenburg whenever I could, but the truth is, I saw them less than a dozen times in those three years. I remember when I heard the news that plague had visited their town. I rode hard for two days until I found them. My captain's wife had succumbed to the pestilence, and more than half the household too, but Magdalena and her mother were strong, and somehow – you would call it the grace of God – it did not touch them. But I could not leave them in the town and so I sent them to Bredenburg, a small but sturdy house in Holstein, garrisoned by some companies of MacKay's regiment under a Major Dunbar. I knew they would be cared for there by my countrymen until such time as I could return for them.' He swallowed down more brandy. 'The castle guarded a pass of no great consequence, and yet Gustav Adolph feared it might be used by the Imperialists, and so he ordered Dunbar to hold it come what may. And what came was Tilly.'

Johan Tserclaes, Count Tilly, General of the Armies of the Catholic League and greatest soldier of the Holy Roman

Empire. Died three years since of battle wounds, leading his army still, at the age of seventy-two. Everyone in Europe knew the name of Tilly.

'It was folly,' Archie continued, 'suicide. Tilly sent a trumpeter to Dunbar, demanding the castle's surrender. It was refused. The Major feared more the wrath of Gustav Adolph than he did the ten thousand men who surrounded him. Three hundred men, he had, and a house filled with peasants – old men, women and children who had come in from the countryside for their safety. That garrison of three hundred held Bredenberg six days, and then Dunbar took a bullet to the head – I would have put it there myself had I been there. His officers, not daring to surrender what he had refused, swiftly followed him through the gates of eternity, and the enemy broke through at last. Their offer of parley having been refused, they had lost almost a thousand men in the assault. They gave no quarter, to man, woman or child. The whole court and lodgings of the place ran with blood.' He was hunched over now, like an old man trying to keep warm. He looked up at me. 'It can be seen to this day you know, on the walls, on the paving stones beneath your feet. Five or six souls escaped with their lives. Anna and Magdalena were not amongst them.'

Though I stood by the fire, I was chilled to the bone, and could feel my body trembling. 'But surely, you cannot be sure? Perhaps in the confusion, the panic . . .'

He shook his head. 'I buried them myself. I had made for Bredenberg as soon as I heard Tilly's forces were marching that way. But I was too late. By the time I arrived, Dunbar had given his answer and the fates of those within the walls were sealed. I tried to find a way in alone, and got this for my pains.' He pulled down his shirt front and I saw the scars of a huge burn that travelled from his neck down the side. Oil. 'When I finally gained the castle, in the wake of the attackers, I found them, huddled in the corner of a stall in the stables, in one another's arms, the straw beneath them red, red.' He pulled from his pocket a small leather pouch and carefully removed from it a packet wrapped in silk. He unfolded the silk and placed it on the table before him. Wrapped inside it was a single blade of straw, stained brown. 'I keep it with me always, that I might remember what I live for.'

I looked from the piece of straw to the bed in which my children slept. I aspired to the ministry of the kirk; I knew every word of all the catechisms, every answer a Christian should give, but a question came to my lips that I could not have asked any other man. 'What is it, Archie? What do you live for now?'

He smoothed the straw with his hand, wrapped it carefully once more in its silken sheath. 'I live to end it.'

I understood him now, the soldier who had become a spy.

'And do you see an end to it?' I asked.

'There is an end to everything, and there must be an end to this.'

'But what end?'

He shook his head. 'I do not know, but even the God of Moses could not have asked such a blood sacrifice as this.'

He seemed weary and almost old. I had never thought I would see Archie Hay old, even had I known him to have lived until now. His fourteen years in the wars had shown him things that I would not see in my lifetime, and despite the kindly light of the fire, the toll of those years showed at this moment in his face.

'How long ago was it? Bredenberg?'

He did not need to think about it. 'Eight years.'

'And in those eight years, nothing has changed. For all you have done, all you have hazarded and lost, nothing has changed.'

'Much has changed,' he said, more animated now. 'The victories of the Swedish king are a memory now. Most of the Protestant princes of Germany have signed the Peace of Prague with the Emperor.'

News of this betrayal of our fellow Calvinists had been greeted with disbelief and disgust in equal measure when it had reached our burgh a few months previously. 'They have abandoned their brethren, and the cause of Elizabeth Stuart.'

His voice was almost contemptuous. 'Calvinist, Lutheran. What does a name matter? And Elizabeth Stuart, Queen of Bohemia? A fading beauty, sitting in the Hague, the widow of a fool and the patroness of a lost cause. Her son will never get back the Palatinate. Europe is full of beautiful widows dreaming of lost kingdoms.' He cast his eye to the stairs. There was no sound other than Zander's breathing at the top of it. He lowered his voice. 'I saw such a woman in Madrid.'

'Madrid?' I put down my glass. 'What in God's name were you doing in Madrid?'

'Alexander, I have told you, I am a spy. I must go secretly in many places. I have sought shady corners in the corridors of the Estoril, sampled the most delicate of pastries within the shadows of the imperial palace in Vienna. I have learned to make myself unseen in plain sight. I have learned to listen without giving the impression of hearing. People will talk in front of me and not realise they have done so.' He watched me carefully. 'As they did once in Madrid.'

'What are you trying to tell me?'

He looked again at the stairs, at my sleeping children. 'Last year, I was in Madrid. You do not need to know where, or why. I had fallen in with some Irish refugees – half Europe crawls with them, Brussels, Lisbon, Rome – but many still cling to hopes in Madrid. They are of royal blood, they tell anyone who listens, descended from kings and princes, driven from their homeland, vowing always to return. I heard tell amongst them of a Scotsman, a scholar, who had come among them once. He too, they claimed, was descended from Irish princes and kings.'

I felt a dread creep through me, of hearing again a tale I had thought long buried. I did not want to hear it again here, in my own home, from the lips of my best friend. 'It is a little late,' I said, 'to hear the drunken fables of Irish beggars.'

'Oh, refugees they may have been, but these men were not beggars, and their tale no fable. They told me of an old woman, Maeve O'Neill, a matriarch of the Irish cause, and of her two grandsons, one an Irishman, another a Scot.'

I looked at him, ready to plead, almost. 'Archie, I do not want to think of these things. It was seven years ago, it was another world and another life that has no place here. My cousins are dead and my grandmother's cause lost. Almost all I knew and cared for in Ulster is gone.'

'Not all though.'

'Do you tell me my grandmother has fled to Spain? I had thought it would take more than one king's army to shift her from Ulster.'

Archie smiled. 'I heard she was a woman of some mettle, your mother's mother. But no, the old woman, I hear, holds fast to her keep in Carrickfergus, and schemes her schemes. It was another woman I saw in Madrid. And this was no grandmother, but a rare and delicate beauty, like a pale flower of spring amid the gaudy colours of summer. She had with her a son, a boy of five then, who was treated with much honour on account of her dead husband, your cousin Sean.'

'Macha? She has left Carrickfergus?' Macha was no pale and delicate flower, but warm, brown and strong. Perhaps the years since I had seen her had wrought a change in her.

But he shook his head. 'This woman was not called

Macha, but Roisin O'Neill. She claimed herself as Sean's wife, but there were those that said she never had been. They never said it to her face, though, on account of her lineage. And her child.' Roisin, the name of the woman from that other world who might almost have kept me there. I swallowed, but could not make myself speak. Archie glanced again at the sleeping children in the bed, Deirdre closest to the wall, her arms wrapped around her little brother. I loved Davy with all my heart and soul, but he had little of me in him: he was the very image of his mother. Archie looked back to me again and fixed me with his gaze.

'Your son is very like you, Alexander, very like.'

11

Encounters

Sleep, when it had come, was filled with images of children. A little girl, bleeding to death in the straw, a little boy, alone, wandering empty marble corridors, looking for his father. I tried desperately to force some noise from my throat that he might hear me. When at last I managed to cry out I woke both myself and Sarah. I sat up, breathing heavily, and she put a hand to my forehead. 'Alexander, you are ill.'

'No,' I said. 'It was a dream, but a dream. A nightmare. I'm sorry to have woken you.'

She didn't appear to be listening to me. 'Your nightshirt is drenched with cold sweat. I will fetch you another.'

'Sarah, I am fine.'

'You are not,' she countered. 'You are shaking and near enough grey. Put that on while I warm you something.'

I struggled into the clean nightshirt and a few minutes later swallowed the decoction of chamomile she had warmed over the embers of the fire Archie and I had left. The drink warmed me a little but, as she drifted back to sleep, I could feel my whole body still trembling.

When the drummer came through the town at six Sarah insisted that I could not go in to the college that day; I insisted that I would. I had little enough time left with my scholars before I would be called to my ministry. That was what I told her, but the truth was that I could not stay in this little house, looking up at the rafters of the roof, and listen to the life of my family go on downstairs as if I was the same man to them today that I had been yesterday.

I thought the morning would never end. When the bell rang for the mid-day meal I knew I could not endure again the questions of concern for my well-being from the other regents and the principal himself, the exhortations that I should go home to my bed. The matter was taken from my hands by Peter Williamson, who had the third class.

'Wander round an empty schoolroom speaking to your-self if that is your wish – but you will have no scholars this afternoon.'

'Why not? I am perfectly able . . .'

Peter silenced my protests. 'Well, that is a matter of debate. However, even you are not able to teach students who are not there. The loch is frozen inches thick. I have secured the principal's permission to take the boys curling. You are not permitted to join us. Dr Dun says if you are still within the college walls in a quarter hour he will come and administer physic to you himself.'

The thought of the principal's concern was too much. I took my cap from the door and pulled on my gloves. 'You have convinced me, Peter – I'm going home.'

But I did not go home; I could not. I needed some time alone with the thoughts that had been clamouring to be heard all day, and most of the previous night.

The streets of the burgh were as full as ever – more so, for Lord Reay's men had begun their search for Seoras MacKay. Not a house nor a backland, a woodshed nor a sty was to be missed. For all the civic pride on which the provost might stand, he was, in truth, powerless to stop them, but could only see to it that they were attended in their searches by at least one member of the council or a burgh officer.

It astonished me that a man like Lord Reay, for all that he had grown up in a Highland glen, could think there was any hiding place in the town of Aberdeen. Whatever he suspected of its nooks and crannies, its outhouses and alleyways, I knew it for a warren in which a man might hardly know a moment's solitude, still less lie undiscovered, captive or at his own will, for nigh on five days. There was to be no turning from the world in our godly commonwealth, no monastic indulgence, no veneration of the life of the hermit.

Not for the first time in my adult life, I questioned whether those who had sought to pass their lives in such solitude could have been altogether wrong. And yet, I realised there was a place where a hermit might find a moment's peace, even here. I had seen it marked out on a plan four days ago, in George Jamesone's studio. A pavilion, he had called it, or summerhouse. Not yet built, but I knew there would be somewhere in that garden, if nowhere else, that I might have an hour alone.

There were parties of Strathnaver's men in every quarter of the town, but I could not see any yet on the Upperkirk-gate or the Schoolhill as I made my way by the old Black-friars' into Jamesone's garden. As I pushed back the rusted iron gate, I wondered what the good burgesses would make of the Doric gateways George planned to erect at the entrances to his Arcadia. There were those, I knew, who would not like his pretensions or the trumpeting of his wealth, but a man who had painted the king was unlikely to care.

Somewhere, away towards the eastern wall of the garden, I could hear the sounds of chopping and hewing – the two Frenchmen busy still at their clearing work. I sought instead some hidden corner on the western side, and followed a rough path down a grassy slope to the seclusion of the pond.

The water had frozen completely, and even the weeds beneath it were invisible to the eye under the inches of dull ice. The branches of the trees around me, denuded now of many of their leaves, were powdered white against the grey skein of a sky that promised an early snow. Autumn was barely a few weeks old but already the promise of a hard winter was settling on the town. Looking around me I saw now what I had missed in the night, a moss-covered seat set into the high stone wall. At intervals in the wall, George had already marked where niches were to be hewn out and statues set, but today there were no eyes of stone to watch me. I brushed away the accumulated muck of many autumns, as much as I could, and doubling my cloak carefully beneath me, sat down in that hidden place.

I shivered, knowing I should be at home in my bed. It had all come to this. One man who had thought he could live the life of two and it never be known, had been shown that he could not. Not half a mile from here, on the Gallowgate, a large and respectable house, its rooms still empty, awaited its new minister. In a cramped cottage even closer to where I sat, a woman who had done me no wrong prepared her family for shifting to that fine house. And here I sat, a fraudulent man who had no place in either house, and should have been somewhere else.

A boy in Aberdeen who carried my name but not my blood, another, in Spain, who thought his father dead and did not know he was my son; two women who deserved better at my hands. And the God to whom I must pray had known this all along. I besought Him to give me the reason, to show me how I should begin to right these wrongs. My head was in my hands and I did not know I begged aloud until I heard a woman speak my name.

'Mr Seaton.'

I knew the voice but I could not look up. Perhaps if I did not look up she would retreat, back amongst the trees and bushes through which she must have come. But the voice came again, closer, and I jolted as a gloved hand touched my shoulder. The hand was retracted.

'I am sorry.' It was Isabella Irvine. She wore a long green velvet cloak, lined with fur, its hood up against the cold.

Her feet had made little sound on the frosted grass, and she stood directly of front to me now, looking at me with an unwonted concern. 'Is there anything I can do for you? Can I find you some help?'

'You?' I could scarcely believe what she was saying to me. 'You of all people must know I am beyond it.'

She took a step backwards. There was no hostility in her face, and I felt almost sorry for having spoken to her harshly. 'I am sorry, Mr Seaton, I do not understand.'

I ran my hand through my hair. 'I think you understand me too well, as you made clear at our first meeting.'

I saw that it gave her some discomfort to remember it, and I wondered what could have occurred in the last twenty-four hours that could have wrought such a change in her demeanour to me.

She was thinking carefully over her words. 'It was many years ago, and I did not know . . . you must believe me when I tell you I am sorry for it now.'

I sat up now and looked at her properly, a little startled by this. 'Now? Since when is the "now"? Since when are you sorry? Not before the day of the trials, when I can assure you you made plain to me that I was as constant in your affections as ever I had been.'

'Mr Seaton, I . . .'

I was in no mood to listen to her. 'Whatever has brought on this change of heart in you, I can assure you it is an erroneous one. For you had me to rights, all those years ago, Mistress Irvine, and would do better to return to your former views.' I stood up. 'You may have the seat: I am taking my leave. No doubt the lieutenant will be here soon, and I fear we three would make mismatched companions.'

My remark had hit home, for I saw a brief panic flit across her eyes. 'I am not meeting the lieutenant.'

I had already begun to walk away. 'I have no interest in your trysting, but I would urge you to be careful how you deal with your good name.'

In my hurry to get away from her, I found within a few minutes that I had taken the wrong path, and was walking through ever boggier ground and denser thicket until I was thoroughly lost. At every turn I was faced with overgrown hawthorn or rose run wild. There was nothing to do but retrace my steps until I found the place where I had made the wrong turn. After much frustration, I came, at last, to a small clearing where two paths crossed. By one I could see my way to the centre of the garden, where Jamesone planned to erect his pavilion high up at the end of an avenue of fruit trees leading to the amphitheatre; by the other, narrower, more overhung with the branches of old and stubborn shrubs, I could see back to the pond. The sky had darkened still further, ponderous with snow, and the place looked bleaker than even I had rendered it. Isabella Irvine was still on the bench where I had left her, but she was no longer alone. A man sat by her, his back turned partly towards me and his head close to hers. They were deep in conversation, and kept their voices low. I could not have told what they said anyway, for the handsome, well-built man who had his hands over hers was not Lieutenant Ormiston, but Guillaume Charpentier, and they spoke in French.

As quietly as I could, I left them to their conference. I wandered further into the garden. The amphitheatre, over-hung at each edge of the semi-circle by two huge horse-chestnuts, seemed still emptier and more silent than it had done the last time I had been here. A dead place. It did not seem possible that people had gathered here once to laugh and wonder and be entertained, or that they ever would again.

I could hear no sounds of activity now from the thickets to my left where Jamesone's maze was planned and I had no wish to come upon St Clair. The man's face seemed locked in a sneer, as if he hated every soul he had ever met, and he discomfited me. I was unsure which way to turn. It seemed that even here there was no peace or solitude in which to seek to comprehend what Archie had told me last night: I had another son and he was a refugee with his mother in Spain, dependent on the charity of strangers. My hands and feet were cold almost beyond endurance: the answer to these new troubles would not be found here, or in a day, or indeed on my own. I would seek counsel from God, but I knew I also had to talk of it again with Archie. For now, my body was weary, and I turned for home.

I went up the pathway of the planned orchard, and came out eventually at the clearing George had marked out for his pavilion, his summerhouse. My quickest route out of the garden would be through a narrow gate in the eastern wall that gave onto a vennel that came out on the School-hill. I quickened my pace in that direction, but was brought up short by the sight of the old, recently restored work-shop ahead of me. Through the yellow light of its one window, I could see my artist friend there, poring over a large book and talking animatedly to Christiane Rolland. Standing a little apart from them, looking intently where Jamesone pointed on the page, was Jean St Clair. Just at the wrong moment George lifted his head to point to an area of the garden and I was seen. There would be no hurrying on; George gestured largely with his arm, and there was nothing for it but to go into the little stone hut and join them.

A small hearth at one end and the stout, lime-washed walls made the place a haven of warmth in the bleak wilder-ness surrounding it. It smelled of old iron, musty sacking and fresh earth. Wooden planking that looked to be of recent construction provided deep shelving up one of the walls, the shelves ranged with wooden boxes, many labelled. Heaps of bulbs of differing size and shape had been sorted into separate sections, and a series of smaller, labelled drawers suggested that what gleaning of seeds could take place at this late time of year had already been done.

'Alexander! You are here more often than I am myself! You are half-frozen, man. Come in to the warmth and tell me what it is that you seek so earnestly in my garden.'

I nodded to Christiane, who looked no better today than she had done the previous afternoon in Baillie Lumsden's house, and ignored St Clair, which was as he seemed to prefer.

'Only a place for reflection, George,' I said, my breath rising in the air in front of me.

'And in a few months, my friend, you will have it. Look here.'

He beckoned me over to where Christiane Rolland, her fingers red with the cold, was bent over a sheet of foolscap, onto which she was copying notes by the light of a small lamp by her elbow. 'Christiane has been labelling the areas for planting, according to Guillaume and Jean's ideas, naming the flowers as you and I would understand them.'

I leaned over, the closer to see the plan. The notes from which she copied and translated were in a different hand which I knew not to be her own. They were in a very precise italic, the Latin perfect, some of the names of the plants familiar to me from notes belonging to William Cargill's botanist uncle that I had examined years ago. I glanced at St Clair, who was now carefully cleaning some tools at the far end of the workbench, and back to the notes.

'These are the work of the gardeners?'

'Of Guillaume, not Jean – I do not think the fellow can read or write, but he knows his business all the same.'

'Guillaume Charpentier has been very well schooled though, it would seem.'

'Yes,' said George, 'and it makes our job much the easier, does it not, Christiane?'

'I do not see how we could accomplish it without him,' she said quietly, without raising her head.

I looked to George, who pulled a face that told me he had not the slightest idea as to what troubled Christiane. Clearly she had not confided her discomfort regarding Seoras MacKay to him.

I sought to cheer her a little, but wished a few moments later that I hadn't. I pointed to an area of the planting scheme she had already filled in. 'That will be a very pleasant meadow, come summertime.'

He nodded. 'It is somewhere where the children might play, and run and laugh and be happy. "Let all things smile and seem to welcome the arrival of your guests." An injunction from Alberti,' he said, pointing to the tome at his elbow. 'I am going to paint it over the *loggia* to my pavilion. I hope we shall have many summers there, we friends, and watch our children grow.'

His words pained me, and he could not know why. 'It is difficult to believe that the place I have just walked through, so desolate as it is now, so absent of life, could ever become a place so vibrant.'

He put an arm on my shoulder. 'You spend too long in your classroom with your musty books. The world will be a different place when you learn to distinguish what is merely dormant from what is dead.'

Christiane's hand stopped moving over the paper and I

regretted that I had ever come in here, for my visit had done neither her nor me any good. St Clair had gone out to lock his tools away in the small storehouse next to the workshop and I was about to take my leave when a servant from Jamesone's house came running through the door. 'The Highlanders are in the house,' the man said, when he could catch his breath, 'and when they have finished searching they are to make for here. The constable said to fetch you.'

'You did right, Patrick. Alexander, will you see Christiane here safe home?'

'Of course,' I said.

The girl had already covered her inkpot and begun to set aside her work. 'But what of Guillaume? If they come upon him in the garden . . . should I not go and find him? If the Highlanders come upon him, they will neither understand the other.'

'Guillaume is a hearty chap,' George reassured her, 'and could break a Highlander in half as easily as he breaks a rowan branch. Besides, it will not come to that. The fellow has a smile that speaks for him in many languages, as I am inclined to suspect you have noticed . . .'

Christiane flushed under his kindly gaze. My heart sank for her a little at the thought of where he was now, and with whom, for it had become plain to me yesterday that she considered Isabella her friend. I would not have had her find them together.

'Perhaps we could send St Clair to let him know.'

George was also better pleased with this plan. 'Will you tell him, Christiane, that some soldiers are coming to search the garden for the missing students, and it would be better if he and Guillaume were in here? Do not worry, I will explain to Lord Reay's men who they are – no harm will come to them.'

I suspected Christiane had as little concern for the welfare of the taciturn St Clair as I had, but she acquiesced and I went with her, that she might explain to the scrawny Frenchman what was required of him, but when we got outside, he was nowhere to be seen. I was only able to dissuade Christiane from her intention to wander the garden herself in search of Guillaume by pleading my need to get back soon to my own home to be with my wife and children.

Her face was desolate as we left the garden, and I thought again of the legend George planned to have inscribed over the gates: Let all things smile and seem to welcome the arrival of your guests. As I pulled the rotting gate to on the dark and forbidding place he sought to make a sanctuary, I prayed that the winter might be a short one.

12

Shipboard

Sarah had dosed me with compounds and decoctions from the apothecary from the moment I had arrived home, before sending me to bed, where she had set a fire in the rarely used hearth. Despite the agitation of my mind, I had slept solidly for six hours and not even noticed her get into bed beside me at the end of the day. Sleep came more fitfully in the remaining hours of the night, as my thoughts ranged, in no good order, over everything from fantastic schemes for finding the son I had never met to sober realisation that he was better off where he was, for there was one thing I did understand: if he was with his mother, he could not be with me.

All the next day it was the same. Sarah had sent word to the principal that I was too ill to accompany my scholars to the Sabbath preaching in the kirk. I was desperate to talk again with Archie, but I knew there was no way of getting a message out to the ship without attracting notice and that he could not risk a visit to my home in daylight, or even in the darkness, on the Sabbath. Come Monday morning, my body, if not my mind, was greatly rested and stronger.

After our early lessons, I did not accompany my class to the common hall for breakfast but went instead up the stairway to the regents' chambers. I had not seen Hugh Gunn since the day of Lord Reay's arrival and the boy's condition had been weighing on my mind. The guards Seoras's father had set on the door of Hugh's chamber subjected me to less scrutiny than I had expected, and I was admitted to the room with little difficulty.

The physician, Ossian, looked up from the small table at which he sat writing. He smiled over to the figure sitting up on the bed. 'You have a visitor, Uisdean.'

Hugh was properly dressed, and although still very pale and thin, with darkened circles beneath his eyes, it was evident that his fever was gone and he was in a much better condition than when last I had seen him.

'It's good to see you so much recovered, Hugh,' I said.

There was no response, just an uneasy awareness from the young man that I was talking to him. I glanced to the physician for explanation.

'He will not understand you. He still hasn't regained his facility for the Scots tongue. It's as if something will not allow him to speak, not permit him to understand.'

I had not noticed the figure sitting in a chair in the corner behind the door. Too large a figure for this small room; too great a figure for this company.

'Your Lordship, please excuse me. I just wanted to see how Hugh was. I will not disturb you.'

Lord Reay stood up. 'You do not. Uisdean has spoken of you kindly – he has had little enough to say of others in this town. It may do him some good to see you, but you must talk to him in our tongue, which I see you speak like an Irishman.'

'My mother was Irish. I learnt my Gaelic in Ulster. It is much out of use with me, but it passes.'

MacKay nodded. 'It passes well enough.'

I turned to the doctor. 'Is he well enough for me to speak to him?'

Ossian nodded. 'The swelling of his tongue is almost gone, but he still has difficulty with some sounds, and you might have to listen closely. In the main though, what ails him is in his mind, and it will not be got out if he will not speak of it.'

Looking first to Lord Reay for permission, I took up the chair beside Hugh Gunn's bed. I began with some pleasantries about his health and about life in the college, and gradually moved on to the matter that was exercising me.

'Have you any knowledge yet of what happened that night after you left the inn? Any memory?'

He shook his head. 'I remember nothing after we decided to get back to the college through the old town gardens. It was Seoras's suggestion. Normally, I wouldn't go near the place, but I was cold and angry and just wanted away to my bed as soon as I could get there. I wasn't sure which path to take, but Seoras seemed to know where he was going.'

'He knew the gardens?'

What might have been a smile came onto Hugh's face. 'Oh, Seoras knew the gardens. He could not tell you one plant from another, but he knows that place like the back of his hand. He has ...' He glanced at Lord Reay and lowered his voice. 'He has been there often enough.'

'You need not scruple for my benefit, Uisdean,' said Lord Reay. 'I know my son's shortcomings well enough, and I daresay Mr Seaton does also. And no doubt he will speak in your favour, if the time should come when you need it.'

The boy looked up and there was a new determination in his face, a light in his eye. 'And I will need it, will I not? For I know they are saying in the town, and even here in the college that I have killed Seoras, and dumped his body somewhere.'

MacKay stood up. 'Who has said that to you, boy?'

Hugh was defiant. 'Is it not so, then?'

The chief's fist clenched. 'It is so, but you should not have been told.' He looked to Ossian. 'Was it that old crone from the town?'

The physician shook his head. 'I got rid of her the day we came. It was one of the regents. He has been at the door every day, asking after Uisdean. A young skinny fellow with a lazy eye, who claims he wants to learn medicine. He told Murdo MacKenzie, and Murdo, half-wit that he is, told Uisdean.'

Peter Williamson. 'There would have been no malice in it, only folly. Hugh, I think I have come to know you well enough. I do not believe you are capable of what you are accused of.'

Lord Reay regarded me thoughtfully for a moment. 'And Seoras?' he asked at last. 'What would he be capable of?'

I hesitated.

'I would have an honest answer.'

'Seoras was a boy who readily gave himself to be misunderstood. He was careless of the feelings of others. He gave slights as jests but they were not taken as such. He trifled with women who did not know they were trifled with. He never understood,' I finished carefully, 'that he was no longer in Strathnaver, and not subject to such tolerance in this town as is accorded to a chief's son in his own country.'

Lord Reay nodded and I realised that nothing I had said was of any great surprise to him. 'And I think there is a woman at the root of this somewhere, is there not, Uisdean?'

The young man looked startled, like a hare caught in the hunt. 'A woman? I don't know . . .'

'You have spoken in your sleep, my boy. Both Ossian and I have heard you several times murmur the name Christiane. You never once had a thing to yourself that Seoras did not try to take from you. Tell me of this Christiane.'

I remembered Christiane's fears, her suspicions of Seoras. Weighing the look I could see on Hugh's face I sensed his reluctance to speak of this to Seoras's father at all, still less in front of me. 'I will leave you to it,' I said, standing up. 'But I will come back whenever you want me to.'

Lord Reay stood also. 'That will be tonight.'

'Tonight?'

'The magistrates of this town are fools who understand nothing of the bond of soldiering. They are convinced that if Seoras is not dead, he is on the troop ship. Ormiston has humoured them so far as to permit a search of the ship tonight. I and some others are to take our dinner with him aboard ship afterwards. I think you should also be there.'

I scrambled in my mind for some excuse. 'The lieutenant and I . . .'

Lord Reay had no humour for the petty dislikes of men of little account. 'The lieutenant is a soldier and will do as I tell him. I will be bringing Hugh with me – this town will see that I have no suspicion of him, or of Ormiston, either. Your presence will show that the college is also of my mind.'

There was nothing I could say in the face of such an injunction. As I walked disconsolately back down the tower steps, it came to me that at least I might find some opportunity aboard the recruiting ship for some private words with Archie.

I had watched, along with my scholars and the other regents, as the recruits were brought to shore each day at intervals to exercise on the Queen's Links. They were put through their training with pikes and swords by a sergeant who looked as if he had faced down more foes than the recruits would ever see. We watched, day by day, as those destined to be infantrymen grew in confidence and aptitude in their handling of the massive pikes – over twenty feet in length – that they would carry with them in their marches and whose spear point could reach the eye or belly of a musketeer before his weapon could be fired, or tumble an unwary cavalier from his horse. Some, with their halberd heads like spiked axes, could pierce armour and disembowel a man with two thrusts. Before our eyes, these raw recruits were drilled, somehow, to march, wheel on a front, close ranks, open ranks, change distance, all in concert and all keeping steady their weapon. In the courtyard of the college, in the streets of the town, where more than two boys were gathered, pikes would be improvised and drills imitated. Methods discovered by the Dutch, perfected by the Swedish king, passed on to his Scottish mercenaries and so played out in the burghs of our small nation. Ormiston was exercising his men as any good commander would have done, but also he was implanting in the next generation a dream of war.

Of still greater fascination than the pikemen were the musketeers. The guns, Archie told me, had been taken on at Dundee. Far from the suffering, there was always money to be made. I wondered how it was that a man such as Ormiston could raise the funds for such an adventure. There were names, we knew, of lesser barons and second sons who had made their way higher in the world of the Dane, the court of the German Habsburgs, the Muscovite, than they ever could have done at home, but Ormiston's was not among them. Every man, I supposed, might have his time and this, it seemed, was his. Archie had told me he was a good soldier, a good leader of men, and Archie was not one to flatter. I had to concede that in this regiment he was raising, there was much to admire.

I did not envy the men their outdoor pursuits in the hard frost or the falling snow that had succeeded it. 'They had better get used to it,' said Peter Williamson to me, 'for they will have no comfort once they light in Germany. More of them will die of starvation or plague than ever come under enemy fire. My cousin has told me of it. Endless days of marching and only an open field to sleep in. Cold that we cannot even imagine. My God, a man's life would have to be hard here before he would go willingly to such torments.'

'They are not all running from something,' I replied. 'Some go for honour, for wealth, for adventure.'

'Aye,' he said, 'and some are dragged from their beds or their prison cells and never seen by friend or family again.'

I laughed. 'You sound like my wife, Peter. You do not think that there are such amongst these surely?'

'No? Then ask yourself why they are marched to the links and back, looking neither left nor right, not allowed an hour at the market, or in an alehouse. Ormiston does not want to risk losing even one of these men, and he does not want them talking to the townsfolk either.'

And so I did watch, and they were marched and closely

guarded by their officers as they went from quayside to links and back again, and into the boats that returned them to the safety of the carrack that in a few days would take them to Germany.

It was not long after five that evening that I myself was crossing over to that carrack, along with Lord Reay, the physician Ossian, Hugh Gunn, Baillie Lumsden – the only member of the town council willing to undertake this exercise – and, somewhat to my surprise, Katharine Forbes, Lady Rothiemay.

Lumsden was not best pleased. 'MacKay has put me in the devil of a position. I know for a certainty that a warrant for her arrest has already passed Dundee on its way to the sheriff in Banff, who will no doubt be well aware, as is half the country, that her Ladyship is residing with me. And now I am escorting her onto a ship known to be bound overseas.'

'We must hope the captain does not weigh anchor until we are safely back ashore,' I said, laughing.

'It is not you and I that concern me. If her Ladyship was to take it in mind to flee her troubles . . .'

'Katharine Forbes will never leave this country of her own accord,' I said, puzzled at Lumsden's concern.

Lumsden looked beyond my shoulder to the boat we were getting ever closer to. 'There is something . . .' Then he smiled and clapped me on the shoulder. 'Pay me no heed. Sea travel puts my head and my stomach at odds with everything else.'

★

Little though I knew of boats, the merchantman looked an impressive vessel to me, and well adapted to the times. Three-masted, square-rigged and of Dutch construction, she must have been about a hundred feet in length and would have taken a sizeable cargo. Whatever she had transported to Scotland across the North Sea – Dutch pantiles, Baltic grain, Norwegian fir – her cargo on return would be men and arms. I could not help but notice the gun ports as we drew alongside; all but one were closed, but through the one that was not could clearly be seen the barrel of a cannon, and it looked to be trained on the town.

'An oversight, surely,' said Lumsden.

'Ormiston does not strike me as a man given to oversights,' I commented, as we prepared to climb the rope ladder up to the main deck.

The lieutenant, the ship's captain beside him, was waiting for us. Following the recruits' salute to Lord Reay, the captain, a Holsteiner, assured us in thickly accented but good Scots that his ship and his quarters were at our disposal. He would show us around his vessel, but he would not join us in our dinner.

Genial though he was, I paid little attention to the captain and neither, I noticed, did Baillie Lumsden. His eyes, like mine, were looking beyond the welcoming party, to what lay behind them: row upon row of faces – some young, healthy, optimistic, others scared, still others older-looking, cynical, with nowhere else left to go. The welcoming ceremonies attended to, MacKay went round them all, looking briefly into the face of every man, giving some a word or a nod, others a dismissive glance. To two or three of the young men, bound for officers' rank, he asked a question. All shook their heads. None of them had seen Seoras or knew anything of him.

I think I was the only one of our party who searched that crowded deck for another figure, and I found him; Archie had been standing to the side of the recruits, the very embodiment of the forbidding Sergeant Nimmo – hunched, hooded, alien to the conventions of society, not inviting conversation. Not even MacKay had slowed his pace when passing Sergeant Nimmo. I thought for a moment that Lady Rothiemay had glanced in his direction, but if she had, her glance had swiftly moved on, and I knew she could not have remarked any resemblance to the long-dead heir to Delgatie, for it was not a thing she would have kept to herself.

Her Ladyship, along with Ossian and Hugh, were shown to the captain's cabin, and myself, Lumsden and Lord Reay invited to proceed to the inspection of the ship and the search for a boy who would not be there. I felt the old familiar sway of the vessel under my feet, the power lurking within the slightly agitated sea. I saw, for a moment only, how ludicrous to a seaman the fixedness of land must seem, how futile the getting and having of the lives of the people within the never-moving confines of the town. The two towns of Aberdeen were still very visible to me – I had seen them from shipboard before, but never before had I been so aware that the weighing of an anchor could take me from them. We started with the forecastle deck, and proceeded, by way of quarter deck and waist deck to the dark belly of the ship: the hold. Ever since my time in Ireland I had been wary of descent through hatches, darkened spaces. Ormiston spotted my discomfort; I saw the curiosity in his eyes but he said nothing.

And here we came to where a hundred and fifty men ate and slept and waited for their transportation across the northern seas to fight in countries they had never seen in the armies of foreign princes. I wondered that they could find enough air to breathe, or stomach the odour of humanity that filled the place when they did so. The light was poor but the lieutenant had provided us with lanterns by which we probed every corner, investigated every shadow. Sleeping mats and blankets were rolled up beside the packs that were all the recruits' own belongings. Crate upon crate of arms were stored down here too – pistols, muskets, powder belts and flasks, lead bullets and musket rests. But for all the firepower, the smoke and flame and burning inherent in those weapons, it was the contents of the other crates that chilled me the most – the horsemen's hammers, stunted square hammer-head on one side, steel pick on the other; maces with flanged heads and pointed steel finials, obscene almost in the intricacy and delicacy of the decoration of their shafts; quillion daggers with double or serrated blades. Through the noise and the smoke of the guns, men would look their enemy in the eye and fight, hand to hand, for their lives, to butcher or be butchered. I wondered what armour might protect them from such savagery.

From here we descended at last to the orlop deck, where cables, powder, salt, kegs of wine and ale, and other provisions for the voyage were kept. I knew half-a-dozen of Lord Reay's men had been left on the upper decks lest any suspicious movements among the troops or, indeed, the fur-hatted sailors, might indicate some subterfuge, but throughout the whole ship, from galley and boatswain's store to gunroom where the cannon were kept and, finally, back on deck, there was no sign that Seoras MacKay was here, or ever had been.

As the search had gone on, and it had become increasingly evident that we were on a fruitless errand, Strathnaver's interest in the undertaking seemed to lessen. The anger in his voice was directed not at Ormiston, but at those who sat on the shore and pronounced upon others. 'I trust you will take your report of our researches back to the council, Baillie.'

'I will, my lord,' said Lumsden.

'And you may tell them,' his Lordship continued, 'that they are to impugn the word of the lieutenant here no longer. As he and I have told them, my son has never signed up to his recruit or been on this ship.'

Lumsden was careful with his words. 'It is, in fairness, the duty of the town to investigate every possibility, and I am afraid this seemed the most likely. I am truly sorry we did not find Seoras here. I begin to fear the truth of the matter will never be known.'

Had it not already been freezing, the look in Lord Reay's eyes would have turned all around him to ice. 'Oh, the truth will be known, Baillie; if others must go before me to the gates of Hell, the truth will be known.'

Ormiston said nothing. There was no triumph over the town, no mockery of myself in his eyes, just the utter subordination, abnegation, of a soldier to his old commander. I had dressed in my best stand of clothes, as had Lumsden, a wealthier man than me by far, but even he could not begin to rival the magnificence of the great chief or the assured elegance of Ormiston. Lord Reay was wearing black velvet breeches and a doublet the colour of claret which was edged in gold brocade, a shirt of white silk showing through the slashed sleeves. Collar and cuffs were edged with finely worked Flemish lace, around his waist he wore a black sash, and in his hat a magnificent ostrich plume. Ormiston was dressed in a suit of the deepest green, almost black, with silver buttons to the jacket and buckles to his shoes. Everything in his bearing spoke quality and elegance, and the fact that he was used to keeping finer company than mine or Lumsden's. I thought at first his great effort was made all on his old colonel's behalf, but when we were at last brought to the captain's cabin, high on the poop deck, I realised it had probably been for someone else.

We had all to stoop on entering the cabin. It seemed an unfeasibly small chamber in which the master of the vessel slept and ate, and yet a table had been laid that would sit eight people. Lamps had been lit, and hung from hooks on the ceiling, huge scrolls that must have been charts were rolled up and stored between the captain's desk and his bed. There were brass instruments attached to the wall, and books firmly kept in place along one shelf. Most, I could see, dealt with matters of navigation, or of port regulations. I committed as much as I could to memory, that I might relay what I had seen to Zander. Already seated and waiting for us was Lady Rothiemay, along with Hugh Gunn and MacKay's physician. It soon became clear that the empty place beside her had been intended for Isabella Irvine.

Ormiston could not hide his disappointment. 'I am sorry Mistress Irvine was unable to accompany you tonight, your Ladyship.'

Katharine Forbes took a long, slow draught of the wine that had been set before her. 'Isabella begins to show signs of a fever, and I have put her to her bed – a crossing of the harbour in an open boat would have done her no good. What the girl needs is a day at the hunt. The cold in towns is not healthy. It is a wonder anyone survives the winter in such a place.' She nodded graciously to Lumsden. 'Always respecting your kind hospitality, Baillie.'

He made a half bow. 'Your Ladyship would be an ornament to any house, winter or summer.'

Katharine Forbes smiled and waved her hand dismissively at him. 'I am too old for such flattery. And as to the summertime, you would not find me then within the walls of a town, for the summers are even worse. Breeding grounds for pestilence. And *other* contaminations.' I could not be certain that Katharine Forbes had not looked at me when she had pronounced this last, referring, I knew, to the reformed religion, which had a much greater hold in the towns than it ever had in the hills and mountains of our hinterland. I wondered again that her evident contempt for our kirk had so far escaped the notice of the authorities. As she and Lord Reay continued to discuss the inconveniences of town life, I reflected that if Lumsden was right, the walls enclosing her come summer would not be those of Aberdeen but the tolbooth of Edinburgh.

I was seated next to Hugh, who understood without asking that Seoras had not been found.

'Was there not even a sign of him?' he asked under his breath.

'None,' I replied.

Our conversation was necessarily in Gaelic, and Lord Reay was evidently keeping an ear to it. 'You must excuse my foster son, Katharine,' he said to Lady Rothiemay, 'for in his illness he has sought refuge in his mother tongue. No doubt he will regain the facility of Scots as his health improves. You might try him in French though.'

'French?'

'Aye, if my money has not been wasted. Seoras and Hugh have been going to lessons with a French master in the town twice weekly these last few months. I have a mind to send them under Huntly to the *Garde Eccosaise* and see what the French court might make of them.'

It was clear that he would not countenance the idea that his son was dead until he saw the boy's body in front of him, and I would not be the man to argue with him here about it. 'Then they will meet in with your nephew, Baillie.'

'Your nephew, Lumsden?'

The baillie looked a little uncomfortable at my reference to Matthew. I should have realised that some of my old college friend's escapades at home and abroad might not be too readily publicised by those of his family in positions of authority. The baillie, who was active not only on our burgh council, but also served as a commissioner to parliament in Edinburgh, clearly had not planned to discuss his rebellious nephew in our present company. He took a good swallow of his wine.

'My nephew is an old friend of Mr Seaton's, and Alexander here helped him out of more than one scrape when they were boys. But Matthew is now a loyal adherent of the Marquis of Huntly and has taken service in the *Garde*. I am sure he would prove a good friend to Seoras and Hugh in Paris.'

Lord Reay seemed well pleased with this. 'And I daresay Seoras will similarly rely upon Uisdean to get him out of scrapes in Paris – there are many temptations in that town. They will have merry times there, the pair of them, but they will not forget the call of home, either, I am sure.'

'Oh,' enquired Lady Rothiemay, 'is there a pretty girl

waiting for our young friend back in Strathnaver, I wonder?'

'Indeed there is,' said MacKay. 'Hugh has been promised these ten years to Elizabeth Murray, a fine, healthy girl of good family.'

At the name of Elizabeth Murray, Hugh looked up, briefly, and I realised that whatever the French master's sister might have thought of him, all his dreams of Christiane Rolland could have come to nothing anyway.

Lady Rothiemay was happy to try Hugh in French. He answered haltingly at first, and she was delighted. She spoke gently, and waited patiently for his answers. It occurred to me that her own older son could not have been much older than Hugh was when he had been burned to death five years ago by his family's Crichton enemies in the tower of Frendraught. Now her son's memory was held in a chalice of poems and her own desire for vengeance. I doubted if even MacKay's grief, should Seoras not be found, could be more tempestuous or of greater duration. I remembered something William had said when I'd told him of Lady Rothiemay's connection to the Highland lord. 'You didn't know he was kin to Katharine Forbes? How can you not have done? There's something in their blood will make them start a fight in an empty room. They say MacKay fell out with all of Caithness and half of Sutherland. There was no one left for him to fight with at home, so he took himself off abroad.'

But Lady Rothiemay did not have that option, and so had to fight her old fights, time and again, at home, and it

was not long before she and MacKay were bandying opin-
ions about persons at court – who was to be trusted and
who not. The former, it appeared, was a very small group.
Lumsden and Ossian had fallen into the easy conversation
of two learned and well-bred men. Only the lieutenant sat
in silence, Isabella Irvine's empty place seeming to mock
his finery. He cut a solitary figure and I thought I saw
beyond the façade for once, to a lonely man.

At a lull in the conversation, he began to ask after Isabella.

Lady Rothiemay's answers were curt, and it became clear
to me that she was actively hostile to any courtship of her
young companion by the lieutenant. It crossed my mind
that Isabella Irvine, regardless of her own feelings for
Ormiston, was very probably not ill at all.

As we set to the dishes that had been brought up from
the galley, Lady Rothiemay paid a special attention to Hugh
and took some time in pressing food upon him that she
thought would do him good. As he demurred, she called
Ossian to her support, and between them, gradually, they
began to draw him out of himself a little, even to laugh.
Her Ladyship watched him a moment, smiling, and she
murmured, 'How he reminds me of my son.'

There was not one of us around the table who did not
know of the terrible death of her oldest son and his friends
in a fire, at the hands of their hosts in the tower house of
Frendraught. Poems had been written of it, ballads sung,
but she would never see her boy again. MacKay put his
hand over hers and gripped it firm.

'I will never forgive them, you know. Never.'

Ormiston looked at her directly. 'Such a death can never be forgiven, only avenged.'

'You also have suffered loss.' It was a statement, not a question.

He took a drink from his glass. 'My younger brother, Duncan.' And he told us of a golden boy who had worshipped him and followed him to the wars.

'In my first recruit?' asked Lord Reay.

Ormiston nodded. 'All my life, he had been at my shoulder before my shadow was, and so it was in this case too. Nothing I could say would dissuade him from coming with me. And while we waited for the transports, we and the thousands like us, we trained, we green boys, and we became comrades. Before we ever set foot in Denmark or saw the glint of a Habsburg halberd, we were comrades.'

Lord Reay took up the tale then and told how these young comrades, his Scots Brigade, had fought together through many vicissitudes. 'And then we went over to the service of the King of Sweden, and so partook of his glory.'

Here a toast, the first of several that night, was drunk to the memory of Gustav Adolph, great champion of Protestant Europe, the fallen Lion of the North.

Lady Rothiemay had been watching Ormiston all through this. 'When did you lose your brother, Lieutenant?'

Ormiston put down his glass. 'At Stralsund, your Ladyship. The city was laid under siege by the Imperialists and had called on us for help. We came in by sea; our ship was struck by cannon-shot and ran aground, but still we managed to make it to the wharves and so into the town. We were there six weeks, night and day defending the Frankentor, the weakest part of the town, scarcely with time to sleep or change our clothes. I did not know what fear was until I entered those walls: the endless torrent of bullets, the roar of cannon that could be heard thirty miles away. I saw comrade after comrade fall. And yet we held firm, and the town was saved.'

'The gratitude of the burghers must have been great,' said Lumsden.

Ormiston's voice was scarcely audible. 'The gratitude of the burghers was not what it might have been.'

Lord Reay saw the lieutenant's discomfort with the subject and, his face set like rock, took up the telling of the story. It was a tale of boys, exhausted from the daily horrors they were called upon to face, given not so much as a roof over their heads at night by the foreign townsfolk who had called them there. 'We lost many good men at Stralsund. I had been back to Scotland to raise further recruits, and the Danish commander in the town handled things very badly. By God, had I been there, things would have been different.'

The mood was now very sombre, and Lady Rothiemay sought to lighten it. 'But all the same, this soldiering of yours is a brotherhood, is it not, regardless of the side on which a man fights? There are Scotsmen on both sides of this terrible war, I know, and I cannot believe that they ever truly forget they are Scotsmen.'

'Indeed they do not, my Lady. Tell me, Lieutenant, were you at Freistadt?'

The lieutenant smiled. 'I was, Sir.'

MacKay spread wide his hands, 'Then the floor is yours, boy.' And Ormiston told us a tale of the Swedish king's capture, outside Nuremberg, of a handful of Imperialist soldiers, amongst whom were Colonel John Gordon and Major Walter Leslie, the two old acquaintances of whom Archie and I had spoken only two nights before. 'Gustav Adolph, as a mark of the esteem in which he held men of our nation, offered to set them free without ransom, but such was their honour that they would not permit it, and so they stayed with us, their countrymen, a full five weeks, and a merry time was made of it.'

The tale delighted Lady Rothiemay, and she went into a long reminiscence of her dealings with the families of both officers. The dinner had become more congenial than I could have hoped for, but it was evident that Hugh Gunn's strength had been tested to its limit long before the meal was half-way through. A little after we had heard the town's bells ring seven, Ossian made plain to Lord Reay that Hugh would need to get back to his bed soon. Ormiston, who seemed to have a genuine concern for the young man's well-being, was not long in making the arrangements for the small boat to be called that would take the boy and his doctor back to the town, while Lord Reay's vessel awaited the rest of us. I would happily enough have gone with them, in the hope that I might manage a minute alone with

Archie while the boat was readied, but it was clear no such thing was to be thought of and so I spent a good two hours more listening to tales of valour, and of squalor, from the wars.

As preparations were at last being made for us to leave the ship, I managed to draw the lieutenant aside alone for a moment.

'No,' he said, eventually, in answer to what I had asked him. 'I cannot bring Sergeant Nimmo to you. When the sergeant needs you, he will seek you out. It is better for both of you that way.'

There was something in his tone that made his words almost a warning, and as I sat alone by the embers of my own fire later that night, I reflected it would not be a good thing to make an enemy out of Lieutenant William Ormiston.

13

Flights of Fancy

I had been bone weary by the time I had reached back to my house from the ship, but there was to be no getting to sleep until a full report of everything I had seen on my visit aboard had been given to Zander, who had forced himself to stay awake until my return.

And so it was with a sinking heart that I read the missive sent early to my door the next morning by the session clerk of St Nicholas. Further alarms at St Fittick's Kirk across the water at Nigg Bay had worsened the state of the minister's mind and given rise to rumours of illicit gatherings and unnatural practices that the session there urgently requested our help in putting an end to. By some justification elusive to us, William and I had been deputed by our session clerk to meet with our brethren at Nigg and there to investigate the nature of the problem.

'Babbling about witches, and fairies and spirits flying through the trees, speaking in tongues, things risen from the dead. They had to pull him from the pulpit. I hope to God he was drunk when they did so,' said William.

I echoed his hope. If John Leslie had been drunk in the pulpit, then he would surely lose it, but if he had been sober and talking of witnessing spirits in flight in the kirk-yard, then a much worse fate might befall him.

It was a cold morning, and the wind whipped right off the sea to find us on the benches of the ferry as it edged its way carefully across the mouth of the Dee from Futty to the southern shore at Torry. I had not drunk to excess, nor anything like it on Ormiston's boat the night before, but all the same, I would ten times rather have been in my unmoving classroom, with its modicum of warmth, than amongst the sway and swell of this open boat. 'It is a wonder they let John Leslie preach yesterday,' I said. 'He'd been babbling five days at least – for it was Wednesday that we heard of it at the session.'

William, struggling despite his wrappings of hide and fur to keep the cold out, muttered his agreement. 'He had come again to his senses by Friday, it seems, and the session thought the episode passed. They have been so afraid that they will lose their minister and not get another one that they've turned a blind to what every man knows: Leslie is a drunkard. I have it on authority from John Spalding, my clerk who has his ear to every rumour in the town, that he swore to the elders that he would not touch another drop. And yet yesterday he was at it again, rambling and railing about the ungodly dead rising and dancing in St Fittick's kirkyard.'

The look on my face must have betrayed my mind as we

passed silently by the recruiting ship on its moorings. There was no sign of any of the soldiers on deck yet.

'What bothers you so much about that boat, Alexander? You cannot still fear the recruiting sergeant is a threat to our boys?'

I turned my face away from the ship. I could not make myself lie to him, but I knew I could not tell him the truth either. 'His presence in the town has made me . . . uncomfortable – that is all.'

I knew William was not wholly convinced. There was little in my past or his that the other did not know and I had a great longing to tell him what Archie had told me, of the son in Spain whom I had never seen, and have his counsel. But I could not, for – for all they had been friends – Archie had sworn me not to tell even William of his return.

I was glad that we were soon landed on the southern shore of the Dee at the fishing village of Torry. It was a harsh living the men here made, and a harsh life for the families whose mean dwellings we tramped past on our way out to St Fittick's Church by the shore of Nigg Bay. Those who looked out at their doors as we passed would have little cause to know a lawyer from the town or a regent from the college, and yet before we had quite left the village for the moor that would take us over the headland to Nigg Bay, the word was passing from hut to hut that the kirk session of Aberdeen was on its way to try John Leslie.

I had preached once or twice in St Fittick's myself during

the vacancy of their pulpit before John Leslie, then a divinity student of some promise at St Andrews, had been called to fill the charge. That had been eight years ago, and I had had little cause to come here since. The small stone church with its short bell-tower had stood by the shore from ancient times – the stones in its kirkyard already worn and moss-covered long before Bishop Elphinstone had ever thought to build his university in the old town. The superstitions of the place were older even than those of Rome, and in the days of Rome had been kept by the people here. A well, St Fittick's Well, was said to have healing properties, and often a rag, an old pot, a coin or some other gift would be left for the saint, or for the spirits that were said to have inhabited the place before him. Seventy years since the trappings of idolatry had been swept from our churches and still the foolish and weak in faith believed such things. Some from Aberdeen would make their way to the kirk and its well, not across the ferry, but by land, over the Bridge of Dee and through the vale of Tullos, stopping at the Elf hillock and the Faerie Brig. Watches were kept on the ferry, checks were made through the town by the session and the baillies on the Sabbath, fines were imposed, but still there were those who would wallow in their ignorance.

I had not met John Leslie more than a half-dozen times, and not at all in the last three or four years. At first, he had gone to some lengths to make himself acquainted with the theologians of our two universities, but soon it became apparent that he found the moderate leanings of our bishop and the learned doctors too lacking in fervour for his tastes. He had married the daughter of one of his old professors and brought her to his lowly parish with him, and there discovered that love alone would not overcome the ravages of poverty. Child after child had been born to them. He came less often to meetings of the presbytery. The town of Aberdeen and, it was said, his worn-out wife, saw less and less of John Leslie.

The man waiting for us in the kirk of St Fittick's in the care, or custody, of his own elders, looked to be at least ten years older than when I had last seen him. Hair which before had been tidy and thick was now thinned and unkempt; a frame once lean and upright had grown skeletal and hunched; eyes that had been clear and intelligent were bloodshot and wild. I saw, though he had not extended it in greeting, that his hand trembled as I had seen those of others broken by drink tremble. This was not the work of a shock of the last few days, of a sudden descent into madness, but of years of abuse of his own soul and body by this minister of the kirk. Whatever William and I had been brought here for, I had no stomach for it.

'This man is ill,' I said, marching up to the wreckage of the minister while his session clerk was still in the midst of intoning his welcome.

'Mr Leslie has not been in his right spirits of late, and we thought well to call for assistance from our brethren of St Nicholas.'

'He should be at home in his bed, not here in this freezing

kirk,' I said, continuing to ignore him as I removed my cloak and put it round John Leslie's thin shoulders. It was the minister himself who stopped me.

'No, Mr Seaton. You must listen to them. If I am sick in heart and body, it was all of my own doing, and I tell you I repent of it, I repent. But there is no sickness of mind: I have seen what I have seen, and that must I tell, that the souls of my people be not imperilled.'

William exchanged with me a look that told me we must stop the minister from talking, for his own sake. 'You are truly ill,' he said, to the shambles of a man before us. 'Let us take you home to the care of your wife. Your elders can apprise us of all that concerns the kirk.'

John Leslie threw off my cloak and went towards him with some vehemence. 'The elders do not know. They were not *here*. *I* was here.'

I looked to the session clerk, who turned away, embarrassed. 'Then sit and tell us,' I said.

We drew closer to the brazier by the altar, a little sheltered from the bitter cold that licked at the walls and snaked under the doors of the kirk, as he began his tale.

'I was here late last Monday night, alone – I told my wife I had business to attend to in the kirk, but she knew as well as I what that business was. I was down below in the vault – that is where I keep my supply.'

'While your wife gleans for kelp on the shore, and looks to the charity of the fisher folk to put food in your bairns' mouths.' The old man who spoke was disgusted.

'Aye, even then,' said the minister. 'But I have been given my warning. I think God has done with me and left me to the Devil.'

The elders collectively drew in their breaths. If it should become widely known that the minister of St Fittick's had spoken like this, then not only would he burn, but others too, for a man who consorts with the Devil rarely does so alone. If the elders had hoped the sight of William and me would bring their minister to his senses, they were to be disappointed. There was nothing to do but let Leslie speak and pray he did not name anyone else as he did so.

He continued. 'I was in the vault. Had been there some time. It was a cold and wet night, the wind blowing. I was in two minds whether to go home at all, for I have made my place down there quite comfortable, and there is no warmth to be had for me at the manse these days. I keep a lamp down there, so no light will be seen through the kirk windows. I think I must have dozed a while, for when I first heard their voices, the lamp was out.'

'Whose voices?' I asked.

He turned impatient eyes on me. 'How should I know? They spoke in tongues – they cried out to the Devil in tongues. There were others who murmured in low voices, but I could hardly hear them over the rolling of sea on the stones of the shore, and the screeching of the horse.'

'Horse?'

'Aye, horse. Whether of this world or another, I do not know, but I never heard an animal make such a hellish racket.'

'Was there music?' This from an aged elder with an eager look.

'None but a manic clanking of chains, that made a hideous cacophony with the squealing and whinnying of the beast and the endless imprecations in tongues. As it went on I thought I would go mad. Perhaps I did. I relit my lamp, and reckoning that I might as well meet the Devil in this world as the next, I came up out of the vault. The kirk door was swinging open and I could see out into the kirkyard. There must have been a dozen of them. One was very close to me, chained in the branks, a terrible wailing and crying out in their devilish words only a few feet from my ear; another danced in the air, a woman with her skirts all pulled up, making horrible, guttural sounds. The horse was in terror, trying to flee from the sight, but could not. The others stood in a circle round the graves, their besom by them, laughing as the flying wench cackled. I have never known such terror in my life. I turned back into the church, ran down the aisle, and made off out by the lepers' window at the back there.' He pointed to the long, low window near the altar, where lepers once had been allowed to come and witness the ceremonies of the church.

'I was out by that window and half-way across the moor before any of them saw me. I heard them shout and a great commotion began amongst them, but I never looked back once. I banged on the door of the first cottage I came to, Doddie Brown's, and once he had let me in I bolted the door myself and bade him let no one in, come what may.

And there we waited, in terror until dawn broke and Doddie sent his boy down to the village to rouse the elders.'

Here one of the elders spoke up. 'The poor lad was scared out of his wits, said the minister had dragged them from their beds and made them watch the night through for witches and warlocks. When we got up to Doddie's, Mr Leslie there was still in a terrible state, not his *usual*, you understand, but as you see him now.' I was beginning to see that the whole parish knew what John Leslie's *usual* state was, and wondered that the man had managed to keep his pulpit so long. 'And so we went down to the kirk, though Mr Leslie would not come with us, said he would not set foot there again until he knew it had been cleansed for the worship of God. Wondrous to hear him talk so, for us.'

'And what did you find at the kirk?' asked William.

'Not a witch nor yet a warlock, that I'll tell you,' said the fellow who seemed least disposed to further humour the scandalous life of his minister, 'but a pile of blankets and empty wine jars, and a vault that stank to high heaven of debauches.'

'And what of the kirkyard? You found nothing there to give weight to your minister's tale?'

Again, there was unease, a reluctance to speak, amongst them. Finally, the session clerk spoke up. 'It would be best, Mr Seaton, Mr Cargill, if you would come and see for yourselves.'

He led us to the door, the rest following, and showed us the branks where gossips and scolds would be chained, their mouth held in an iron halter that prevented the movement of their tongue, at the time of divine service, so that all who passed by on the Sabbath might see their penance and humiliation. The bridle was mangled and the chain that linked the iron manacles to the wall hacked in two, by an axe if not some brutal show of demonic strength. I thought of the incessant clanking of chains, the moaning from the branks of which the minister had spoken. 'What else?' I said.

The clerk threaded his way through the gravestones to a more open space under the old hawthorn that somehow withstood the blasts that came over the sea direct from Norway. 'It was a wet night, last Monday night, and has been a hard frost ever since.'

'Aye,' agreed William. 'The ground has relented nothing in a week.'

'That is right,' said the clerk. 'You see how the turf is trampled and churned here. As if many feet had danced.'

'Booted feet,' I said, stiffening after having bent down for a closer look at the frozen mud. 'I had not imagined witches so careful of their feet.'

I looked up at the tree through which Leslie had sworn he had seen a woman fly. It had nothing to tell. The ground had also been churned by hooves. I pointed the marks out to William. He inspected them cautiously. The members of the session seemed reluctant to come near them. A nervy-looking man spoke for them. 'Do you see any there that are – cloven?'

William struggled to suppress a smile. 'If the Devil danced here, he was remarkably well shod.' He looked beyond the kirkyard towards the path that led up to the cliffs where, year on year, the sea scoured more and more of the rock away and paths crumbled over the edge. He had seen enough. 'Come, Alexander, there is nothing more to be learned here – no witches' sabbath but some young ones, out dancing, and John Leslie too drunk to know the difference.'

I looked around at the old, worn graves, the newer ones with their engravings still fresh, the tranquillity of the place disturbed only by the occasional cry of a sea-bird or the building rumble of the pebbles as the waves rolled gently from the shore. 'It is hardly a place of disturbed spirits,' I said.

'Then you are a fool, Mr Seaton, and you do not know what you look for.' John Leslie, still shivering but no longer hunched, regarded me gravely. 'For at night, in the darkness, with the wind howling and the sea crashing on the shore like a demented beast in search of its prey, familiars of the Devil walk here. I know it, for I have seen them, and I have seen the unquiet dead they leave behind.' The man was stone cold sober, and now I was certain he had lost his mind, for the words he spoke would be his own death warrant.

'Get him away from here, get him home!' I shouted, and frightened by my vehemence, the clerk ordered two of the strongest-looking of their number to take John Leslie to his miserable manse and bid his wife keep him there.

I looked after him, then turned to address what was left of the session. 'This is an offence to the kirk and all that is right. After the way you found him on Tuesday morning, ranting and raving and in a terror, how could you have thought of letting him back in the pulpit again yesterday?'

'We thought at first, as you do, that he had been driven mad by the drink, that the visions he claimed were the product of a mind destroyed. He swore to us then he would never touch another drop. It was not the first time he had done so, I grant you, but he had been so frightened out of his wits we believed him. And then, he did not touch a drop all week, is that not right?'

The man who spoke looked around him for affirmation, and many heads nodded in assent. 'Even his wife confirmed it. He had taken it ill a few days, but by the fifth day, Saturday, he was beginning to look more like a man in health – in mind and body too, and he praised the Lord for it, and begged our leave to do his penance before the whole kirk, in the seat of repentance on the Sabbath. That was what we allowed – it was from that seat, and not the pulpit, that we dragged him.'

I had noticed it earlier, below the altar table, facing the whole kirk, a small, wooden stool. By a kitchen hearth, in a barn, it would have drawn little attention, but in a kirk it drew every eye, for that was where notorious sinners must sit, in shame and sack-cloth, to do their penance. I remembered John Leslie on the day eight years ago when he had been inducted into this charge, and wondered that such a man could have brought himself so low as to be forced to sit before his own congregation in this manner to proclaim his ruin.

'He deceived you then,' said William.

'What?'

'When he feigned sobriety.'

The clerk shook his head. 'He was as sober as you or I, Mr Cargill. Clean-shaven, not the merest taste of drink upon his breath. His wife had sworn that he had taken no drink in five days. She said he had gone early, and with a firmness of purpose she had not seen in him in a long time, to the kirk. He wished to prepare himself in prayer for his public repentance, there was a kind of peace and joy about him, she said. That was an hour before the service. By the time the precentor came in and found him here, his sack-cloth rent and ashes in his hair, he was not in his wits. He was howling to God for deliverance from his torment, from the visitations of the walking dead. The precentor could not shift him, and those of the congregation that arrived first were too terrified to go near him. It took us some time to get him down from the stool and away to the vestry before the people could hear much more.'

'What more was there?' I asked, not certain that I wished to hear the answer.

The others looked to the session clerk. 'It was not easily that we calmed him, put an end to the ranting.'

I was becoming impatient. 'What did he say to you then?'

The man's face was almost defiant. 'That he had seen the dead walk. As sober as I am standing here, and yet he looked me in the eye and told me, in words well measured, that he had seen the dead walk.'

William's face paled. 'When? When did he say he had seen them?'

'Yesterday morning. In the kirkyard. From the grave behind Jessie Goudie's. He saw a creature, dreadful, rotted, rise from it and call to him.'

My mouth was dry. 'What did it say?'

The clerk shook his head. 'He did not know. It croaked at him in strange tongues. He fled to the church for sanctuary.'

'And did the thing he saw not follow after him?'

'He said it never entered the church.'

As petrified as their minister, they pointed out Jessie Goudie's grave, but would not take a step closer to it. It was there, clearly marked, a spinster not dead two years. But behind hers was another, much older stone, tilted at an angle to the ground, beset by lichen. Whatever it told of the body whose last resting place it marked was long worn away by wind and salt rain. The stone showed no cracks, and the ground around it was undisturbed.

William surveyed the ground around, and I was about to turn back to the kirk when his voice stopped me.

'Alexander, the well.'

I looked over to the spring where the waters of St Fittick's Well, that place of resort for the superstitious and the desperate, trickled from the earth. I saw nothing there I had not seen before.

'No,' he said, animated now. 'Not that one. But there, the Lady Well.'

Some way back and off to the right from behind the old and unmarked grave was the vaulted stone casing of a well dedicated long ago to the mother of Christ. No miraculous or magical properties being claimed for it, it had fallen into disuse and been all but forgotten by those who thronged the other. We walked towards it, pulled back the bush whose twigs and branches had recently been snapped and trampled upon, and descended the stone steps down to the spring of the well itself. A foul smell, not just of damp but of animal filth came to us.

'There must be a beast dead in here,' said William. 'Mind your feet there – the steps are covered in slime.' But when we got to the bottom of the steps, we found no dead beast, just the excrement and blood of one who, for its time in this shelter at least, had lived.

My stomach lurched, and I pushed past William up the steps for air. He was up there soon after me. 'Dear God, the stench.'

'Perhaps, if they had done something to the horse . . .'

William shook his head, and said what I knew already to be true. 'Whatever detritus was there came from no horse, and no spectre either. Someone has cowered here, and bled. John Leslie may not be as mad as we have thought him.'

The reluctant elders were brought to view what we had found. Rabbits, foxes, large wildcats, all were suggested, the latter beast thought most likely to have been that seen and heard by the deranged minister on the morning before. The question of why such an animal might have come from the mountains to the very edge of the sea did not much trouble these good men of Torry, now that they had an explanation for the deranged visions of their minister that left the Devil happily to his devices elsewhere.

It was agreed that John Leslie should not be allowed back in the kirk until after the matter had been brought fully before the presbytery. I volunteered to do that myself, determined that Leslie should face his brethren on charges of drunkenness and not witchcraft. In no way did I believe that the kirk of St Fittick's had been the site of any demonic Sabbath such as its minister claimed to witness. Yet, as William and I readied ourselves to leave Nigg Bay for Torry and the ferry that would take us back to Aberdeen, I could not persuade myself that what the terrified minister had seen on that early Sabbath morning had been a wildcat, nor any other dumb animal.

'One thing more,' said William, as the session clerk shut the kirkyard gate behind us. 'Has the horse been found?'

'It was found wandering about over by Dounies. It's a wonder the poor beast never went over the cliff. It took three men to get it by the bridle. It's stabled now at Brown's Inn, and if no one claims it within the week, it will be sold for the poor box.'

Back down in the village, we made our way to the inn, which was hardly worthy of the name. The innkeeper snorted.

'Sell it, they think? no one will ever saddle that beast again. Boiling for glue'll be the best they'll make of it.'

He showed us round to the stable where the miserable creature whinnied and tried to rear back in its stall. It could only get up so far, as a rope tied its bridle tight to an iron pole.

'I cannot think that rope will help calm the poor beast,' said William, making soothing noises as he approached the horse.

'It was on him when they found him, eight feet of it trailing behind him. We managed to cut away a length of it, but couldn't get close enough to get the rest untied. You may try if you wish, but he'll knock you senseless.'

'Not I, but Davy Durno,' murmured William.

'What?'

'This is Davy Durno in Woolmanhill's horse. The one that he accused his neighbour of stealing. I've seen it trail a cart behind it up to the Stockethill often enough.' He turned to the innkeeper. 'Let no one else claim this horse. It is the property of Davy Durno in Aberdeen. He will be here before tomorrow night to collect it.'

'And welcome he is to it,' grumbled the innkeeper as he went back to his duties. 'And mind you tell him to bring the money for its stabling.'

I was not sorry to get back on the ferry, away from Torry

and the grim things we had found at the other side of Girdle Ness, yet had I known what awaited us when we set foot back in Aberdeen, I would have bid the ferryman tarry longer in his work.

14

A Killing Frost

We could tell there was something amiss before we even stepped off the ferry at Futty. Two of the burgh constables were at the landing shore, and there was nothing in their aspect that suggested they were passengers waiting to make the crossing. As the ferryman docked at the pier, the taller of the two constables called down that he should come up but that no one else should leave the boat until given permission.

'What has happened?' asked William Cargill.

'We are searching after two people who might have tried to leave the burgh by night.'

'Who?'

'The French master's sister, and George Jamesone's gardener, who lodged with them. Neither has been seen since last night.'

The constable was able to tell us nothing more, and neither the ferryman, nor any of the other passengers, had any information of use to offer. 'This is very bad,' I said as we headed back in to town as quickly as we could.

'Louis must be going out of his mind,' said William. 'But what is this about the gardener?'

Assuming it was Charpentier and not St Clair who was the man in question, I told him briefly what I knew of him, and of Christiane's liking for him.

'Surely you don't think the girl would have gone away with him?'

'No, I don't,' I said. 'But the baillies obviously do. I should have listened to her, I should have paid her more heed.'

William stopped for a moment and turned to me. 'Alexander, what on earth are you talking about?'

I told him then about Christiane's fear of Seoras, her belief that he was watching her.

'Surely,' he said, 'Seoras MacKay is dead.'

'I wish I could be as certain. I am going to George's. I think they must search that garden.'

We found at George's house that searches were under way in every quarter in the town as well as at the entrance gates and the harbour and ferry landings. The artist himself had gone with Christiane's distracted brother to question Jean St Clair on what he might know about the disappearance of the pair.

We found them in the workshed. George was pacing around the small floor space while Louis was hunched before the fire in front of a tight-lipped St Clair. George was greatly relieved to see us.

'Alexander, William. Thank goodness you are here. I

think we will go mad with this fellow. Louis can get practically nothing out of him.'

'What have you been able to find out?'

'Louis was out at Pitfodels last night. He goes every Monday evening to tutor Menzies' daughters. Menzies himself was at home and invited Louis to stay for a hand of cards. It was after eleven before he got back to his own house. He could hear snoring from the schoolroom – where the Frenchmen sleep – and assumed they were both in there.' Almost as an aside, George said, 'Guillaume had been here with me, working on the planting schemes until well after seven. Then we had left together and said our goodnights on Schoolhill. He went his way towards Louis' house and I turned into my own. Anyway, it also didn't cross Louis' mind that Christiane would not also be safely sleeping in her own chamber. He went straight to bed and did not wake until after eight this morning. Of course, at that hour there was nothing strange in St Clair and Charpentier being long gone to their work, but he was surprised that Christiane had let him sleep so long. When he went to look for her, he could not find her in the house. She had not been seen out in the street, or the marketplace either. That is when he began to worry. He went to Lumsden's house, thinking Lady Rothiemay or Isabella might have sent for her for some reason – for she has been much in company there of late, despite her failure in the trials.'

'And they had not,' finished William.

'No,' said George wearily, 'they had not. The baillie began

to organise a search – on a small scale at first, and only because her Ladyship was almost as concerned as Louis – and Louis came to me, looking for Jean and Guillaume. I took him down to the maze, where they were to be working, and found Jean there alone. He said he had not seen Guillaume since last night. I sent word of this to Lumsden and that is when we took Jean up here, to try to get something sensible out of him.'

Louis stood up. He looked dreadful, despite the night's sleep that appeared to have cost him so dear. His face was almost grey and his eyes set in dark hollows that had not been there the last time I had seen him. Apprehension was sketched deep in his face, and when he spoke he sounded hopeless.

'I think she must have gone away with him.'

'Non.' It was the first word I had ever heard Jean St Clair utter.

'But what else can it be?' Louis almost yelled in frustration, and in English. 'After all you have told me, what else can it be?'

The Frenchman sat impassive once more.

'Come and sit down,' said William, pulling a stool out from beneath the workbench, 'and tell us what it is he has told you.'

Louis was shivering, and George took down one of the gardeners' capes from its nail behind the door and set it about his shoulders.

'He says he returned to my house at around six last night,

that Guillaume was to be labelling plants and seeds that he had already sorted and then was to work on the planting schemes with you.' He looked at George, who nodded.

'Christiane had already written the necessary translations. We managed well enough between us and finished sometime after seven.'

'How did Charpentier seem to you?' I asked George.

George considered. 'Perhaps a little quieter than usual. We could never converse very much, but there was always a geniality about him that made our time together very pleasant. Last night though, when I think about it, he did seem to be a little more pensive than usual, and in a hurry to get away.'

This revelation did not cheer Louis. 'Well might he have been. Jean St Clair says that sometime before seven, while he and Christiane were having their supper, a note was brought for Christiane. A town's urchin. St Clair has no clue what it said, but at the stroke of eight by St Nicholas Kirk bell Christiane put on her outer clothing and went out, not telling him where she was going, but only that she would be back in an hour, and he was to tell me not to concern myself if she was still out when I arrived home.'

'He had no clue where she was going, or who the note was from?'

'None.'

'And he did not try to dissuade her?'

Louis voice was tinged with disgust. 'He said it was not his business to be my sister's keeper. Dear God, I knew he took little enough interest in the lives of others, but to let her go out like that alone . . .'

He put his head in his hands and was wracked with sobs. George put an arm around him. 'Come now, Louis. If she has indeed gone away with Guillaume, it is not the worst, for he is a good man, and would treat her kindly, you know that.'

The French master nodded and rallied himself to continue. 'I know he would – if she is with him. He never went back to my house last night, and St Clair says as far as he can tell what Guillaume has of belongings are still there.'

'And St Clair thought nothing strange that he did not come back? That he was not there in the morning?'

Louis shook his head. 'He simply shrugs and says Guillaume goes his own way and he his. He has not seen or heard anything of either my sister or Charpentier since and he is completely unperturbed.'

'And yet,' said William, 'he seems certain that they have not gone away together. Why is that?'

Louis shook his head hopelessly. 'I don't know.'

'Well let us find out,' said William. With a look on his face usually reserved for appearances in court, he went across to St Clair and barked something at him in French – a language that it had never occurred to me he could speak. St Clair stood up instantly, like a man used to the voice of authority. William asked him a question slowly, and very clearly. Unlike George and Louis, I had no idea what he had just said, but it was clear from his tone that an answer would be given before either he or St Clair ever left this workshed. The Frenchman opened his mouth to speak, closed it, and then laughed in derision as he made his reply.

'What? What is it?' I said.

Louis turned to me. 'He said that if we truly think Guillaume Charpentier has the slightest interest in my sister, then we know nothing about him at all.'

Just then, we heard voices coming down the path towards the workshed and opened the door to be met by Baillie Lumsden and four men of his search party.

Louis was at them first. 'Is there any news? Have they been found?'

'No.' said Lumsden. 'George, we need to search this garden.'

'Of course,' said George. 'Let me show you the plans.' Within two minutes they had a plan and instructions set out for a thorough search of the gardens, beginning at the maze in one corner and the small wooded area between Jamesone's back wall and the Blackfriars' gate on the other. The parties were to work their way in opposite directions up and down the garden and meet again at the centre, where George's summer pavilion was to be.

We wanted Louis to wait in the warmth but he would not, and so George, William and I took him out with us. We also made St Clair come with us. Nothing in what he had said had convinced the others that he did not know a lot more, or indeed that what he was telling us was anything near the truth. As for me, all I could think of were the fears Christiane had expressed to me about Seoras, and I believed every word the unsettling little man had said.

Our party went first to the area of George's planned herb garden, where already stones of granite had been laid out in the form of a wheel. George tried to cheer Louis a little by talking of his sister as if she might just have slipped away on an errand. 'This is Christiane's favourite spot, you know. The planning has been nearly all hers. The centre-piece, Alexander and his blessed session permitting, is to be a small statue of the goddess Ceres, surrounded by lavender, to match your sister's pretty eyes.'

Louis attempted a smile, but his mind was too distracted to give much attention to what George was saying. Mine too was distracted, by the mention of a statue. One of several statues George had planned for the ornamentation of the garden, but most were to be elsewhere. His nymphaeum.

'They will not have met here,' I said.

'What?'

'Christiane and Charpentier. If they met, it would have not have been here,' and I started to run across and down towards the north-west corner of the garden, and the pond.

Images flashed through my head as I ran. Memories of images. Isabella Irvine and some unknown man disappearing through the trees in the darkness. Isabella Irvine coming upon me as I sat, alone, on the stone bench on the far side of the frozen pond. Isabella Irvine and Guillaume Charpentier sitting, only a short while later, on that same bench.

The frost in the air burned my throat as I ran and hurt my lungs so that my chest felt it might split open, but despite the shouts of those behind me to wait for them, I could not stop until I got there. I knew well enough now the best way through the trees in the tangle surrounding the pond and hardly had to look down to avoid roots and boulders that had found me out before. But then, as I pushed my way between the last of the branches into the clearing around the frozen water, I did stop, as if a wall of glass had appeared between me and what was in front of me. For there, suspended in the air like a jewelled doll above the ice, her hair and lips frosted, her head limp and the skin on her arms and her bared neck blue, was Christiane Rolland, more dead than any other thing in this wintered place.

I forced myself to take control of my thoughts. And turned, arms outstretched, to stop whoever might be coming behind me, to stop Louis, from coming upon what I had just seen. I opened my mouth to shout at the others to stop him, but I was too slow, I was too late. The sound that filled the air was not my voice, but his. It was not a shout but a howl. I watched as William and then George tried to pull him back, but he wrestled them away. And then he was pushing past me, shouting her name.

I caught him just as he was about to go out on to the ice. He sank to his knees and I did also, putting my arms around him and turning slightly so that his head was pulled against my chest and his eyes averted from the dead form of his young sister.

William and George came to a halt behind us. 'Oh, God. No.' Our shouts had brought Lumsden's search parties running in our direction and the baillie and two of his men were very soon with us.

'Cut her down, for God's sake,' said Lumsden to the man next to him. Only then, when I looked up, did I see that standing a little behind him, her hand covering her mouth in horror, was Isabella Irvine.

Half an hour later, I was sitting opposite Isabella in the parlour of Baillie Lumsden's house. George had sent for a physician to see to Louis Rolland and had gone back to the French master's house to wait with him there. William had gone with Lumsden to his chambers off the Castlegate to further question Jean St Clair about the events of the previous night, and whether he knew of any relationship between Christiane Rolland and Guillaume Charpentier. I would have to officially report Christiane's suicide to the kirk session, although the news must already have been in the mouths and ears of half the town. For now, though, all my interest was in the woman who sat, shivering and hunched in upon herself, three feet away from me. Neither of us had spoken a word on the way up from Jamesone's garden.

My first words jolted her out of her distraction. 'Did you never imagine she might take her own life?'

'What?' she said, as if I could not actually have asked what she thought I had just asked.

I was in no mood to further humour this woman, and repeated my question.

'You and Charpentier. When he played on her affections and you betrayed her friendship. She was a fragile young girl, whose state of mind had already been thrown in to disarray by the disappearance of another man who had courted her. It never occurred to you that her cruel treatment by two whom she thought her friends might drive her beyond what she could withstand?'

Isabella looked confused, desperately seeking to understand what I was saying and to find an answer for it. She seemed to stumble over her words.

'But he – Guillaume – he never played on her affections. He never encouraged her feelings. And there is nothing – nothing, you must believe me – between him and me.'

'You would have me believe that you never betrayed her friendship?'

She did not answer me, but worked at her bottom lip. I had never before seen Isabella Irvine so vulnerable, but I was too horror-struck by what I had seen in the garden to be put off. 'For one of your station, Madame, you have made yourself very familiar with a gardener.'

'You do not understand,' she said, as if any fight had gone out of her.

'Oh? Do I not? After all the years of spite – deserved,

I'll grant you – you have harboured for me, do you not think I know a tryst when I see it?'

This had been truly unexpected. 'A tryst?'

I had not the patience to humour her. 'Dear Lord, Isabella, did you think no one would observe you going into George's garden? Heavens, you have rarely been out of it. Who were you to meet there today? Guillaume Charpentier – a common gardener? William Ormiston, whose touch seems so to thrill you – and oh, I saw that touch. Or is it someone else?'

It was only when I said the words aloud that it came to me. 'Archie Hay.'

Below her pallor, her face became paler yet. I knew it then.

'Archie? Is it Archie you hoped to find there? Archie Hay, come back from the dead? How long have you known, Isabella? Have you always known?'

The eyes that had looked on me in times past with such disdain, were brimming now, pleading. 'I did not know, Alexander. I swear to God, I did not know.'

The sight of this woman, scared, sorry before me, shocked me out of my anger. My voice became hoarse. 'But you know now, do you not?'

She nodded once, then lowered her head, a scarcely audible 'yes' escaping her lips.

Into our silence came the sound of footsteps on the stairs. Not of Lumsden, still busied with his duties at the tolbooth, nor yet Lady Rothiemay, who on hearing of Christiane's disappearance that morning had taken herself to the old town, thinking to find news of the girl there. It was some relief to me to see George Jamesone shown into the parlour by the young servant.

He enquired briefly after Isabella, but it was soon clear that it was me he had come to see.

'I am on my way up to the Castlegate with this for Lumsden. Louis found it in Christiane's chamber when we returned to his house.' He held towards me a small piece of paper, neatly folded in half. I opened it out to find a short message of some sort, neatly written in words I assumed to be French. But what was clear enough in any language was that the note was addressed to Christiane Rolland and purported to be from Guillaume Charpentier. I looked at it and turned to George.

'This is his handwriting? His signature?'

He nodded.

'Then some at least of what St Clair claims is true. He did send her a note.'

I rang for the housemaid and asked her to stay with Mistress Irvine until Lady Rothiemay should return, then George and I went quickly across Broadgate in the direction of the Castlegate and William's chambers.

'I cannot understand it,' said George as we turned in to the end of Huxter Row. 'Guillaume was with me until well after seven last night, and yet this note from him, asking Christiane to meet him at the pond, arrived at Louis' house before seven, delivered by a boy who had just been given it, according to St Clair. I swear to you, Alexander, I never saw him write it nor hand anything to any message boy.'

'It is definitely his hand?'

'I could show it to you. It tallies exactly with that on his labelling on my plans.'

I had noted Charpentier's neat careful hand before, marvelled at his very exact Latin. It had not seemed quite right to me even then, to find a gardener so well lettered. 'And does he express himself well?'

'It is just a brief note, Alexander, and my French none the best, but it looks well enough to me.'

Lumsden was still with William and St Clair when we arrived at William's chambers.

The baillie was flustered on being shown the note. 'So where is the fellow?' he demanded, after having it explained to him. 'Four hours now we have searched, and not the hint of a sight of him. Perhaps he never went there to meet her at all.'

It was a possibility we considered amongst ourselves for a good while after Lumsden had gone to the tolbooth to check on the progress of the search.

'He must have gone there,' said William. 'Why would she have taken her own life if he had not thoroughly rejected her? Hardly a reason, even that, but I do not know what goes on in a young woman's mind.'

George also was at a loss. 'But it was an attraction, an infatuation such as we have all been prone to from time to time. I never saw Guillaume give the slightest sign of returning it. Only kindness and perhaps a degree of affection. Christiane was a sensible girl – surely she cannot have read it as anything more?'

'But why would Charpentier flee? He would hardly have allowed her to hang herself in front of him?'

'Unless he went back to the spot later and found her and panicked . . .'

William and George were going further and further down a road that led nowhere, trying to work out an order of events that never happened. But I was scarcely listening to them for I was thinking of her dress, her pristine blue dress, unmarked save for a little mud around the hem. I looked at St Clair, silent in the corner of the room.

'She would hardly have taken a rope. Ask him, William, ask him if she had a rope.'

'What?' said William.

'Ask Jean St Clair if Christiane took with her a rope when she left Louis' house last night.'

The Frenchman had looked up at the mention of his name and seemed to be thinking before William even spoke to him.

No. She had no rope. What young girl would walk through the streets of the town in her prettiest dress with a rope over her arm?

'It was not dirty.'

Now it was for George to look utterly lost. 'Alexander, what are you talking about?'

'You keep ropes somewhere in the garden?'

'Yes, for hauling cut trees and the like. They are in a store near the workshed.'

'And we are to think Christiane hauled a rope from the store all through the garden down to the pond, where she then climbed that tree, set a noose round her neck and let herself fall. Think, George: her dress – pale blue. Scarcely a mark and not a tear nor a caught thread on it.'

William was staring at me. 'What are you saying, Alexander?'

But he already knew. The girl in the spotless pale blue dress whom we had found hanging above the ice less than two hours ago had not taken her own life over a rejected love. She had not taken her own life at all.

Fifty yards away in the guard room of the tolbooth, Lumsden understood instantly. He took William with him for an inspection of Christiane's clothing and then sent me to fetch Dr Dun from the college. Within twenty minutes the principal had arrived and completed his brief examination. We should have seen it ourselves from the start.

'Her neck has been broken, all right, but not from hanging. Did you not notice her eyes, her tongue, the lack of lividity in her face?' I thought of the face, so pale it had almost matched her dress. Dun closed her eyes tenderly. 'The child was dead before she was ever hung from that tree.'

15

'Will I Tell You of Your Brother?'

A night's sleep and a hefty measure of George's best port wine had done little to diminish the sense of shock among us as he, William and I met together once more the next morning in his studio. St Clair, at his own request, had been allowed to return to his work in the garden, albeit under the eye of one of Lumsden's men. Every so often one of us would lift our heads as if to speak, but our words only went in circles, and we had all but given up.

'But, he is a *good* man, I would have sworn it. I cannot believe he would have done this.'

'Perhaps he did not,' I said.

William was almost annoyed at me. 'Oh, come, Alexander. You cannot still be at this nonsense about Seoras MacKay. That boy is lying dead somewhere, and anyone with any sense knows it. When we finally get Hugh Gunn out of the precincts of that blasted college of yours without twenty of MacKay's men around him, we will have the truth out of him.'

'MacKay will never let you near him,' I said, 'and without a body, they can hardly charge Hugh with murder.'

'We have Christiane's body, though,' said George, returning to the matter at hand, 'and Guillaume fled or killed.'

'Or pressed,' I said.

They both stared at me. In fact, up until I had said the words, I had not considered the possibility myself.

Comprehension spread over their faces. 'Ormiston?'

I swallowed some port. 'It's possible.' I remembered the night in Downie's Inn, and how abruptly the two Frenchmen had left when I had been engaged with the lieutenant.

'But why just him? Why would they not take St Clair too?' asked William

I raised an eyebrow at him.

'Well, apart from the obvious. Do you think it was a question of chance?'

I pushed at a log in front of the fire with my foot. 'I think it is possible that Guillaume was pressed because of Isabella Irvine.'

George sat back in his chair, opened his mouth as if he would speak. Closed it again.

I could not help but laugh. 'It is not often I render you speechless, my friend.'

'It is . . .' He was still struggling. 'I thought I was out in the world more often than you, Alexander, saw more of its secrets, but I see that for all I know of the doings of marquises and kings, I know very little of what goes on under my very nose. I had never considered there could be any connection between Guillaume Charpentier and Isabella Irvine. They met in my garden only last week – indeed, "met" is hardly the apt expression, for it was to Lady Rothiemay that Guillaume spoke, and Isabella did not appear to take any particular interest in him, nor he her. Mind you,' he said, almost shielding his face with his glass as though he might be caught in an indiscretion, 'my wife never tires of telling me what a handsome man Guillaume is considered, and I would not put it past Isabella to bestow her affections on a gardener while treating every other man that comes near her with disdain.'

'So it is not just me then?'

He put down his glass, shaking his head. 'Granted, you seem to be an especial object of her contempt, but she scarcely gives more encouragement to men she has never before encountered.'

'There is something between her and Ormiston, I know that for certain, and if he suspected anything at all of Charpentier, he may well have taken measures to remove him from her circle.'

I told them what I had witnessed by the pond on Saturday afternoon, and of the tryst I had come upon in the garden in the darkness not long before our own scrap there on the previous Monday night.

'Ormiston?'

'Probably.' I told them also what I had glimpsed in the mirror at Baillie Lumsden's house. 'The lieutenant was greatly disappointed that she was not in attendance at his ship-board dinner the other night. She had been put to bed with a fever. Lady Rothiemay seemed distinctly against any encouragement of the lieutenant from what I could see.'

'Well, pity help Ormiston, then, for Katharine Forbes is not a woman prone to ambiguity.'

'No, but she is evidently not averse to the odd lie when it suits her purposes,' said William, again in lawyer mode.

'How so?' I asked.

'Well, did Isabella Irvine look to you like a woman who had been put to bed of a fever only the night before when she appeared in George's garden yesterday?'

My unnecessary answer was interrupted by the arrival of the exhausted-looking Baillie Lumsden.

'I think I must question this St Clair fellow further, George, and whether he knows anything more or not, I do not think it good that he should wander the town freely when there is a murderer abroad. Will you take me down to him?'

George agreed, and while William reluctantly went to his own duties in the Castlegate, I, already having sent word to the college that I would not be there before dinner, went down into the garden after them. We went through the gate in the wall of the backland of George's house and made our way towards the place St Clair had last been working. We found him with little trouble near the site of the maze, at his favourite pastime of hacking down trees.

In a clumsy approximation of the French language,

George told St Clair what the baillie wanted of him. The gardener still had the axe in his hand, and gestured in the direction of the workshed that he should return it.

George himself was slow to move. 'What has become of my sanctuary, Alexander? How can I think of making this a place of pleasure now?'

'It was God's will that Christiane helped you here. She worked with you to accomplish something good, and she took a delight in that work. You must do so also, so that her coming here was of greater significance than simply to find the place of her death. The spring will bring new life, and a memorial to her. You must reclaim this place from evil.'

He smiled and put an arm around my shoulder. 'You are right, my friend. Thank you.'

Avoiding any glance in the direction of the pond, we followed Lumsden through the trees and out to the clearing between amphitheatre and pavilion where George planned to plant his avenue of fruit trees. It was a relief to be out in the open, and the greater light, further away from the place of yesterday's grim discovery, but the relief was short-lived, for just as we were bidding farewell to the baillie with his charge, a party of a dozen armed men, headed by Sir Donald MacKay of Strathnaver, Lord Reay, came down the hill towards us.

'Your Lordship . . .' began Lumsden.

'Where is the body?' shouted MacKay.

Lumsden appeared a little shaken. 'Taken to the kirk, but it is not Seoras, your Lordship, it is not your son.'

MacKay's pace slowed only a little, and only for a moment. As he came closer I could see jaw muscles working as if he was trying to hold in some rage. The men behind him looked equally determined. They drew up in front of us and I saw that all the good humour of the night on shipboard was gone from the Highlander's face as he addressed Lumsden without even acknowledging George or me. He spoke slowly, and in his voice there was something chilling.

'Where is the body?'

Lumsden tried again. 'I sent it to lie in St Ninian's Chapel. I can assure you, Sir Donald, the body is that of a young girl, the French master's sister. George here will confirm it, Alexander too.'

Lord Reay turned flaming eyes upon me. 'The girl Christiane? The one of whom Uisdean spoke? Is everyone my son knew to be assaulted? Murdered? And I have to hear it on the street? I have seen better order in a Spanish brothel!'

Visibly shaken, it took the baillie a moment to find his reply. 'I am sorry, your Lordship. You should have been told. We have been busy . . .'

'No doubt,' said MacKay, his outburst evidently having calmed him. 'But I would still see the body, and the place where it was found. I have read the dead often enough, and I may see something that you do not.'

'Of course,' said Lumsden.

'And my men will search this garden, Jamesone.'

The baillie was perplexed. 'But if they have done so already . . .'

'Aye, well they will do so again. If this is to be a dumping ground for the murdered of this town, I will not have my son rot here. And if the man who put that child to death be still hiding here, he will not escape my vengeance!'

There was nothing more to be said, and George and I fell reluctantly into line behind Seoras's father and his men, the unfortunate Lumsden trailing behind them in the direction of the pond.

'You come too,' called George.

I had forgotten about St Clair, as had the baillie, but I saw him now, stopped in his tracks on the way to the workshed. His face was a picture of uncertainty.

'*Venez*,' George said eventually. '*Suivez*.'

The party ahead of us had paused for a moment when George had called out, but seeing it was an issue of no consequence, had soon continued on their way. All but one of them, a stocky, scarred man who might have been anything between thirty and fifty years of age. He did not follow his companions as they picked up their pace again, for the sight of the gardener had caught his attention. Like a man suddenly finding himself in the wrong place, he stared at Jean St Clair. His mouth began to move, almost silently, as if he was speaking to himself, testing the words on himself, and I could not hear what he said. But then, somehow satisfied, he repeated them, louder, and the men closest to him also stopped.

'Johnny Sinclair.'

I stared at him.

'Johnny Sinclair, from Wick. You cowardly, runaway son of a whore.'

St Clair gaped for a moment as if he had been struck to stone, but he quickly regained his wits, and before I fully understood what was happening, he had turned and begun to run. His hand still gripping the axe, he was making at speed in the direction not of the workshed but the east gate, and the centre of the town. But for all his knowledge of the overgrown garden, and the strength that years of physical labour had given him, he was no match for the barefooted Highlanders with ten years of fighting in the field behind them, and it was far from certain that he would be able to make his escape into the morning bustle of the town before they were upon him. Even so, it was not one of Lord Reay's men who caught him, but Lieutenant Ormiston, who was just coming through the gate as St Clair reached it. Unlike myself, Ormiston needed no time to understand what was going on, and had the gardener lying on his back, the point of a sword at his throat, before Lord Reay's men had come within twenty yards of them. St Clair, recognising a man for whom killing would not be a novelty, did not even struggle.

By a small movement of his sword, Ormiston brought the gardener to his feet without ever giving him the chance of retreating from its point. The Highlanders had halted in their pursuit now and, regaining their accustomed order, waited.

'What would you have me do with this detritus, your

Lordship?' The lieutenant prodded St Clair in the chest with the end of his blade, forcing him backwards towards the waiting soldiers.

'Bring him to me that I might look at him. Neil Ross, come and tell me what you know of this man.'

The soldiers parted to make way for Ormiston and his prisoner. Ross, having first spat at the ground before St Clair's feet, walked ahead of them. St Clair himself looked neither left nor right. They stopped six feet in front of Lord Reay, and Ormiston forced the Frenchman down onto his knees.

I glanced at George Jamesone, whose face was such a picture of astonishment I knew he understood no more of what was playing out before us than I did.

'Well, Neil? What will you tell me about this wretch?'

Ross never took his eyes from the gardener, who appeared now to fully comprehend his situation as one lost, and had therefore once more adopted his wonted expression of contempt.

'It is Johnny Sinclair, your Lordship, that I have known since we first fought over crabs amongst the rocks of Wick Bay, neither of us higher than your knee. I should have put a knife through him nine years ago, the day I saw him turn up at Cromarty to board the ship that was taking our regiment to Gluckstadt, for he never did a good turn in all his life, and would as like take the last drop of water from the lips of a dying man as give him comfort. I warned him that day that if he ever stepped out of line or brought shame on our regiment I would kill him.'

Lord Reay briefly glanced at St Clair before addressing himself once more to Neil Ross. 'And yet he is not dead. I do not imagine that is because he brought glory to his colours instead.'

Ross's face contorted in disgust. 'Indeed he did not, but I'll put an end to him this very minute if your Lordship will but give the word.'

'I suspect I shall have cause to, but tell me first what he is doing here on his knees in George Jamesone's garden, instead of marching behind our colours or lying dead on a German battlefield.'

Ross nodded, and it was clear that his anger now was tempered by memories clouded by grief. 'Two years, Sinclair there kept himself out of my way and out of my notice – for where the service was hot he was rarely anywhere to be seen. But then we came to Stralsund, and at Stralsund there could be no hiding place.'

The name was familiar to me from Archie's stories, and also from Ormiston.

'Mackenzie was in charge of the regiment.'

'Aye, for your Lordship was on the way back from Scotland with new-raised recruits. An honourable and brave commander Captain MacKenzie was, Sir, and much loved by his men.'

'I know it. But had I been there myself, perhaps . . .'

'Saving your honour, Sir, there was nothing you could have done that Captain MacKenzie could not, unless perhaps make the Danish governor of the town have a better regard for the needs of our men, but that is away on the wind and cannot be changed now.'

George had found his voice at last. 'What did Jean St Clair – Sinclair – do at Stralsund?'

Another of Lord Reay's men spoke up. 'I will tell you, for I remember him now, filth that he is. He left his comrades to die. I saw it myself. At the very moment it looked as if the enemy might break through the Frankentor and all be lost, Johnny Sinclair emptied the pockets of a comrade with his arm blown off that was screaming for his mother, and turned his tail and ran. Had I not been looking a German pike in the eye I would have put a bullet in him myself. Six weeks we were there, hardly a minute or a place to lay our heads, to change our linens; I hear the noise of those cannon now when I close my eyes at night. Five hundred of our regiment dead – more than lived to hold the place, and of those, few above a hundred were able to walk uninjured from its gates. Yet Johnny Sinclair plundered and fled over the bodies of his comrades. Give me the word, Sir, for if Neil Ross has not the stomach for it, I have.'

Ross rounded on his comrade. 'A word more of that and I'll fillet you first, Eoin MacRae.'

Lord Reay lifted his hand. 'Enough. Lieutenant, you lost your own brother at Stralsund, though I can scarcely believe that you and this worthless pustule sailed in my regiment on the same ship. That he should live while your brother lies dead and honoured puts this man's life in your hands, not mine. Death would be a release undeserved for such filth. Will you press him?'

Throughout the soldiers' narratives, Sinclair's face had remained impassive, but now every feature came to life, and he tried to struggle to his feet between the two men who had moved to stand at either side of him. They took him by the arms and forced him back down to the ground, but he struggled to break free of them again.

'You'll not press me, Ormiston. You'll not get me back over there again, do what you will to me. I would rather rot in the ground in this God-forsaken town than set a foot again upon German soil. Marching for weeks on end without pay, without food, without a blanket to cover us, and all while the likes of him trade us by numbers and take their dinner with kings.'

At this, Ormiston, his gauntlet removed, gave Sinclair an almighty slap to the face that sent him collapsing back to the ground. To my surprise, the gardener, covered in dirt now and bleeding from a gash in his cheek, righted himself and began to speak again.

'You don't remember me, Ormiston, do you? Too busy shining your buttons and waiting to step into the next dead man's boots, to get your next promotion. But I remember you, and I remember your brother, and his honourable death.' He smiled, a horrible smile. 'Will I tell you of your brother?'

Ormiston's face went white, and I saw the hand that held his sword begin to shake. I think Lord Reay saw it too, for slowly, he took the pistol from its holster at his side and handed it to the man beside him.

'Load it, Urquhart,' he said, without looking at the man to whom he spoke.

When it was done, and it was done with expert speed, he took the sword from Ormiston's hand and replaced it with the gun.

'Remove that blemish from my regiment, Lieutenant,' he said.

And without a word, before all our eyes, in the middle of that late autumn afternoon, William Ormiston blew John Sinclair's brains out.

16

Things Dormant

'Dear God.' Sarah sat down, almost as worn out by hearing of the events of the morning as I was by witnessing them. 'Was Archie there?'

'No. I haven't seen him since I glimpsed him last night on the ship, and not spoken with him since he left here five nights ago. He doesn't go in to the town with the lieutenant or any others from the ship during the day.' I had had no chance to speak to him on the evening of Ormiston's dinner, and none to search him out since. The report for the presbytery of our visit to St Fittick's the day before remained unwritten. Events in the town since then had sent all that to the back of my mind. Sarah was still speaking, as if to herself.

'But Christiane . . . I cannot believe it. And the gardener – he seemed so kind. Surely he could not have . . . and the other one . . . ? That the lieutenant just executed him there, in the garden . . .'

I had been over and over the same ground with George and Louis that morning, for the news of more horrors in the garden had brought the French master running up from his house. I had seen men dead and men tortured, but I had never seen a living man all but slaughtered before my very eyes, and the sight had emptied my stomach. It had taken an hour in George's studio, and half of a bottle of brandy between us, before I had even been fit to think of going home. And after the initial horror of what we had seen began to pass, it was Louis who realised it first: with St Clair, or Sinclair – it hardly mattered which now – had gone all knowledge he might have had of Guillaume Charpentier.

'What an ending,' George had said, 'for a man who had worked in the Infanta's garden in Brussels, to die like a dog in an overgrown scrap of land here in this poor town.'

'Brussels or no, when he ran from Stralsund, he was never going to be able to run far enough,' I said. The late autumn sunshine glinting though the panes of Jamesone's window spoke of a world more tranquil than that we knew to be outside our doors. We could turn our eyes – our minds – from the horrors suffered by our brothers in other lands, but they would find us out anyway. There was nothing to be seen of the garden through the bare branches of the trees but golden, brown and red leaves piled one upon the other. You could not see the blood, darkened from red to brown, that stained those leaves. A man could only guess at the rot, the decay taking place around him and beneath his feet, and trust in God for the renewal that came, every spring from the dead remains of what had gone before.

Going over it all again at home with Sarah brought me no nearer to an understanding of what was going on in our town. Eventually, I stopped even trying, and turned my mind to something I could at least achieve: my report to the presbytery on what William and I had learned at St Fittick's Church the previous morning.

Sarah attempted to persuade me to take some rest. 'It will make little difference, I think, to the presbytery or to John Leslie if they receive your report tomorrow or the next day – the man is lost, and for you to make yourself ill by toiling over it today will do neither of you any good.'

'I must finish it,' I said impatiently. 'I must finish something. Anything to dislodge the images of Johnny Sinclair and Christiane from my head.'

Sarah hesitated. I avoided looking at her and kept my eyes firmly on the writing in front of me, but she was not to be thrown off. 'It's not just what happened in George's garden today, is it? You haven't been yourself since Archie returned.'

'I, it has been . . . it's nothing. I'm just tired.'

'Tired?' she raised her voice in frustration. 'I have known you nine years, Alexander. Do you not think I know it when there is something wrong? You cannot shut me out of your troubles, however much you might wish to.'

I put down my pen and tried to think what I could say to her.

'It's just that . . . it's no small thing to know that one

dear to you, whom you thought dead and mourned, has been alive all that time.'

'I know,' she said. There was a strange expression on her face as she watched me. 'But it has been a few days now, and what you have learned seems to trouble you as much as it brings you joy. Will you not talk to me of it?'

I leaned towards her and took her hand. 'What I must say, I must say to Archie.'

'Are you angry with him?' she asked.

'No, not angry, not that. But there are things I need to ask him, things I need to understand.'

If I had hoped she would not pursue it I was to be disappointed. 'What things? Do you mean?' She swallowed. 'Do you mean his sister?'

'What? No – oh, no.' I got up and went to her, putting my arms around her, but she did not crumple, and she did not want my comfort. She pulled back from me.

'Is she here, Alexander?'

I stepped back.

'What? Katharine Hay? No. No.'

'She is not at Bailie Lumsden's house, with Lady Rothiemay?'

I sat back down. 'Why would you think that?'

'Because I know who *is* there. I know of Isabella Irvine, who she is. I know that you have seen *her* there, so why not her friend?' Her voice was steady and relentless. 'I know you've been more often to George's garden than you've told me. Do you think that now you are to become a minister no one brings gossip to my ears? Do you think me a fool?'

I was stunned, guilt-ridden at being caught in a crime I had not committed. I could only wait until she had finished. 'Never,' I said. 'I have never thought you a fool, and I have never sought to deceive you. I didn't mention Isabella Irvine's connection with the Hays because I didn't want to hurt you, and yet I see I have done so anyway, and in truth, I take no pleasure in her society or our past connection myself.'

She was not to be so easily mollified.

'And the garden?'

'I went to the garden to look for Seoras, and later for Christiane and Charpentier. Any other time it was that I might think. It seemed a place where I might be alone.'

She nodded, as if finally I had given her the answer she had been looking for. She lifted her warm shawl from the back of a chair and put it round her shoulders. 'Before Archie returned,' she said, as she picked Davy from the floor and went out in to the yard to call Deirdre, 'you had no wish for such solitude.'

I wished I could have gone after them, to gather brambles on the Woolmanhill, but Sarah's face had made it clear that our conversation, for now, was finished. Archie's return had indeed placed a barrier between us, but Sarah did not know the truth of what it was. Whilst she could not see beyond my years-dead love for his sister, it was his revelation that Roisin O'Neill had borne my son that haunted my waking and sleeping hours. It was five nights now since

I had spoken with him, and my need to see him became more urgent with every passing hour.

Tensions in the burgh were such following the events of the last two days that I knew there was no possibility that I might go out into the darkness later that night to look for Archie. What I had to ask him could not be asked in front of Sarah, who now watched my every movement. But Isabella – she had seen him, and perhaps, through the lieutenant, offered my only way of reaching Archie. Isabella played too much on my mind. I could not believe that she had been complicit in the murder of Christiane Rolland, but of the disappearance of Guillaume Charpentier I was convinced she knew more than she had told. I was resolved to go and see her one more time.

My report for the presbytery at last written, I sat a while in my chair by the fire to arrange my thoughts. Of all that had crowded into my mind these last two days, as I closed my eyes I saw not the destroyed face of Jean St Clair, but that of John Leslie as he had babbled about a creature flying through the air and speaking in tongues. I heard his voice. I heard the voice of Christiane Rolland, her terror that she was being watched in her coming and going from her brother's home, in her working with Guillaume in the garden. She had even thought she was being watched in Baillie Lumsden's house. I had dismissed her fears and now she was dead, and the man she had loved was missing. The half-hour that remained to me before I must leave to take my afternoon class was not a peaceful one.

17

Host

In the late afternoon, my students' appetite for a continuation of our lessons in Hebrew grammar was not what it might have been. There was not a soul in town who did not know that I had discovered Christiane Rolland hanging in George's garden, or that Sinclair had been shot right in front of me. Of the girl's death, no one asked me, but Sinclair's seemed to be regarded as a spectacle provided for their fascination, to say nothing of the theories they exchanged over the disappearance of Charpentier. They had persisted with their questions until the six o'clock bell released us from one another's company. As they trudged, dissatisfied, to their supper, I heard one of them mumble to another, 'Never mind, Mr Williamson will be sure to tell us.'

I knew that Peter Williamson, who lodged in the college and was nearer in age to the boys than he was to me, would indeed be sure to tell them all he and the other regents had been able to glean from me. Even the principal himself had been unable to feign lack of interest in the gruesome tale of Sinclair's execution. I recounted for them the barest details, and yet had been unable to look at the food before me. I was consequently ravenous when I walked out of the college gates shortly before seven, and I should have gone home. But I could not face Sarah until I knew more of the truth from Archie, and once I did, I would find a way of telling it to her. There was word in the town that the troop ship was making ready to leave within the next two days, and I had to see Archie one more time before it did so. If I must reach him through Ormiston and Isabella, so be it.

A freezing fog was descending on the town, and even a man who thought he knew his way might easily have got lost. It muffled the sounds of my own footsteps to something ghostly. Voices half-familiar came through the mist to me as I made my way to Baillie Lumsden's house on the Guest Row, the *Ghaist Row*, so called for the unquiet spirits of the kirkyard towards which it led.

The figures who stood their pikes by their sides at the front door were no ghosts but armed men of living flesh who were more watchful for the living than they were for phantoms.

'What is your business here tonight, Mr Seaton?'

I considered telling them I was here to see Isabella, but was not certain that that would be enough to gain me admittance. 'I have come at the request of Lady Rothiemay.'

The one who had spoken to me nodded, but the other

did not move his weapon. 'Have you her note with you?'

'Her Ladyship does not like to commit anything to writing.' I answered. 'In the present circumstances.'

The man still looked unsure, but his companion had seen me come and go from the house on several occasions now, and persuaded him to let me past. The young girl who answered the door at their command was unfamiliar to me, and, as soon became evident, the house.

'I am sorry, Sir – there are so many stairs here, and I only began my duties today. The rest are at the . . . are busy,' she said confusedly.

'If you could just tell me where Mistress Irvine is at the minute, I will find my way there myself.'

She looked greatly relieved. 'They are all in the Long Gallery.'

I smiled at her. 'Do you mean the Great Hall?'

'No, Sir,' she shook her head, quite clear. 'The Long Gallery, on the floor above the Great Hall, up this stair.' She indicated the narrow turnpike, and turned away, vindicated, when I set my foot on them. I had never been up to the Long Gallery before, for all the times I had been in this house. In fact, I was not certain that I had ever heard it mentioned, although at the back of my mind there was something Jamesone had said about painting work he had been unable to do for Lumsden. I had not paid him any great attention at the time. I wondered what purpose Lumsden might have in a Long Gallery, usually the preserve of the castles and strongholds of the powerful of the land, not of burgesses, however wealthy and influential they might be. I could not imagine a busy merchant such as he was, with all his additional duties on the council and as a baillie of the burgh, would have the leisure to play at bowls or shuttlecock or indulge in the other pleasures for which these places were intended.

The sound of the housemaid's footsteps returning to the kitchens had long receded, and I was conscious of nothing but silence emanating from the rooms I passed. I was still not convinced that the girl had the thing to rights, and so when I came to the landing between Lumsden's wife's parlour and the Great Hall, I knocked upon the doors of both. Getting no reply at either door, I tried them both in turn, but found only deserted rooms lit by ochre light from low-burning fires in the hearths.

Apart from the young girl who had let me in, I had not seen another living soul since I had entered this usually busy house. As I emerged once more from Mistress Lumsden's parlour onto the west stairway, I thought I could hear some very faint sound emanating from above me. Something in it made me slow my pace, take greater care to make no sound by my own steps, and I went quietly up the remaining stairs towards the Long Gallery like an intruder in fear of discovery. The whole household must have been in the gallery, but there was no sound of clinking glasses or clattering of knives and forks, and instead of companionable chatter or even polite conversation I could hear only one, low voice, and from the one or two words

I caught I could tell the man spoke in Latin. It felt too as if the fog from outside were seeping through walls and under doors, clambering the stairs with me, finding my throat. I wanted to cough at the sickly sweet perfume of it, but a deep foreboding now told me I should not draw attention to myself, and I fought down the urge.

I could see the door now. The murmuring stopped for a moment, to be followed by a scraping noise of chairs being pushed back and a shuffling of feet. Although much of the house that I had travelled through was in darkness, bright light flooded underneath the doorway ahead of me. A heedless determination came over me, and without knocking, I pushed open the door.

Everything in front of me stopped as if I had broken in to some enchantment, some scene from another world. After the murky darkness of the street and the dim light that had attended me through the house itself, I found myself suddenly dazzled by light and colour. The place was ablaze with candles, in sconces on the walls, on window ledges, and in candelabra hanging from bosses in the ceiling, and what that candlelight illuminated took my breath away. The gallery was a field of images. Everything from the ceiling boards to the plaster of the walls told a story, against a sea of sapphire blue, of the life of Christ and of the baillie and of every other person in that room. All around and above me was painted, in panels framed in gold, scenes from the Annunciation to the Ascension; the tale of our Saviour's suffering, even the sickening sight of the Crucifixion itself was depicted there in gaudy colour for any who might lift their eyes. Seldom, even in Ireland, had I seen such flagrant, shameless idolatry. Years, decades ago, throughout Scotland, such images had been painted over, torn down, destroyed, burned, and yet here, in the house of one of the foremost men of Aberdeen, their brightness blazed. My mind hardly paused to consider that this room, at the top of a merchant's house, had somehow been missed, forgotten, hidden even from the iconoclasts who had first heralded the coming of the Reformation of religion to our town over seventy years ago, for the images assailing me were fresh and bright, not in the least worn or faded, in the style, if not the handiwork of Jamesone and his peers. Amongst the images, clearly displayed, were the arms of Baillie Lumsden himself.

Towards the back, the north end of the room, stood the servants of the house, all of them, I suspected, save the new, unknowing maid who had shown me in. In front of them, seated on wooden benches, were some burgesses of the town – a handful of craftsmen, merchants, magistrates, who must spend half their lives in keeping each others' secrets and who now looked aghast that I too now knew their greatest secret. In front of them, seated upon two rows of high-backed, finely carved oak chairs, were Baillie Lumsden, his wife, Lady Rothiemay, and the woman I had come in search of, Isabella Irvine. The women were all veiled: Lumsden's wife modestly, Lady Rothiemay magnificently in golden lace, but it was Isabella who, amidst all the colour, the grandeur and the beauty, drew the eye. The lace mantilla that draped her hair and hung from her shoulders was edged with silver thread so fine that it might have been a spider's web bedecked with dew drops. The light from the candles glanced off the silver candlesticks and the jewels at the neck of her elder companion to reflect in her own brilliant eyes. The pallor of her face was greater even than it had been in Jamesone's garden the previous day, and as she turned her startled eyes on me, I did not think I had ever seen a woman look so beautiful.

This was not the time though, for the contemplation of the art of man, nor that of God. Beside Isabella, exquisitely attired in black velvet, was William Ormiston, the shimmering light dancing from his buttons and buckles to the hilt of his sword. He also turned to look at me, and instead of surprise, I saw the makings of a smile on his face. To Lady Rothiemay's left knelt another man, also richly attired, his form too, I thought, familiar to me. But it could not be, for only five days ago Baillie Lumsden had told me that his young cousin and namesake, my old college friend Matthew, was in France, in the Scots Guard of the French king. He did not wear the uniform of the *Garde Eccosaise,* and yet I knew, as soon as he started to clear his throat, and turned to look at me, that I was not mistaken; it was indeed my old friend Matthew, whom I had not seen in more than six years.

I had no time to process even this revelation, for it was not he, but the two figures at the front who took my eye.

Kneeling at a wooden altar, before a richly robed priest who held the host above his head – for this was a Popish Mass, I had known it from the moment I had stepped through the door – was Archie Hay. He, and the priest, were the only ones in the room who had not turned at my disturbance, though both must have been aware of it. I saw, rather than heard, the priest murmur the words 'Corpus Christi', and I watched in horrified disbelief as the blood companion of my boyhood crossed himself and took into his mouth the blasphemous host of the Church of Rome from the hands of the man I had known as Guillaume Charpentier.

18

Nimmo

The enchantment was broken, and before the priest had finished giving his blessing Ormiston and Matthew Lumsden were on their feet. Archie had at last turned and begun to call my name, but I could not watch any more of it, could not listen, would not hear him. I pushed through the door and out to the corridor, black now after the startling light of Lumsden's secret chapel, and stumbled my way back down the many stairs of his house and out to the street, ignoring the shouts at my back.

I ran and ran until I thought my lungs would burst, the guards on the door having at last come to their senses and begun to follow me, in the van of at least half-a-dozen men who had spilled from the doors of Baillie Lumsden's house. Shapes looming towards me out of the fog might have been innocent townsmen or spirits risen from the kirkyard for all I cared; anything that came in my path was barged out of the way regardless of age, sex, or dignity. By the time I had turned into our pend off Flourmill Lane, only one runner still pursued me, and I knew without turning to look whose was that peculiar, uneven gait. Archie called my name again and again, careless it seemed whether the fog hid him or no, but whatever he might have to say to me, I no longer wished to hear. I carried on to my own door and was through it and had it locked before he could catch up with me.

I stood against the door, my chest heaving and my throat burning. The group I broke in upon looked no less stunned than those I had come upon only ten minutes before: Sarah, in her chair by the fire, Davy asleep in her lap, Zander at the table showing Deirdre how to scratch the letters of her name on his tablet. A small, warm place, little room amongst the pots, pans, ladles, the vegetables that hung from the ceiling, the shelves and cupboards on the walls, for painted images or rich hangings. Such few pieces of Delft or pewter, such cushions or drapes that were of some quality had been hard won and were well cared for by the woman, the unadorned woman, at the centre of this home. Honest, defiant, more than the poverty of her surroundings, and better than I ever deserved.

At the sight of me she stood up and laid Davy gently down in his bed, telling Zander to go upstairs now, and take his sister with him. His thought of protest was banished with a look.

Now home, I found I could not move from the door.

She came over to me, put her arms around me like a mother with her child, and I buried my head in her chest. 'Alexander!' she said, dismayed. 'My darling. What is it?'

I could hardly lift my head to look at her, to speak.

'All is false,' I said eventually. 'Everything. And it always has been.' I looked at her. 'You, you are the only thing that has never been false.'

She shook her head. 'I don't understand.'

'No,' I said, 'you do not. Thank God, you do not.'

Her eyes betrayed her complete lack of comprehension, but she asked nothing else as she led me over to my chair and bent to take off my boots.

'You do not need to do that,' I said.

'Hush, don't speak. You are as white as a ghost. Take a minute here to calm yourself. I will fetch you some brandy.'

Once I had swallowed the drink and she had warned the children to stay upstairs, she knelt before me and took my hands. 'Now tell me what's wrong.'

'Archie,' I said.

'Archie?' She drew back, alarmed. 'What has happened to him?'

'Nothing. Nothing has *happened* to him. He has turned Papist.'

'Papist? When? Did he tell you this?'

'No, he did not tell me: I saw. I saw the lie of his life, the latest lie, and I do not know how many others he has told me.'

Just then came a gentle knock on the door.

Sarah started to rise, but I caught her arm. 'Don't answer it.'

She ignored me and went to the window. 'It's him, with another man I cannot see properly.'

'Don't let them in,' I said.

'Alexander, for all that has happened, he is your friend.'

'I don't know who he is.'

She stared at me a moment and then began to lift the latch on the door.

'Sarah! I forbid you . . .' I started to rise from my chair but it was too late. The door was open and she was stepping back to give access to Archie. Behind him in the doorway, stood Matthew Lumsden. Archie said nothing; it was Matthew who spoke.

'Can I come in, Alexander?'

I looked at that other friend of my abandoned youth, the one who had never pretended to be other than what he was, though it got him into trouble time and time again.

'You are always welcome in my house, Matthew. You know that.'

'And I?' said Archie, watching me.

I looked at him for a long time. 'I do not know who I welcome into my house when I open the door to Sergeant Nimmo,' I replied.

'Will you at least let me tell you?' he asked.

'I have no interest in hearing further lies.'

'There will be none.'

Sarah had quietly shut the door behind them. 'Listen to what he has to say, Alexander. There can be nothing lost from that now.' She came over and kissed me on the forehead before making for the stairs. As she put her foot on the bottom step, Archie caught her hand. 'Thank you,' he said.

She looked at him directly, honestly. 'I did it for him, not for you.'

When she was gone, Archie sat in her chair opposite me, and Matthew drew up a stool from the table.

I could not help but smile at him. 'I thought you were in France, serving the Marquis in the French king's *Garde*,' I said.

'Oh, I was intended for that service, and indeed, had fully made up my mind to take it up, but on my journey towards Paris I found much conviviality amongst our fellow Scots at their college in Douai, and fell in with other very genial fellows who were on their way to the Scots College in Madrid.'

'You fell in amongst the Jesuits,' I said.

He shrugged, affected the grin that he had always believed would get him out of trouble and which rarely had done. 'Not all of the Jesuit fathers were entirely taken with my temper, or my manner of devotion, but they found me to be,' he paused, 'useful, and so our purposes complemented each other, and we were able to tolerate each other for the sake of them.'

I could well imagine how the Jesuits had found my old friend useful, for Matthew had the ear of the Marquis of Huntly, and the Marquis, like his forebears a Papist to the core, had the ear of our king. From the mouth of a priest in Madrid to the ear of a king in Whitehall was but a matter of three whispers.

'It cannot be safe for you to show yourself here. I suspect it will do your cousin, and indeed his house guest, Lady Rothiemay, little good were it known that you were lodged under the same roof.'

Matthew shrugged. 'My cousin knows the risks, and what they are taken for. He is not quite of my politics, but his faith is strong. And as for her Ladyship – she was instrumental in arranging for Father Guillaume a safe means of travel north. By the way, you must not condemn the painter – he knows nothing of Guillaume's true calling. There are many amongst Lady Rothiemay's kin and friends who do, in the mountains and the straths, and who thirst for the sacraments. Many who will happily shelter him.'

'A murderer! I do not think it.'

Matthew smiled again. 'Alexander, when will you get past this idea that our Mass is a . . .'

'I am not talking about the Mass,' I said, aware that I was raising my voice. I lowered it again. 'I am talking about the cold-blooded murder of a young girl whose only crime was to fall in love with him.'

Archie's brow furrowed. 'What are you talking about, Alexander?'

And so I told them of Christiane's death, in every detail I knew. 'And her murderer is harboured in the house of the very man charged with finding him!'

Archie was ashen-faced. 'This girl – the French master's sister – has been murdered?'

I was disgusted. 'Are you going to pretend you didn't know? It was the night of Ormiston's dinner.'

Archie leant closer to me. 'I didn't know, Alexander, I swear to you, I did not. But,' his mind was working quickly, tying one piece of knowledge to another, 'Father Guillaume did not kill her. He cannot have done.'

'How can you know that?'

'Firstly, he is a good man – he is truly a man of God, however you may suspect his faith and his order. But more than that – you tell me the girl was seen alive at eight o'clock that night?'

'Yes.'

'At eight o'clock that night, Father Guillaume was robed and preparing to say Mass in a private house in the old town, two miles from here. I know, for I was there – I was his escort. If you do not believe me, you may ask Isabella Irvine – she too was at the Mass. While we were there, we had intelligence that a warrant was on its way to Banff for the arrest of Lady Rothiemay. It was decided that it would not be safe for Guillaume to return to the new town by day. His friends urged him to leave for Strathdon there and then, but he insisted he would hear confession and say Mass in the new town, as he had promised Baillie Lumsden. That is the only reason he was still here tonight. I swear to you he cannot have killed that girl. He will grieve for her, I know it, for he had become fond of her.'

'And St Clair? Am I to believe that he, too, was a priest?'

Archie lip contorted. 'He was a gardener, nothing more. His presence detracted from any suspicions Guillaume might have aroused on his own. He travelled and worked with Father Guillaume in that respect alone. If I had known his true identity, I would have shot the man myself.'

I laughed. So did Matthew, if a little nervously, but Archie was not fooled.

'What is it?'

'Do you know,' I said, 'I always liked Katharine Forbes. For all that was ever said of her, for all the havoc she has wrought throughout the countryside, I always admired that woman. I would defend her against her detractors, and now I see they were right – she is a threat to this very nation.'

It was Matthew who replied. 'No, Alexander, no. You malign her there. She brings in priests that they might minister to the faithful, but my uncle the baillie has warned me well: she is not a woman who would countenance the . . .' He seemed lost for the appropriate word.

'Invasion of our kingdom?' I suggested.

He made a conciliatory gesture. 'I was going to say "interference" of external powers. She will happily separate matters of religion from matters of state.'

'And you?'

'I don't see that it can be done,' he said at last.

He must have gauged the disappointment on my face. 'Come, old friend, you have known me long enough. Did you really expect to find me altered?'

I took the hand he held out to me. 'No, never, and it does my heart good to see that you're not. But you must know I cannot condone your politics, Matthew, nor countenance your religion.'

'I know it,' he said, 'and that's why I have never spoken of it to you until now, nor ever would have done, were it not for Archie. I'll be gone from here tomorrow. I ask you for that one night's grace.'

He was asking me to keep what he thought to be his secret a few hours longer, to let him slip, unnoticed, from the town once more and to go in to the hinterland where the Jesuits found refuge and a base from which to spread their poison, and meet with them there in the houses of our wealthy and high-born recusants, or those who had never made any show of professing the Protestant faith at all. He was asking that I would not hand him over, this very hour, to the authorities, and see him die a traitor's death, the man I had known since we were boys of fourteen.

'You will have your twelve hours, Matthew, and longer. It would hardly be news to anyone that agents of the Marquis and those of Spain roam from house to house across Strathbogie and Glenlivet almost with impunity. For me to see you condemned would change nothing of that. But you must tell your uncle to get rid of his priest tonight – if it were known that such abominations were being carried out in his house . . .'

'I understand.' He stood up, readying his hat to go outside

into the mist again. 'Will you embrace me as a brother, Alexander, and will you tell me that come what may to our land, you will remember me always as a brother?'

'I will.'

With a curt nod to Archie, Matthew left, to go once more into the spider's web of the councils of his masters. Archie looked after him, long after he had closed the door behind him, and there was something in his face that told of an alteration between my two old friends. We were alone now, in the near silence of my kitchen, where the gentle hiss of the fire, the even breaths of my sleeping son, and the ticking of the clock on the mantelshelf could not even begin to span the chasm of silence between us.

At last Archie spoke. 'Will you condemn me for a Mass, Alexander? Is all we have ever been, one to the other, to be lost for the sake of a Mass?'

I could hardly believe he was speaking those words to me. 'Do you think it means nothing to me?' I said at length.

He spread out his hands, beginning to relax. 'Not nothing, of course not nothing. But not so much surely, that you're lost to me?'

I saw in his face that he truly believed what he had said. 'Archie, you have known me my whole life, almost. I have loved you my whole life, but you and I, we are nothing, we are dust. Dust and ashes in the hands of God. A man cannot place the love of friends, of family even, before his obedience to God.'

'And yet you embraced Matthew . . .' His certainty was beginning to falter.

I leant towards him. 'Archie, with Matthew we always *knew*; there was never any attempt to dissemble. His whole life, we knew what Matthew was, and I have prayed daily to know that he might be amongst the saved. But you . . . you and I, we've been different from what Matthew and I ever were, different even from what William and I have become.' I could see the slightest pain, even now, after all, at the mention of William who, over long, constant years, had begun to fill Archie's place in my life, as if that one thing, in all that had changed and happened over time, mattered more than the rest to be left unchanged. 'For all we were ever different, for all your recklessness, you were never reckless in *that*. Your faith was as sure as mine.'

He rubbed at a cord at his neck that I had never noticed there before. I remembered, long ago, in Ireland, a time when I had come in to that habit myself, and I imagined the crucifix that must lie against his chest as it had done then, against my will, on mine. He was only aware of the gesture when he saw that my eyes noted it.

'When I was young, all I knew of Rome was the catalogue of vanities, blasphemies, idolatries our ministers and teachers warned us against, and I knew that my father had faced exile and the near loss of his patrimony in its name.' Archie's father had known disgrace, in the days of King James and the old queen, Elizabeth, in England, for too close an acquaintance with the Spanish plotting of Scottish

Romanist noblemen. He had nearly lost Delgatie over it, and had resolved never to glance at a rosary again. 'But in the war,' he continued, 'I learned a different tale.'

I stared into the fire and said nothing.

'Will I tell it to you?'

'Will there be any truth in it?'

'All of it.'

I was as loath to hear Archie's truth as I was any more of his lies, but I had not the energy to argue. 'Go on, then.'

'I told you how after I recovered from my injuries at Stadtlohn I travelled until I found the Protestant forces under Count Mansfeld, and what a wretched collection of humanity I found there.'

'I thought,' I said, my voice strangely dry, 'that you all went to the wars for honour.'

'Did you? I do not think so, Alexander. You see enough in this small town, in the country around, when harvests fail or debts are called in, when the only other choice is jail or the House of Correction, why men and boys throw in their last chance with the recruiters. And the men recruited by Mansfeld in '24 were the absolute worst, the most desperate dregs of humanity you could ever hope to see. Almost a hundred shiploads he brought from England with the thought to relieve Breda from the Spanish, but our French allies withdrew their permission to land on their shores, and so away to the north he sailed. But the Dutch liked the look of his recruits no better than the French had, and they were left a fortnight at anchor at Flushing, to starve, to die from the cold, from thirst. The bodies of the dead and the nearly dead were thrown overboard. By the time the rump that was finally let ashore reached Breda, the town was beyond help, and when it fell, the Dutch no longer wanted Mansfeld's ragged mercenaries. And so we marched north and north, and those who should have succoured us would give us none, flooded their own lands that we might find no sustenance, and so we were forced to plunder those we had thought to help. We never did meet up with MacKay's regiment as had been hoped. They came too late. Wallenstein decimated our forces at Dessau in April of '26. Over half of our men were taken prisoner, and most of the Scots and Irish amongst them went over to the Catholic side.'

'And you went with them,' I said. 'Your faith could not sustain you through defeat.'

He went over to the sideboard and poured himself a goblet of my wine. I wanted none. 'My faith, or something, some deadness in me perhaps, sustained me through defeat often enough. It was victory I couldn't stomach. I wasn't amongst those taken prisoner at Dessau, I didn't join the enemy's forces then. All that I told you up to, and a little beyond that point was true.'

I did not know whether I believed him or not, but he seemed intent on telling out his tale. 'And beyond which point would the truth not advance?'

He sat down opposite me once again.

'It was at Weisskirchen.'

'You already told me of Weisskirchen,' I said. 'The horrors you witnessed. They were reported even here. The slaughter of man, woman and child by the forces you had fought with. You told me you ran from it.'

'And so I did. But it was Weisskirchen that changed my faith.' He turned the goblet in his hand. 'No, that is not true: it is what I saw at Weisskirchen that gave me faith.'

'I don't understand you.'

'How would you? You've always been so certain. So assured.'

'Archie, I . . .' But he would not be interrupted now, and so I left him with his illusions.

'I had seen many things, many acts of brutality before we ever came to that town, and whatever had been good or noble, if ever there had been, in the men with whom I had soldiered for a year by then, it had long been destroyed, and the taking of that town gave vent to everything, the most base vileness of humankind, that was left. When I could stomach it no more, when my sword arm was rendered useless by one of my own comrades whom I had tried to turn away from his evil purpose, I turned from that town and I ran. But before I was through the gates, I saw something I had never thought to see in those wars.'

I waited while in his mind he seemed to see it again.

'I saw a vision of peace. An old woman, gouged by an axe when she had been trying to protect her grandchild, was very close to death. A young priest, somehow unscathed by the venom being unleashed all around him, knelt over her and spoke to her in Latin. Quietly, in the midst of all the sound and fury, he murmured to her that her sins were forgiven, and he sent her to Paradise with the peace of Christ in her eyes. I was covered in blood and dirt and I went down on my knees before that young priest and asked him to give me absolution too.'

'It was not his to . . .' I began, but he stopped me.

'Yes, I knew you would say it was not his to give, but I felt the weight of my sins lifted from me as I knelt before him and he told me they were forgiven.'

'And from that day you have been a Papist.'

'Yes, Alexander, from that day to this and until my last.'

'And yet you fight for the Protestant cause?'

He was looking right into me, unblinking, leading me to something I had not been able to see. 'My God,' I said at last. 'Oh, my God.'

I had been blind. Stupid. He had all but told me more than once. He and Ormiston – Ormiston, who had been waiting to take the host after him, were not recruiting for the Protestant forces at all.

'I wanted to tell you, I started trying to tell you, the last time I was here, but then the child woke up, and the moment was gone. I did not want to lie to you.'

'Spain?' I said at last, my voice scarcely audible.

He nodded, seeing that I had it now. 'Of late, yes. But for most of the last nine years I have served in the Habsburg armies of the Emperor. When I left Mansfeld's rabble, I joined with the other Scots and Irish in Wallenstein's

Catholic army, under Colonel Daniel Hepburn. You see, there are thousands of us on both sides, and it is not always what we have left behind that shapes the choices we make.'

'And Ormiston? When did he make his choice? Did he ever sail with MacKay's regiment, or was that a lie too?' It seemed to me that Ormiston was brazen enough to lie to the face of Lord Reay himself.

Archie took another draught of his wine. 'He is not the man you think him to be, Alexander. He has greater honour than you give him credit for.'

'And yet he raises troops to die abroad under false promises. They think they go to fight in the Protestant cause, for the King's sister, and all the while they are but fodder for the cannons of the Habsburgs. And Ormiston has the gall to receive honour from Lord Reay.'

Archie's face hardened. 'He well merits it. He fought for six years in MacKay's forces, saw his brother die . . .'

'Is that what turned him?'

'Turned him?'

'Is that what sent Ormiston scuttling over to the Habsburgs? That his brother died in the Protestant cause?'

Archie regarded me a while. 'You see it all in such simple terms.' He sighed. 'No, he did not come over then. The first time I met him, I was with Colonel Butler's Irish forces, defending Frankfurt an der Oder against the armies of Gustav Adolph. Ormiston was still with MacKay's regiment then, and though they were victorious, his own commander praised the valour of Butler's defence.

Ormiston told me of it when next we met, and I think it created a kind of brotherhood between us, despite the slaughter we had both witnessed in that town.'

Within me yet, for all my anger with him, for all the distrust of him that had welled up within me in the last hours, something winced at his talk of brotherhood with the lieutenant, a brotherhood I knew I would never be able to share in.

'It was two years after Frankfurt, at Freistadt, that we met again. By that time, I had met in with two of our old acquaintance, Walter Leslie and John Gordon, risen high in the Imperial armies. We were in a stand-off near Nuremberg, and one afternoon, while on reconnaissance, we were captured all three of us by a party of Scots in MacKay's regiment, serving under the Swedish king. With Leslie and Gordon I had been openly Archie Hay, but as a captive I was again humble Sergeant John Nimmo. Five weeks we stayed with our captors, until ransom was paid, and a merry five weeks they were.' I realised it was the tale Ormiston had told us aboard his ship two nights before, but he had not told all, as Archie did now. 'The causes for which we fought were put aside, and we revelled in our shared nationhood, and a comradeship of arms far from home. While Gordon and Leslie were royally entertained by their fellow officers, I was under the watch of a young ensign. That is how Ormiston and I came to meet again. We spoke over our memories of many shared battles; in time we came to speak of what we had lost through the war – he of his brother, I of all my family and friends at home, and finally, as men will do, of what faith we had. And so, in time, he conceived a desire that when Leslie, Gordon and I should finally be released to rejoin the Imperial forces, he should come with us, and so he did, and he and I have fought and travelled together ever since.'

I saw now that Ormiston was far from the mere acquaintance that Archie had first presented him to be, and that the officer's knowledge of and dislike of me probably stemmed from the same roots as did mine of him. I went over to the window and looked out at the murky darkness. 'And so all your talk of spying, of travelling across Europe, of Brussels, Madrid, that was just a fantasy for my amusement, my entertainment.'

'No, Alexander. The difference is that I walked openly, was welcomed in Vienna, in Brussels, Madrid, but that in other places I had to pass with caution, in the shadows, not make myself known. And the lieutenant . . .'

I spun round. 'I do not care about the lieutenant. What I want to know is . . .' I swallowed, cast my eyes up the stairs to where Sarah was probably still awake. ' . . . Is what you told me about Madrid true? '

'The child?'

I nodded.

'It's true. What's more, Matthew Lumsden saw him too.'

I went back over to the fire, my voice lowered. 'Matthew?'

'It was he who first spotted the boy. I have to confess, my eye was more taken by the mother, but it nearly stopped my heart when Matthew said to me, "Is that child not the image of Alexander Seaton?" It was all I could do not to take the boy in my arms and whirl him round the room. In the years since the loss of my own darling child, it was the greatest joy I have known.'

I wanted to be where he had been, in that room, in that Jesuit house, in that city of heat and wonders, and see what he had seen. Not Roisin, for I had never cared enough for Roisin and could only with difficulty picture her face, but my son.

'Are you certain?' I said, my voice almost a whisper.

'As certain as I am looking at you. I asked the woman outright. She dissembled at first, but she was no good at it. And so she told me that yes, he was your son, but she begged that I should tell no one else, for she and her child were dependent on those who believed he might one day follow in the footsteps of his father, and that that father should not be a university teacher from a cold Scottish town.'

I sat down, my head in my hands, my heart thumping so loud I could hardly think. Archie crouched down in front of me. 'They are cared for there, Alexander, safe and honoured in your cousin's name. And these Jesuits whom you so despise, and Lady Rothiemay and all the other recusants, here and in Ireland, see to it that they and many others like them will not go hungry, nor dishonoured, nor without shelter. Nothing you could do would make life any the better for them, or for you. You are a great one for the will of God. Accept it in this.'

And so we talked on, and I came to understand, I think, what drove my friend. He had not lied to me before when he had said his one aim was that the war should end, and that he believed only a victory for the Habsburgs could end it. And so he recruited in that cause. By the end, I was no longer angry with him, no longer disappointed, and I wondered even that in the life he had led since our youth, it should still matter to him that I thought of him at all. I felt, as we sat across from one another in the warmth of my small kitchen, that the night had strengthened our friendship, not destroyed it.

'But there is one thing, Archie. You know I cannot let you take those boys you have on the ship away to fight for the Empire. You know they must be released. And I must name you, and Ormiston.'

He was resigned. 'I don't know whether to be sorry or proud that you are still so incorrupt, so constant. Proud, I think, but I also would beg of you one day's grace.'

I shook my head. 'No. Not a day. You must be gone tonight, and in the morning I will go to the sheriff and have them name you, and Ormiston, and Charpentier, and what your purposes have been. The sheriff's officers will board your ship and those boys will be taken ashore and sent back to their own parishes and towns, or put under Lord Reay's charge to go south with his men if they still wish to fight. This will be their last night aboard that ship, and you – I care not for Ormiston – but you must leave this town tonight, and you know you can never come back.'

It was as if I had not spoken. 'One day's grace, Alexander, that's all I ask.'

'What? So you and the lieutenant can spirit that ship away, with its unsuspecting cargo?'

'No,' he said quietly. 'So that I might go and see my father. Come with me, Alexander. To Delgatie. Let us go the old road together one more time.'

19

St Ninian's Chapel

The town was still a mire of darkness and fog when I set out early the next morning for the college. Already, Lord Reay's men were abroad, continuing their futile search for the son of their chief. Nodding to them as I passed, I did not go directly to the Broadgate, but rather took the path down St Katharine's Hill until I came to Shore Brae from where I could reassure myself that the recruiting ship still sat steadily at anchor off Torry. It did, and I offered a silent prayer of thanks to God. Others around the harbour had less to be thankful for, anxious as they were for the arrival of some cargoes or the departure of others. It was a fog of the sort that could lie over the sea for days, or be burned off in two hours. I must have been the only man in Aberdeen who wished to see it last.

Sarah had still been awake when I went to bed late the night before. It might have been tiredness, nothing more, but there was a look on her face that was almost haunted. I did not think she could have heard the conversation that passed between Archie and me, and yet I had found myself unable to talk of small things, things of no consequence that might put her mind at rest. She asked me, almost blankly, if we had made up our differences, and I told her that we had. I told her too, of Archie's wish that I should go with him to Delgatie.

'Do as you will,' she had replied. 'My blessing will alter nothing.'

She was cold through, and though I held her through the night, I do not think she ever got warm.

'I love you, Sarah,' I had said as I left.

'Maybe that will be enough.' She turned and smiled at me at last. 'Be safe, Alexander.'

I was not to meet Archie until the afternoon, and had my classes to see to in the morning. I drove my scholars hard, setting them exercises of translation from Latin to Greek and thence into Hebrew. I allowed them to discuss any difficulties with one another, and soon enough there was a steady murmur that covered the silence of the room. For there *was* a silence, emanating from the bench where Seoras MacKay and Hugh Gunn had always sat together. This silence seemed to accuse me, for I had hardly thought of them these last few days, so quickly had they faded from my concern in the face of the other things that had happened in the town.

When the bell went for the midday meal, I dismissed my scholars quickly and left the college the back way, through the gardens. The image of Christiane Rolland as we had found her had haunted me for two days and nights, and I did not wish to remember the girl that way. Before I went to meet Archie, I was resolved to look upon her one more time, at rest, where she lay in St Ninian's Chapel on the Castlehill. As I went out at the back gate, I was met by the figure of Ossian coming along the path towards me. I had to look twice to be certain it was him. Instead of his usual tunic and plaid, he was dressed in a long, belted, academic gown and wore a cap over his usually free-flowing locks. His face registered my surprise, and he broke in to a smile.

'Is it my attire that confuses you, Mr Seaton?'

'No, no,' I began and then, 'well, yes. Until now, you've been every inch the soldier. I hadn't expected to find you today in the garb of the learned physician.'

He looked down at his garments. 'A soldier on the march is a soldier on the march, and must dress accordingly. But here in your college, I have the leisure to attend my patient in a proper room, with a bed in it and clean water, linen, and abundant medicines to hand. It seemed more fitting and respectful that I should dress here as Dr Dun, Dr Gordon and Dr Johnston do. I am on my way now to eat with my good colleagues while I have the opportunity.'

'Hugh can manage without you, then?' I asked.

'He manages better every day. But I haven't left him entirely alone. Your young friend Peter Williamson has been assiduous in his attentions.' He laughed. 'Neither knows a word the other says, but they seem to manage together well enough. He tells me he has a desire to study medicine, and I think he may have some aptitude for it.

I'm of a mind to put in a word to Lord Reay that he might assist him, for I have the impression he has not two pennies to rub together.'

'I'd be surprised if he had one, never mind two,' I said.

Ossian looked down at my own clothes, my academic gown replaced by a riding coat, my cap by a hat.

'You are making a journey?'

'I have some business to attend to out in the country,' I replied. I could not tell him the same lie I had told Dr Dun to cover my absence – that I had heard word someone of Seoras's description had been sighted in the town of Turriff. 'But first I thought to take a moment's prayer in St Ninian's Chapel to seek God's guidance in all these troubles.'

Ossian nodded. 'Then you will find Hugh there, where I have just left him. He keeps a vigil over her. This has been a heavy blow to him, after all that has already passed.'

I bade farewell to the physician, and as he went his way through the winter vegetable garden back into the college, I went out past the backlands to the chapel in the precincts of the long-gone castle that had once guarded our town.

I was glad to see two of Lord Reay's men at the chapel door. Despite Ossian's confidence in my friend, I did not much like the idea of Hugh Gunn out and about in this burgh with only Peter Williamson to protect him.

The chapel – no longer used as a place of worship – was familiar to me from its occasional use as a court, and as a common meeting place of our presbytery. It was also, increasingly, the favoured place of lying in rest of the wealthy and influential of this town. In the normal run of things, a girl like Christiane Rolland would never have been placed here, but Baillie Lumsden had done it as a mark of respect to Louis, and in some way to comfort him.

Inside, the place was almost bare of any adornment. There was a bleakness to the sturdy walls and flagstone floor that gave it a special solemnity as the resting place of the dead. The only furnishing was at the far end of the chapel, where the chairs of the consistory court were ranged along the side walls, and the massive carved oak altar, endowed by a burgh provost over a hundred years before, had survived the destructive rage of the iconoclasts.

It was before this altar, on a simpler table, that the body of Christiane Rolland had been laid. The mortcloth, the town's best, had been pulled back and folded down at her waist, so that her hands rested on top of it, and it looked for all the world as if the girl were sleeping. At each end of the bier was a candle, as if their light might keep her warm. Beside her, like a sentinel, stood Hugh Gunn, his head bowed. Like me, he was no longer in the clothes of a scholar, but unlike me, he was dressed in the saffron shirt and coloured plaid of his north-country kinsmen. He was no longer the boy I had thought I'd known over three years, but every inch the soldier. As he stood there, oblivious to my presence, I realised I had never looked at him properly on his own, for it was always Seoras that took the eye. Seoras, compact, dark, strong, eyes that danced with mischief and sometimes something more, a small mouth

that could be cruel when it wanted to. Hugh had always
been the other one, quieter, tall, more strongly built, handsome even, with pale grey eyes, fine cheekbones and a long
nose, balanced by straight fair hair that fell to his shoulders. A watcher, a listener, better – it seemed to me – than
him he had had to watch and listen to. And now, as the
search for that other probed ever-deeper into the secret
places of the town, and stretched wider into the hinterland, the rivers, bridges, fields, woods, it was as if he had
imposed this new silence on himself for fear he must step
out of the shadows now and become the one who must
talk and do.

So taken was I with the image of Hugh and Christiane
that I had not noticed Peter Williamson standing in the
near-darkness of the doorway, by the old baptismal font.
His voice startled me.

'He has been like that an hour. Not a movement. Not a
word.'

I kept my voice low, as he had done. 'And you have been
here with him all that time?'

He was downcast. 'Much good may it do him now. If I
had watched them better, him and Seoras that night after
Downie's Inn, we might none of us be here now.'

'Come, Peter, you cannot think that had a part in Christiane's murder?'

'Have you a better explanation?'

'No, but yours is no explanation at all. Does Hugh
remember nothing yet?'

'I don't know. He has erected a wall of silence for himself. I cannot penetrate beyond it.'

It was clear that Peter had no wish to pursue our conversation, and so I left him to his thoughts. The sound of my footsteps going up the aisle were out of place in the quiet stillness of the chapel and they roused Hugh from his vigil. It was as if he had forgotten, for a moment, that there was anyone but himself and this dead girl that he had loved.

'Mr Seaton, I, I didn't hear you . . .'

'I haven't come to disturb you, Uisdean, I just wanted to see her a moment for myself. At peace, as she should be.'

He shook his head and I saw that his eyes were filled with tears. 'She was sixteen years old. She should not be at peace. She should be laughing and singing and lighting the world as she always did. She should be dancing, flitting from one thing to another, free, like a bird in that garden.' He had been standing rigid but now his shoulders sank. 'That garden, dear God. If only she had known.'

'Known what?'

'About Charpentier. That he was a priest.'

And so the word was out already. It had not taken long. My first act on arriving at the college that morning had not been to go to my classroom, but to take two reports to Dr Barron, Professor of Divinity and Moderator of our presbytery. One told the sorry tale of John Leslie, Minister of St Fittick's Kirk at Nigg Bay, the other gave notice of hearsay, that an unknown seaman, drunk in an inn, had been heard to say George Jamesone's gardener was known from all the ports of Spain to this as a Jesuit. For all that they might have warranted it, I could not call down the forces of retribution of law and kirk upon the Baillie, nor Lady Rothiemay and Isabella either. What Archie had told me of my son's welfare in Madrid stopped my hand at that, and though my conscience forced me to denounce him, I had given Charpentier a twelve-hour start.

I could see Hugh's hopeless thought. 'If Christiane had known he was a priest, she might never have loved him.'

He was certain of it. 'No, and she would have had no cause to go in to that garden to see him, nor meet her death at his hands.'

I cleared my throat. 'I don't think Charpentier killed Christiane.'

This shook him out of his stasis. 'What? Who else could it have been? She found out his secret and he resolved to murder her, and now he has fled.'

I shook my head. 'He fled because I discovered his secret. And he cannot have murdered Christiane because he was . . . elsewhere, when she met her killer in that garden.'

He crumpled his brow. 'But how can you know that?'

'I cannot tell you, but I had it from one whose word I trust. He wouldn't have lied to me about this.'

'But then, who . . .?'

'I don't know.' I hesitated to go on, but things could scarcely be made worse – the worst lay before him now, in this chapel. I took a deep breath, and kept my voice low, although I knew Peter Williamson would not understand a word of what was said between us anyway. 'Uisdean, did you ever see Christiane after the night you were attacked and Seoras disappeared?'

His face lightened. 'Yes, she came to see me, twice, in my room in the college. The first time, Peter tells me, I was insensible, and did not even know she was there. But she left a book for me – something in French that she thought might entertain me. Rabelais.' He smiled. 'I don't know what Louis would say to her even knowing of such a fellow.'

'Nor I,' I said, glad to see him cheered for a moment, but it was only a moment.

'The second time, I was awake again and the fever passed. When she spoke to me first, I didn't have a word of Scots to answer her. But then she tried me in French and the wonder of it was I could follow and answer every word.'

'I think you enjoyed your lessons at the French master's house.'

'They were happy times for me.'

'And your mind has stored them in a place for such times, where there's no room, it would seem, for the rest of your life in Aberdeen.'

'I mean no disrespect, Mr Seaton, but this is not my place – I don't belong here, and I will be glad to be away from it and amongst my own people.'

'Your own people? Even in the wars?'

'There will be more of them there than there are here,

and Lord Reay won't make me stay here with Seoras gone.'

'You don't want to gain your degree?'

'I have no interest in it. I will go abroad and serve where Lord Reay tells me to serve, and that gladly.' He stroked Christiane's cold brow. 'There's nothing here for me now.'

Still I was hesitant, but I had to know. 'When she came to see you that second time, did she tell you of her fears?'

He looked up at me. 'About what?'

'About Seoras,' I said. 'She had got it in her mind that he was watching her, following her.'

'Yes, she told me, and I told her it could not be. Mr Seaton, I have known him all my life. I know him better than I knew my own mother. For all his faults, he would not do this thing to me. He would never have taken a trick so far. He would have tired of the business by now.'

It was this last that seemed most like Seoras to me. 'You think he would have tired of it?'

He nodded. 'He was already beginning to, by that last Monday night. We saw the two Frenchmen in the inn and he said he was of a mind to leave Christiane to the gardener.' He ploughed his fingers through his hair and gave a laugh with no humour in it. 'The gardener. It never crossed his mind that she might think of me. And that is what I told Lord Reay, when he finally got to the bottom of Seoras's trifling with Christiane. I told him nothing of my own feelings for her – there would have been no point.'

Because Lord Reay already had a wife marked out in Strathnaver for his foster son.

I remembered MacKay's insistence on seeing Christiane's body. 'How did his Lordship react?'

Hugh shrugged. 'As I had expected him to. He cursed Seoras for a knave, and many other things. It angered him that she should have had cause to fear him, but at the same time it gave him hope.'

'That his son might still be alive?'

'Yes.'

'You mean he did not dismiss Christiane's fears – that he thought it possible Seoras might be tormenting her still . . .?'

'Yes. I told him it was wrong, that it could not be. Seoras is gone.'

'Are you so certain he's gone?'

He put a hand over his heart, in the manner of one making an oath. 'I don't feel him any more. Here.' He pressed the hand harder. 'These last few days, something has gone from my spirit. Seoras has gone.'

'Since the night I sent you away from Downie's Inn, the night you both went missing?'

He shook his head. 'No. Since Sunday morning. I slept late – after the others had all left for the kirk. When I first woke, I knew he was gone.'

I could not understand him. 'Are you telling me Seoras had been with you until then? In the college?'

'No, no. But I had felt the sense of him.' He looked down again at Christiane. 'Those close to me are being taken. Is it me, do you think? Is it me that's the cause?' I was about to tell him 'No,' when he continued. 'But why then was I returned? To suffer more perhaps?' He put a hand to the hilt of his sword, which, as a student, he should not have been carrying. 'Well, they shall not see it, whoever has done this thing. I will be away from this town as soon as Lord Reay leaves, and go to France as soon as he will let me.'

His mind was made up, and I wondered whether in his determination he would even allow himself the time to grieve. I wondered if the wars would change this young man as they had changed Archie Hay. I thought he had begun to change already.

There was less than an hour before I had to meet Archie at the other side of the Old Town, at the Brig o' Balgownie, and I could not afford to stay much longer, but there was one more question I wanted to ask him.

'Uisdean, when you and the doctor left Ormiston's meal early the other night, did anyone else leave with you? I mean, go ashore in the boat?'

There was no hesitation. 'Yes,' he said. 'It was the recruiting sergeant.'

20

Delgatie

He was waiting for me in a small wood not far from the Brig o' Balgownie, where he would not be seen from the road. Earlier in the day, all roads from the town, but especially this one, had been crawling with men sent out in search of the reported Jesuit priest, known as Guillaume Charpentier. I suspected that by now Charpentier would be with my friend Matthew Lumsden in some Popish fastness in Strathbogie or Strathdon, and that he would never be caught.

As I approached the appointed place, Archie stepped out from between the trees to greet me, but the smile on his face died when he saw the look on mine.

'Don't tell me you come to say you'll not come with me?'

'I don't know. Will you tell me the truth, now?'

He laughed, a little nervously. 'But Alexander, I have already told you.'

'Not all, though.'

'All that you asked. What else would you know?'

'Did you kill Christiane Rolland?'

His face blanched. He looked away and then looked back, angry almost. 'I? Murder a girl? My God, Alexander, how low your opinion of me has fallen if you think me capable of that.'

'Then tell me where you were on Monday night, when I was on your ship with your lieutenant?'

He started to say something, but my question had unseated whatever easy reply he had been about to make. 'I . . . I told you, I was at Father Guillaume's Mass in the old town. I was his escort.'

I shook my head slowly. 'Do not lie to me, Archie. Do not lie to me any more.'

'I swear to you, Alexander, I'm not lying.'

I felt the ire rising within me. 'For God's sake, it was after seven when you left the ship. You could hardly have got ashore and up to the old town much before eight.'

'No, that's true. Guillaume was already robed and preparing to say Mass when I got there.'

'Why didn't you go before, if you were to be his escort?'

He sighed heavily. 'Because I hadn't known I would be needed at all. Isabella was to take him up to Old Aberdeen, and she did, but a note that Lumsden had brought aboard with him meant I had to see Guillaume myself that night.'

'What did the note say?'

'That there was a matter Guillaume urgently needed to discuss with William Ormiston or myself.'

'And what was that matter?'

'He could not tell me until after the Mass. And by then it was too late.' He took a breath. 'Christiane had spent a good deal of time at Baillie Lumsden's house – you know that, don't you?'

I nodded.

'It seems she had been . . . aware . . . of persons there who did not wish to be seen. She got it into her mind that it was the son of Lord Reay – the boy that has not been found.'

'I know that,' I said, becoming impatient.

'She went looking for him, Alexander. In Lumsden's house.'

'You are not going to tell me she found him?'

He shook his head. 'She found, or rather overheard, someone else – Matthew.'

'Matthew Lumsden?'

'Yes. In conversation with Lieutenant Ormiston about the recruit – the true purposes of the recruit.'

My heart sank for the young girl. She had gone in search of imaginary dangers and found a real one. 'And they decided to silence her.'

He nodded. 'I did not know of it, and neither did Ormiston, I swear to you, until Isabella's note came to us on the night of the dinner. Christiane had confided in Isabella, who had persuaded her not to tell anyone else until she should have a chance to speak to Guillaume. Guillaume was certain that he could persuade Christiane to say nothing of it until after the ship sailed. He would send her a note and ask her to meet him in the garden the next morning at eight . . .'

'I saw the note. It said nothing of morning.'

'I know, but it was not to have been delivered until later that night, long after eight in the evening had passed.'

'A boy brought it well before eight in the evening though.'

'Yes, that's what I have heard.'

'So who gave it to him?'

He held up his hands. 'I don't know. It had been sent down to the new town before I ever got up to see Charpentier, and I never thought to ask.'

After that, very little was said between us for the first few miles, but the further we got from Aberdeen, and the ship, and Lumsden's house and all that that entailed, the easier things became between us, so that when we at last rode in to the bounds of Banffshire, it was almost as if the last thirteen years had never been. There was scarcely a landmark we passed that did not recall for us some escapade, some scandal, some golden hour. Only as we approached Turriff did Archie become quieter, more withdrawn, in body as well as speech. We were entering upon the country where the Hays held sway, over which he had roamed as unquestioned heir, and where he was remembered still and often. I watched as Archie Hay disappeared before my eyes, to emerge as Sergeant Nimmo. He sat more hunched on his horse, the reins lay less easily in his hand, and even I would have sworn he did not see so well from his left eye.

All the same, we took the back roads for the last few

miles to his father's castle, spurring our horses quickly past anyone who might appear at their gate or the door of their cottage to watch us pass, acknowledging no greeting on the road. And then, in the falling darkness, above the black spikes of the trees, we saw it, waiting for us, challenging us at last to face our return: Delgatie.

Our horses slowed, as if they, too, understood this was no light step we undertook. I let mine fall a little behind Archie's, let him look upon the sight in silence and alone. He brought his beast to a stop and looked on for a full two minutes, then I saw him square his shoulders and turn to me.

'Well, Alexander, what think you? Shall we show them Archie Hay is back?' and with a whoop he dug his spurs into his poor beast's flank and galloped towards the old place like the returning hero he once would have been.

As we approached the gate, Archie at last slowed to a more dignified pace, and I, relieved, drew up behind him. The castle rose above us, every window a memory, every water spout and gargoyle a forgotten adherent or foe of childhood games. The place was not in darkness, as I had expected, but lit up, a candle burning at every window. It was only then that the realisation struck me. 'You are expected,' I said.

He raised his shoulders lightly. 'By some, who are in there, but not by all. It was necessary, to make some arrange-ment. But the old man doesn't know.' He gave a boyish smile. 'It's an indulgence, I know, but I wanted to see his face for myself, to see the honest face, and my father's love in it.' He took his gauntleted right hand from the rein and clasped mine. 'Wish me courage, Alexander.'

Even through the gloves, I felt the warmth of my old boyhood friend. 'You have it, more than any I have ever known, and I love you for it.'

His eyes were gleaming, the troubles, the knowledge of the darkness of the world gone from him for this short while, and I followed him as he walked his beast under the archway and in to the courtyard of Delgatie Castle. It had been fourteen years since he had last passed under that archway, the hero going to the wars, and ten since I had done so, the disgraced, reprobate ingrate who had dishonoured the daughter of the house and turned the love of her parents for him to ashes in their mouths.

We took the horses around the side to the stables – no lad or groom to be seen, but eight or nine fine mounts well tended in their stalls. The sweet smell of the hay and the warm odours of the horses brought my every sense flying back over the years to the hours we had spent here, in the loft, hiding from his sister or planning our adventures. I watched Archie's memory make the same journey as mine, and then his eye lighted on the magnificent grey in the furthest stall from the door, the best stall, and his face came alive. 'My Lord of Balvonie.' He strode over to the beast and stood before it, as the old stallion lowered his head to sniff and then nuzzle his master's son.

'It is him,' I said, in a kind of wonder.

'Of course it's him,' said Archie, laughing. 'Balvonie will be here as long as the old man can put foot to stirrup.' He murmured sweet words in to the creature's ear. 'The King of Sweden himself never sat a finer horse.' He patted the beast's neck and then put his fingers to his lips in an old, long-forgotten whistle.

'Archie, what are you . . .?'

'Sh,' he said. 'Wait.'

And so I waited, and soon there came the sound of footsteps in the yard. The stable door was opening, and Lord Hay's stable master was holding up a lantern and peering down the stalls to where we stood.

The man looked, then took a step closer. 'Is it you? Is it really you, Sir Archie?'

'Aye, Ronald, it is me.'

The old, strong man, who had more than once in our boyhood lifted both of us by our collars from the ground, began to shake his head. 'She said you would come, but I did not think it possible. The Lord be blessed that I lived to see this day.'

Archie was still, silent, as if twenty years had fallen back and he was a scared child awaiting censure from one of the few people in the world whose approbation mattered to him. 'I'm sorry,' he said at last, almost swallowing the words down, and then again more clearly, 'I am so sorry.'

The stable master came over to us and laid a hand on Archie's shoulder. 'It's the proudest thing of my life, to know that my son died fighting at your side. I wept for him, although I should not have done, but I give thanks to God every day that he died in honour, and for his faith.'

Archie looked to the ground and could say nothing. Ronald nodded at me and became gruff, as I had always remembered him. 'And now, if the pair of you would leave me to see to these horses, they've been ridden hard, no doubt, and have stood here patiently long enough.' And so we left him, removing the tack, emotion dispensed with, fulfilling his function in this world.

Once in to the house, I would have turned to the right, and down the steps for the kitchens, but Archie stayed me.

'No, Alexander, you would not make me do this alone?'

'Your father will want none of me,' I said. 'I wouldn't wish to mar the lustre of your homecoming, or bring a moment more grief to that man's heart. I will wait down here; there'll be a warm corner in the kitchen somewhere where I might pass the night.'

His face was pale and I saw that his hand trembled. 'Please. I don't think I can do this without you. Think what I have done to that man.'

And so, with my heart beating hard and my whole body shivering as if from the cold, I mounted with him the stone stairway to the great dining hall. I had expected silence. I had thought somehow, with his wife dead, and his son and daughter gone, old Lord Hay would keep his state alone, at the end of the long table in an empty hall, under banners of his family's past glories. And at first, silence was what accompanied us up those stairs – not a servant, not a guard to be seen. It was like an abandoned castle. And then I heard a murmur, a low tide of voices, lapping and retreating. I turned to Archie to ask him, but his eyes were fixed straight ahead, and so we went on.

I was a little surprised to see an armed man at the door to the hall. Just as I was placing his livery in my mind I heard the voice, a woman's voice, strong, certain, accustomed to being listened to. I turned to Archie in disbelief. 'Katherine Forbes is here? Lady Rothiemay, here?'

He grinned awkwardly, and raised his eyebrows as a wave of laughter broke out of the dining hall and sped towards and past us in the wake of a young spaniel trailing a hunk of meat. And then we reached the top of the stairs, and the guard stood aside for Archie, and all laughter from the dining hall stopped. Four people were in there, seated at the end of the great oak table that had seen forty gathered round it before now. At its head, as ever, aged by more than the ten years it had been since I had last seen him, was Lord Hay of Delgatie. His attention had been turned towards Lady Rothiemay, seated on his left, but now something had drawn his eyes straight ahead, to the doorway. I saw his mouth begin to form a word it could not manage. His hands gripped the edge of the table, he forced himself up and tried again. This time the word but no sound. And then the sound, a call from the depths of himself, from the grief of his stomach, to sound in our ears. His goblet went over, his chair was thrown back. A dog yelped as the old master started to stumble and then run to the lame, scarred, weary soldier who had at last come home.

I kept back, in the shadows. I had no place here, but as father and son held each other, I thought my heart might break and I could not take my eyes from them. At length, the old man released his grip a little, just a little, and stepped back to survey his son. He passed a hand over the hair that as yet showed not a fleck of grey, to run it down the scar that cleaved the left side of Archie's face. He took the hand, freed of gauntlet now, and turned it over in his own, larger, calloused ones. His boy's hand. He moved his head in wonder and said, 'My darling boy. My only boy.' He clasped Archie again, then turned his head towards the table. 'Look, Katharine. See who has come home to me.'

From my place in the shadows, I watched Lady Rothiemay. But it was not her to whom Lord Hay spoke. Across the table, closest to the door, was Isabella Irvine, and Lord Hay was looking past her, to the woman who had been sitting on his right. I had not seen her until now, had not looked her way. As she rose from the table, Lord Hay's eye at last lighted on me. A sudden recognition, a mild confusion, but the anger that should have come did not. Instead a smile, a kindness in the eye of the man who had done so much for me and whom I had so long ago wronged. 'And Alexander Seaton with him.'

He held out his arm to me and drew me also into his embrace, and then one of us on each side, took us into the dining hall. Lady Rothiemay remained seated, her face a glow of happiness in the candlelight. Isabella Irvine was seated also, but I could not see her face, for it was turned towards the woman next to her, who remained up from her seat but unable to move. Isabella put a hand on her friend's arm. 'Katharine . . .'

But Katharine Hay did not hear her, did not seem to feel her touch. She started to say my name, but her body swayed and then gave way under her. I was half-way across the room when the guard who had been behind Lord Hay's chair caught her before she collapsed to the stone floor.

'The lassie has had a bit of a shock, that is all,' said Lady Rothiemay, lifting the cup of brandy to Katharine's lips where we had seated her before the roaring fire. A marten rug had been brought and set over her, and Isabella Irvine sat anxiously at her feet, gently warming Katharine's hands in her own. The women had moved me aside and I could not get near her. I felt my entire body shake, and struggled to master my breathing. A strand of pale blonde hair, a glimpse of her foot in its red velvet of her slipper, a hint of the scent of her. I was a boy again, engulfed in the proximity of her. Had anyone asked me, I could hardly have told them my own name.

Lady Rothiemay looked up a moment from her attentiveness to Katharine. 'Matters will hardly be helped by you looming over her like a thundercloud of misery that doesn't know what to do with itself.' She passed the cup to Isabella and, taking my arm, eased herself wearily to her feet. 'Come 'till we get you some food: I never yet met a man that was any use on an empty stomach.'

She led me to the table and sat me down before calling for a clean plate and filling it up herself with items of food for me. Archie and his father sat together at the end of the table, and I caught a few words and phrases as Archie told his father what he had told me only a few nights ago, in our old burrow on the Heading Hill. Every so often Lord Hay would exclaim, 'But surely', or 'How could you have thought it?' The same useless words that I myself had uttered in trying to understand why our love had not been enough to bring him back from the wars.

Lady Rothiemay watched them. 'If his mother could have seen him again, just once . . .' She sighed. 'But that is not in God's plan for us, which is why we give birth in agony, that we might be prepared for all that is to come.' The minister in me might have opened my mouth to correct another woman, on another night, but tonight, in this place, the minister in me was utterly gone. 'You, though, that is another matter.'

'Me?'

'Yes, Alexander Seaton, you. What is to be done about you?'

My eyes must have registered a sudden suspicion that I had been led in to some trap, for she reassured me. 'Ho, do not tell me you think you have been brought here that you might be done away with, before you can give away the recusancy of the good baillie, Isabella and myself?'

I groped awkwardly for the right words. 'Your recusancy, your Ladyship, would hardly be a great surprise to anyone of this country, or the baillie's either, I think, if truth be told.'

She laughed. 'I always liked an honest minister. Cannot be doing with snivelling sycophants.'

I put down the chicken leg I had been holding. 'But I would like to know why I *have* been brought here.'

'Hmmph. Well might you ask. I suspect it is because Archie Hay has not a grain of sense in his head. Katharine knew her brother was coming, of course. She has known for years that he was not dead.'

'Years? How many years? How long has she known?'

She pursed her lips. 'I could not tell you, for she made none privy to it that he did not require to be, which was few enough, and it is not my business to ask her. What you ask her is another matter. Anyhow, Katharine knew Archie was coming, and Isabella and I have known about it since we first saw him at Lumsden's, with Lieutenant Ormiston.'

'When was that?'

'Friday night last, very late.'

'The day of the schoolmistress trials.' After Archie had left my own house.

'Indeed.' She became brisk. 'Now, as you know, my enemies have conspired against me so that there is a warrant for my arrest speeding its way northwards as we speak. I am on my way back to Rothiemay, and they can haul me from its ramparts with ropes and horses if they wish. Isabella is refusing to leave me, but she is too young to tie all her fortunes to a cause that is lost, or to lose that pretty head from her neck. She thinks she is coming with me to Rothiemay, but I will be gone by the morning' – she nodded in the direction of the two guards and I knew now exactly why I had recognised their livery – 'and Delgatie here has undertaken to have her safely delivered to her aunt at Straloch. Anyhow, that is not the matter in hand. The only reason you are here tonight, I presume, is because Archie Hay wanted you here. He was always a determined boy, and thought that if he wished something to be so, then it would be so, and others would see the rightness of it eventually. I could scarcely believe it when Katharine told me he had insisted on his father not being forewarned of his coming – why, the man might have taken a turn and died at this table before our very eyes just at the sight of him. But as to bringing you here, when he knew his sister also would be here, and not forewarning either of you of it . . .' She shook her head. 'But the thing is done now, and must be got on with.'

Sensing that she might have said what she had intended to say, and was waiting for an answer of some sort to a question she had not asked, I sought some words.

'I truly do not know what I am to do, what I am to say. I never expected . . .'

'No,' she nodded, 'I can see that. Well, remember one thing, Alexander Seaton, what happened between you and Katharine Hay is ten years past, and we do not live our entire lives for one moment that will not come back. You were free once, but you are not free now.'

'I know it.' I ate and drank then in silence, for there was nothing else I could say, but I knew she had not finished with me.

'And the recruits?' she said at last.

'The recruits?'

'Those boys on Ormiston's ship that think they are going to fight for the honour of Elizabeth Stuart and the Protestant cause. What will you do about that?'

I glanced at Archie and then looked Lady Rothiemay directly in the eye. 'I cannot let him take them, your Ladyship, were the King himself to command me.'

She smiled, satisfied. 'Good, for if you did, I would trust no man again.'

This I had not expected, and she saw it.

'Do not confuse my faith with my loyalties, Mr Seaton. I will be loyal to the House of Stuart until the day I die. I will never see a Spanish standard planted in the soil of Scotland, and there are many, many of my faith who will tell you the same thing. Lieutenant Ormiston is lost – I have told Isabella, and I thank God I have got her away from him – and he will take Archie Hay with him. No one with the scrap of a position to hold on to will take my word on anything, but you get back to Aberdeen tomorrow and denounce the pair of them. Archie has made his choices, and his father has had his moment.'

She got up then, and pausing only to say something

privately to Isabella, she bade the rest of the company a goodnight that none of them heard.

The withdrawal of Lady Rothiemay left me awkwardly alone for a time, and I pretended to eat food I had no appetite for, but then Archie noticed me and called me up to join himself and his father. The knowledge of Katharine just six feet rather than hundreds of miles from me, made me almost insensible of anything else, and yet the other people in the room – Archie, his father, Isabella, the guard – erected by their very presence a barrier as impassable as all those miles would have done.

There were words of kindness to me from Lord Hay. Words of sorrow from me on the passing of his wife. Unspoken words of regret by both of us for all that had passed in those ten years.

We sat an hour, he trying to take me on his side in persuading Archie not to return to the wars, and with all my heart, in spite of everything I knew, I joined him in those efforts, but I knew it would be to no avail. So, eventually, did Lord Hay. He sighed heavily. 'So I must live till Mark is of age then, and pass Delgatie safely into his hands.'

'Safer in his than in mine, Sir,' said Archie with a twinkle, 'for you know it would go on gambling and women.'

'Surely,' said his Lordship, partaking in the game, 'Alexander would keep you from such snares?'

'Alexander? He never could. I only ever kept him by me father, that the ladies might see how well I looked in comparison. He also stopped me once or twice from wagering away my horse.'

But I could not join in their laughter. I could hardly hear it. 'Who is Mark?' I asked.

'What?' said Archie, refilling his glass and his father's.

'Who is Mark?'

Lord Hay's voice was gentle. 'Mark is my grandson, Alexander. Katharine's son. He's nine years old. When I'm gone, he will be the laird of Delgatie.'

I could not conceal – what? My distress? Shock? Some other emotion that should not have been mine. I tried to put my own glass down on the table, but my hand shook so much that half the wine spilled on to my knee.

Archie, helpless for once, looked at his father. The old laird stood up.

'Isabella, it has been a long day. I think perhaps you should take Katharine to her chamber.'

All this time, Katharine Hay and I had exchanged not one word, and I found myself getting to my feet, fearful that any chance I had to speak to her would now be lost. At the same time Katharine looked helplessly from me to her father.

'Please father, I . . .'

He put an arm round her. 'Hush, now, lassie. It will be all right. I promise you. You go with Isabella.'

'Please . . .'

'Go now.'

All the while, Archie had me by the arm, but I had not

the strength to pull away from him anyway. I felt my feet would not move and that I might be sick. He guided me back into my chair.

'A few minutes, Alexander,' said his father, 'and then you can go to her. What you must say to one another is between you two alone.'

It was perhaps ten minutes later, perhaps two, or an hour, I did not know, that I finally walked from the hall and down the stairs to the chamber that had been Katharine's all her childhood. It felt as if every step I had taken in the last ten years, no matter how far I had run from the place, had been leading me here. At the accustomed turning, I stepped from the turnpike and down the three stone steps that would take me to the door of her room. I lifted my hand to knock, but drew it back at the last minute. I had not the first idea what I could say to her, what I might do. I pressed my fist to my mouth and muttered, 'God help me,' but as I brought it to the door at last I knew God's work was done with Katharine and me.

21

Katharine

The door opened slowly and I found myself looking into the eyes of Isabella Irvine. She was startled and seemed about to close it again.

'Please,' I said.

'Think what you are doing.'

'I just want to talk to her, Isabella, please. I must see her.' All my defences were gone, and I did not care who knew it. 'I beg of you, please.'

Then Katharine's voice, quiet from the dim candlelight. 'Isabella? Who is it?'

'It is no—'

I pushed past her. 'Katharine, it is me.'

She got up from the footstool by the low fire, and let the rug she had round her shoulders fall.

'Alexander . . .!'

Isabella took a step towards her. 'Katharine, do not . . .'

But Katharine wasn't listening. She was looking at me as if she could see no one else.

'Leave us, please, Isabella.'

'Katharine, think . . .'

'Just go.' Her voice was quiet, flat almost. 'Just go, and leave us.'

And so Isabella left, giving me a look I did not wish to understand, a look that spoke of my wife and the hundred other reasons why I should not have come to that room.

And then, we were alone there, alone but for the child who slept on a couch at the bottom of the bed. I did not go to Katharine, but to the couch, and looked down upon the sleeping boy. He was slighter, paler than my Zander, and like all children looked younger than his years in sleep. His hair was neither Katharine's white gold nor my own ebony, but a muted red that in a horse would have been bay. I guessed that behind the slumbering lids the eyes were as pale a blue as his mother's. There was much of her in him, nothing of me. I reached out a hand, wanting to stroke the cheek.

'He is not yours, Alexander.'

I turned my eyes from the boy to his mother. 'Are you sure of it?'

'Certain.' She came and stood beside me. 'I hoped, you know. I even prayed, but I had my answer soon enough: my wedding night brought on my courses, and my husband was well pleased, thinking it something else. I bled again the next month, and then I knew that there could be no hope. Mark was born a full year after I last saw you.' She bit her bottom lip and seemed to be gathering strength in herself. 'When my husband saw me safely delivered of a son, a brother to all his bastards, he went back to the cook, and the scullery maid and his stableman's wife, for he said he did not like the embrace of a skinny whore. And so, at last, God showed to me His mercy.'

A tear had fallen from her bottom lash to her cheek. I lifted my hand to brush it away.

'Katharine, please, I'm so sorry.'

She brushed my hand away. 'I don't want your pity.'

My voice was hoarse. 'It's not pity. I cannot bear it.' I sat down on the bed. 'I cannot bear to think of another man . . .'

'You did not want me.'

'Not want you? Dear God!' The grief was ripping through me. 'That you could believe that I ever did not want you.'

She stepped back from me with a look as if she hardly knew me. 'You cannot have forgotten, can you? That day when I left here and rode for Fordyce, with my mother's cries in my ears and the eyes of half the country on me, to plead with you?'

'I haven't forgotten.' I did not want to hear it, but she would have her saying of it.

'I pled with you, in the dirt, on my knees, to have me. I pledged you everything I had, I turned my back on every other soul that loved me, to throw myself on the ground before you.'

I had my eyes closed now, as if that would stop me hearing. 'I was on the *ground*, Alexander. I was begging you, but you would have none of me.' Her voice became quiet and she said, almost to herself, 'and I have spent every day since being told by my husband what an honour it is for me that he took up a schoolmaster's leavings.'

The memory was seared into my mind, of how I had thrown away that last chance for us. Forbidden to see me, she had yet defied her parents and come after me, offered herself, body and soul, to me, and I, consumed with bitterness at my public shaming, had rejected her. My head was in my hands, and she supported herself against a post of the bed. For a moment, neither of us could speak, and all the sound in the room was the gentle crackling of the fire and the soft breathing of the sleeping child.

'I was taken by a madness,' I said at last, 'and by the time I came out of it, it was too late.'

She returned to her footstool at the fire and began absentmindedly to rake at the coals. The boy on the couch stirred and she laid the poker back down on the hearth. Whatever she had endured, ten years looked scarcely to have altered her. Her hair was loosed and hung down her back as it had done when she was a girl, and she was slim and delicate still as a young girl. The long, pale fingers had not been roughened by work as my wife's had. But for the truths I knew, she might still have been the princess in the tower.

I had no good cause to be there, but I could not make myself leave. 'How long have you known? About Archie?'

She did not turn, but continued to look into the fire. I

thought at first she had not heard me, and so began to repeat my question, but she had heard.

'Years,' she said.

'How many years?'

'Does it matter?'

'It matters to me,' I said, eventually.

'I did not know on that day on the road from Fordyce, or not many days later, when I became that other man's wife. How long after that does not matter.'

She was right. There could be no good purpose in her telling me, and yet I could not leave it. 'How long, Katharine?'

Now, at last, she turned to face me. 'Seven years. I have known seven years.'

'What? When?'

'I told you: seven years.'

'The month!'

She rounded on me now. 'Why, Alexander? What would you have done? Would you have told that servant girl with her bastard child that you would not marry her after all, because you had another man's wife to rescue from an old man's bed?'

That was what I, in my turmoil, wanted to know – would I have done that, had I known Archie wasn't dead? Would I still have married Sarah? But Katharine's anger brought me back to myself. 'Do not speak of Sarah like that.'

'Why not? When she has what should have been mine?' I had never seen her like this, never heard such bitterness in her voice. 'Do you really not remember the last time we were in this room together?'

I looked away. 'Of course I remember.'

'And do you remember what you promised me that night, in that very bed, over and over again?'

I said nothing.

'I remember, Alexander, even if you do not. You said that you would be—'

'Yours, and only yours until the day I died.' I remembered it. I remembered her face as I'd said it.

'And how long,' she asked now, 'before you forgot those words? Did they fly before dawn? Was it my mother's discovery that chased them away?'

'Katharine . . .'

'When, Alexander? Was it at Fordyce, when my father denounced you? Was it when I wept before you? Was it the first time you saw Sarah Forbes? The second?' She was pacing the room, wringing her hands, angry.

'The child, Katharine.'

'*My* child. Do not use my child as an excuse – I will have your answer, you owe me that.'

I stood up. 'Isabella was right. I should not have come here.' I started to walk to the door.

'What?' It was like she had snapped out of that other person, the anger gone from her. 'No, Alexander, please.'

I shook my head. 'There's nothing more that can be said between us, and nothing that can undo what's done. But you should know this, Katharine: I have never forgotten what I said to you that night, and in all the days of my life, in all that is to come to me, be it Heaven or Hell, I will never feel for another woman what I have felt for you.'

And I left, having betrayed my wife with the truth I had been struggling ten years to deny.

22

Between Darkness and Dawn

I should have gone down to the kitchens but, unthinking, I let my feet take me to Archie's old room. There was no sign of him in it, but the bed was made up and a good fire burned in the hearth. I took off my boots, and without lighting any candle, lay down on the heavy damask cover and stared up at the ceiling I had looked upon so often. Painted figures and mottos, images of fabulous trees and grotesque creatures which had terrified me as a child, exhortations to firm morals and true friendship gazed down on me. I closed my eyes and hoped for a clear vision of something, but could only see a muddle of faces and hear the repetition of words I should not have spoken. I began to pray, but the words left my lips with so little power that they had vanished in the cold air before my sentences were fully formed. In truth, I did not know what I prayed for, for no answer from God could put right now what I had put wrong. I tried to call up to my mind some portions of scripture, but they were dead in my mouth before I spoke them.

I thought to lie there until Archie came in, but it was many months since I had been on such a long ride and the generous dispensations from Lord Hay's cellar had rendered me sleepy when I should have been awake all night. I must have slept, I could not tell for how long, but I woke, cold, with the fire burned down low and a crick in my neck. Archie had still not come in. I was loath to raise myself from the bed despite the chill air, but persuaded myself eventually to get up and put more coals on the fire, then get myself, fully dressed, beneath the covers.

This time, I could not sleep. I tried to picture Sarah, at home with our children in that small house. 'What should have been mine,' Katharine had said, but I could never have asked Katharine Hay to live the life Sarah had lived. And yet here, now, I felt I was in my own place, somewhere more home to me than even that manse that waited for us on the Gallowgate. It was as if the ten years had never been, as if Archie had never been away, as if all were yet possible. And she was only a few feet away from me, through walls, up stairs I had walked before. My prayer now was not to God but to myself, the one word uttered in desperation, in warning: 'No.'

It was useless, and so I got up and went to sit by the fire, in my hand a volume of Tacitus that might have been a laundry list for all the sense I could make of it with a mind that was engaged elsewhere.

At last I heard footsteps on the stairs and coming towards the door, but I knew they were not Archie's, limp or no, for he could never walk so light. I stood up, my back to the fire, and waited. But God showed me His answer, for it was not Katharine.

Isabella Irvine almost stepped back in to the darkness when she saw me.

'Archie is not here,' I said. 'I'm sorry he has missed your rendezvous.'

'There is no rendezvous.'

'Oh? Poor Archie; changed days for him that he cannot tempt a woman who gives her attentions as easily to a Scottish lieutenant as she does to a Jesuit priest.'

Another woman might have been offended, disconcerted by such a greeting, but it seemed nothing I said truly touched Isabella Irvine. 'That is cheap, Mr Seaton, and I am not. I understand that you and I will never be friends, but you should know that I have never spoken a word of you that is not true, and all my dislike of you is because of what you did to Katharine.'

I put the book down on the floor and rubbed my hand over my eyes. 'I know that, and I'm sorry. I shouldn't have spoken to you that way, although you know there's cause for what I said. Will you sit? Archie will surely be here before long, and I should go down to the kitchens.'

She came over to take the other seat by the fire, and I saw for the first time how truly tired she was. Her eyes were reddened through lack of sleep, the candlelight capturing the dark circles beneath them.

'Please don't go,' she said. 'You are as well here as not. Better, perhaps. He might listen to you.'

'Archie?'

'Yes.'

I laughed. 'Archie listens to no one.'

'Then he is lost and so is William.'

'Ormiston?'

She nodded.

'Why did you and he pretend not to know each other?'

She took a moment to work out the words. 'Because I knew Lady Rothiemay did not like him, and also I feared that too close an association with me, and therefore her, might cast doubts on his faith and his loyalty.'

'Doubts which would have been proved justified.'

'Perhaps,' she said.

'How long have you known him?' I asked.

She smiled. 'A month, less maybe. I met him in Edinburgh while he was recruiting there. I was staying with my cousin on my way back from visiting Katharine in the borders, and I met him at a dinner in the home of my cousin's friend.'

'And the good lieutenant dazzled you with his fine manners, I suppose?'

She looked at me directly, the old look that did not mind what it said to me. 'There's nothing wrong with good manners, Mr Seaton, and it's a pity more men did not have them.'

I could not help but smile at my adversary. 'And yet Lady Rothiemay is not so particular?'

'I am fonder of her than I was of my own mother, but

her Ladyship has not always been the best judge of persons, or causes.'

'You stand by her though.'

'I would not see her alone.'

I was learning that there was much more to this woman than I had ever allowed there could be. Perhaps I should have realised it before now. 'Why does Lady Katharine not like the lieutenant?'

'She did not trust him from the start. She knew he dissembled about something.'

'And she was right,' I said. 'You know, don't you, that he and Archie plan to take that ship full of recruits and hand them over to fight for Spain?'

She looked down at her hands. 'I did not believe it, until tonight. Even when Christiane came to me. I thought she must have misunderstood – I tried to explain to her that being of the Catholic faith was not the same thing as being a supporter of Spain or the Empire in this war, that many of our religion had died in the cause of Elizabeth Stuart, of the Palatinate . . . but I could see she was not convinced, and I thought Guillaume would be able to explain it to her better.' Tears were splashing now on to the hands she was wringing in her lap. 'You must believe me, I had no idea she had the thing aright and it was I who was wrong. I had no idea that they were indeed planning to take these recruits to fight in the Habsburg cause. If I had known the truth, I would never have told Guillaume, I would never have given his note for her to . . .' The colour drained from her face. 'Oh, God.'

I leant towards her. 'Who, Isabella? Who did you give the note to?'

Her lips scarcely moved. The words were only just audible. 'Matthew,' she said, bleakly. 'I gave it to Matthew Lumsden.'

The shock went through my whole body. Matthew whom I had permitted every indulgence for the sake of my memories. And in his stead I had accused Archie. Archie had told me, had shown me, how the war had changed him; I had never once stopped to consider that it might also have changed Matthew. Matthew, who had never been near the *Garde Eccosaise*, but who these last two weeks had hidden in his uncle's house and, overheard by poor Christiane Rolland, had intrigued with Ormiston in a treason that if known would have cost them both their necks – and the discovery of which had cost Christiane Rolland hers.

I remembered our last embrace and knew Matthew had played me for a fool. 'He has gone with the priest, hasn't he?'

Isabella nodded.

Gone with my blessing and my twelve hours' grace, to be absolved by Guillaume Charpentier who without Matthew would be lost in our country. I thought of the times we had shared, Matthew and I, over the years, all the allowances I had made for the love of him, and I felt the wreckage of my memories tumble through my fingers.

I looked at the woman opposite me. 'And you support their cause? How can you stomach it?'

'No, no,' she said desperately, 'you are wrong.'

I could not believe what she was saying. 'Dear God, Isabella, you truly think me a fool: I saw you at the Mass in Baillie Lumsden's chapel. I *know* you for a Papist.'

'I am faithful to the Church of Rome, but I could never countenance murder in its name. And Christiane . . . But as for wars and causes, I do not care for them one way or another. There is enough death, here, daily, over nothings and wrongs that will never be righted. But if Archie and William are found out to be conspiring against the king, they will hang.'

'And you have come here to ask me to let them slip away, with those boys on board, to their unwilling deaths?'

She smiled at me. 'I have known of you for more years than you have of me, Mr Seaton. Katharine forced me to listen to tales of your many virtues long before she ever even took your eye. I know that nothing I could say could persuade you to bend from your purpose. It was Archie I came to plead with.'

'Would your lieutenant not listen to you? Is he so enamoured of the Habsburg cause?'

'You make light of it, and of him – for his clothing, his manner – but he has suffered much in these wars. As much as Archie.'

'How can you say that? There is but one thin scar on Ormiston's face.'

'And you think all scars can be seen? That all scars are of the body?' Her eyes travelled to my forehead, and then my neck. 'Are those the only wounds you carry? I think there are others. I watched you tonight, in the dining hall, when you saw Katharine. Do not try to tell me you do not still love her.'

'I – that has nothing to do with Lieutenant Ormiston.'

'Does it not? Perhaps you should not condemn what you do not know. William lost a brother at Stralsund seven years ago. They had travelled to the wars together, fought together, he says they should have died together. He carries his loss every day, his scarred heart.'

'I know of his loss, and believe me, I'm sorry for it.'

She shook her head. 'You only think you know. You think he was killed in battle, don't you?'

'I . . .' I shrugged. 'Wasn't he?'

Her voice was low. 'He was hanged by his own comrades, on the orders of his commander.'

'What?'

'He and two Danish soldiers. Hanged, at Stralsund, in punishment and expiation of their crimes.'

I thought of Jean St Clair, Johnny Sinclair, his final challenge to Ormiston: 'Will I tell you of your brother?'

'Was he a deserter?'

She shook her head. 'He had had the boldness, after four days of sleeping in the street of the town they were daily risking their lives to defend, to go with some other young soldiers to the home of the burgermeister and demand that they be given suitable billets. For this "mutiny", the Danish military governor, whose blame the lack of proper quartering was, had them court-martialled. They were found guilty, and Governor Holck decided that three of the men should be hanged as an example to their comrades. They were forced to draw lots, pieces of paper out of a hat. All but three of the papers had a blanket drawn out on them. A grim joke: those with the blankets on their paper would sleep sound and warm that night.'

'And the others?' I asked, my mouth dry.

'Gallows.' Her eyes became hard. 'Lots, Alexander, to see whether they should live or die. William had to watch as his brother pulled out his ticket. He had to watch as his brother, whom he loved, was hanged in the square of that foreign town. All for asking for a roof over his head from the people who had called them there in the first place.'

I felt sickened. 'But could the Scottish commanders do nothing?'

She looked into what remained of the fire. 'The Danish officer had superiority. Had Lord MacKay been there, he would not have allowed it, but he arrived from Scotland too late. Duncan Ormiston was eighteen years old, and William has never got over it.'

'He told you all this?'

'Not him, Archie. He was trying to warn me, I think, that I should not set my hopes on William ever settling and coming home until this war is over, for it is a thing very personal to him, and his wounds will not heal until he has avenged his brother's death.'

I could see a sadness in her that, for all the antagonism

between us, I would not have had her subject to. 'And yet the lieutenant has courted you, and his feelings for you are real – I have seen it myself. On the night of his ship-board dinner, his disappointment at your absence was very genuine.'

'I know it,' she said. 'And I think I might, in time, pull him back from this course of life that is bent only on vengeance and destruction. I think I might persuade him to make his future with me. But that future will never be if he is hanged on the Heading Hill of Aberdeen for treason.'

'No, I see that.' Her honesty had brought me to a decision. 'If they let the recruits go, I will tell no one what I know, Isabella.'

She got up. 'Thank you. And I will keep your secrets also, Mr Seaton.'

After she had gone, I sat a while in the chair and thought about what she had told me. Ormiston's shooting of Jean St Clair at the mention of his brother's name made some sense to me now, but I did not think that would be enough to give him peace. The clock on the mantelpiece sounded three o'clock, and I could not think that Archie and his father could still be up talking in the Great Hall. I wanted to talk to him before taking a few more hours sleep, and so I left his room and went to look for him.

All was silent in the castle, and only a few candles remained lit, to lend their dim light to stairways and corridors. I made my way quietly back to the Great Hall, but the guards were gone from the doors, and on pushing them open I found the place empty and in darkness, save for the last red glow of the coals in the hearth. I was about to go out again when I heard a slight stirring from beneath the south window. I moved closer, and saw that a figure slept there on a couch. It was Katharine, wrapped in a rug. Her breathing was soft and regular, and I knew that if I made my way quietly from the hall and back to Archie's room, she would never know I had been there.

That is what I should have done. Perhaps, in the light of day, with a clear head after a good night's sleep, it is what I would have done. But it wanted four hours or more until the break of day, and I had slept but very little. In sleep, she looked almost like a child again. She was the girl I had known all my life, the girl I had fallen in love with, without any hope of release, at the age of seventeen. I walked to the doors of the Great Hall and closed them. A basket of coals had been set by the fire and I carefully placed a few on the glowing embers, raking them gently to stir them back to life. I went over to Katharine's couch and knelt down by it. I lifted my hand to touch her cheek, stopped myself, withdrew it. I cursed my weakness, told myself to get up, to walk away, but then she moved a little in her sleep and the rug began to slip from her shoulders. I bent again to shift it, and felt the warmth of her breath on my cheek. She was so close, and in that moment, my everything.

'Katharine,' I said. 'Katharine, wake up.'

She moved a little again, opened her eyes, squinting, confused, in the candlelight. 'Alexander?'

'Katharine. Listen to me.'

She sat up now, pulling the rug round her for warmth. 'What's wrong, Alexander?'

'I need you to listen to me. I need you to know that I love you. That every day since that day on the road to Sandend I have regretted walking away from you. I love you and I have never stopped loving you.'

'Nor I you,' she said. She tilted her face towards me and I bent and kissed her lips, gently, softly, before drawing back in some sort of shock at myself.

'And does this end it?' she said.

My breathing came hard and my hands were shaking. 'I cannot, Katharine. Do not ask me to end it again.' I bent my face to hers again, and this time I did not draw away.

23

Tempest

'Wake up, Alexander. For God's sake, wake up.'

It was Isabella Irvine who was shaking me by the shoulders and shouting urgently in my face. I turned slightly but there was no sign of Katharine on the couch behind me. Isabella was thrusting my boots and clothing towards me.

'Katharine?'

'Katharine is not here. She is gone. They are all gone.'

I sat up, mindless of my bare chest and shoulders.

'What? What are you talking about? Who is gone?'

'Lady Rothiemay, Katharine and Archie.'

I shook my head, as if some sense would be let loose in it. 'Her Ladyship has gone to Rothiemay – she does not want you to share in her troubles, Isabella. You are to go to your aunt's at Straloch.'

'But . . .'

'She knew you would be full of "buts". Allow her this autonomy at least, and do some good to yourself. But Katharine?' I looked behind me uselessly again, looked around the large, cold room. 'She will be in her chamber, surely. She will have gone to her son.'

'No,' said Isabella, beseeching, frustrated. 'She's taken him with her. She has gone with Archie.'

'But where to?'

'Oh God, Alexander. How much of a fool *are* you? She rides home to her husband's tower house, and Archie to Aberdeen. He's going for the ship. They're leaving.'

'With the recruits?'

'Yes, with the recruits. Why do you think he has taken a two-hour start on you? They told me at the stables – they were gone by five this morning.'

I could not believe it. She must have left very soon after I had fallen asleep. I pulled off the rug and Isabella hastily turned away as I began to throw on my clothes. 'I may still catch them. The child will surely slow them down, and it may take him some time to get out to the ship from the quayside.'

I noticed that Isabella was weeping, the first time I had ever seen her do so. She must have realised now that Ormiston was lost to her. I reached out a hand and gently lifted her chin. 'I may be in time. I may stop them before they do anything that cannot be undone.'

A husky voice came from the doorway. 'You will not stop them.' It was old Lord Hay, ashen-faced, broken, all the light of last night gone from him. 'Archie told me he would take precautions – a surety for your silence. I am sorry, Alexander. I am truly sorry.'

★

Lord Hay's own old horse was too aged now for the ride that I had to undertake, but he gave me the next best mount in the stables. 'I love my son, but it were better that he had never come here. The boy I bade farewell to fourteen years ago would never have countenanced what Archie plans to do today. Make haste, Alexander – I would not have him bereave other fathers for a lie.'

The stable master had the horse ready for me in minutes, and I rode from Delgatie without once looking back. I rode like the Devil. My oldest friend had played me for a fool and I did not know what he had told me in the last week had been truth and what a lie. I knew there was one truth in all that he had spoken, the one he had told me at the first that I had refused, utterly, to believe: the Archie Hay I had known and loved all my life had died twelve years ago on the field of Stadtlohn, and the one who walked in his place was hardly worthy to bear his name. Of Katharine, I could not bear to think.

The morning was grey and windy, but clear of fog, thank God, and the ground firm underfoot. By Fyvie they were telling me that Katharine Hay and her son had ridden past twenty minutes after a lone horseman who had driven his mount on as if his life depended on it. By Oldmeldrum the gap was nearer an hour, and I came upon her myself outside Newmachar. I reined in my horse, only for a moment.

'You knew.'

It was clear that she had not expected me to follow so soon. 'I did not seek you out, Alexander.'

'He put you up to it.'

'No.' She looked anxiously at her son and back to me, lowering her voice. 'It was you who came to me.'

'But he told you what he planned and you did not warn me.'

Her face paled then became defiant. 'They will send him back, once they have got clear. Why would I have told you? What difference would it make?'

I dug my spurs into Lord Hay's horse, calling over my shoulder to her as I did so. 'All the difference. All the difference in the world, Katharine.'

'But why?' she cried after me. 'The boy is not yours. Everyone knows he is not yours.'

I did not look at her, did not turn to see her face or hear what other words she might have to say. At that moment, I knew I never wanted to set eyes on Katharine Hay again.

I must have covered the miles to Old Aberdeen more quickly than I had ever done before, but it seemed to me that the road would go on for ever, and that I would never come within sight of the Cathedral of St Machar, rising high above the old town. At last though, when it seemed that the poor beast under me could have little left in him, the twin spires of the church came within my view, and I was crossing the Brig o' Balgownie.

The watchmen on the Bishop's gate told me that yes, a horseman calling himself Sergeant Nimmo, from the recruiting ship moored off Torry, had come by nearly two hours ago, riding hard. At each port on my way down to the new town I was told the same thing, and my heart sank further with every telling of it.

Once through the Calsey Port into the New Town, I headed down the Gallowgate, but instead of continuing on to the harbour, I urged my beast towards my own house. There was little traffic on Upperkirkgate, at this time on a winter's day, and I was soon dismounting in Flourmill Lane. I ran to the door of my house, and although I found it locked, I banged hard for a moment all the same, cursing myself for losing time I did not have. The sky was darkening and the shutters above me rattled in the rising wind. I left the exhausted horse where it stood and ran on foot to William's house. I met my friend on the path on the way back to his chambers after taking his dinner at home.

'Alexander . . . you were not expected back yet. Had you any luck finding Seoras?'

'Seoras?' I had forgotten the pretext for my absence from the town and had no idea what he was talking about. I did not slacken my pace but ran past him. 'Where is Sarah? Is she here?'

'Yes, of course, but . . .'

I could not stop to hear him and barged through the door of the kitchen, with William now in my wake.

Sarah was there, with William's wife Elizabeth. They looked up from their work, surprised by my sudden entrance. 'Alexander . . .'

'Where are the children?'

'Deirdre is in the henhouse, looking for eggs. Davy is

sleeping.' Sarah indicated my youngest child curled up in a corner with William's dog. 'Alexander, what is it?'

'And what about the boys?' I said to Elizabeth.

'James is back at the school – they finished their dinner an hour ago . . .' Her voice trailed off and she glanced, a little frightened, at Sarah.

My heart went cold. 'Sarah, where is Zander? Is he at the school?'

Her face paled and she shook her head slowly. 'No. No he is not.'

I gripped her by the shoulders, so hard it must have hurt her. 'Where is he?'

'Arch . . .' She glanced at Elizabeth and back to me. 'Sergeant Nimmo. He sent word just when they came home for their dinner, for Zander to meet him and go out and see the ship. I thought there could be no harm.' Her eyes were filling with panic now. 'Alexander, what is it? Alexander, tell me. Where has he taken him? Where has Archie taken him?'

I ran out of the house with William close behind me. The kitchen door banged shut behind us – the wind was working itself up to a gale. William was shouting at me, but I had not the time to turn round, until I felt his hand heavy on my shoulder, bringing me to a halt.

'I have no time . . .'

'What is going on, Alexander? Why would Sarah let Zander on to the recruiting ship, and what did she mean about Archie?'

'He is back, William.'

'Archie? He cannot be. Alex—'

'He is back. He is Sergeant Nimmo, and he has my son.'

I tore myself from William's grip and began to run once more. There was no time now to go to the Castlegate and summon up the magistrates. Every moment would be a moment lost. I ran down Ragg's Lane to the Broadgate, pushing cursing and bemused townsfolk out of my way. Two of Lord Reay's men, engaged in buying supplies of some sort at the market on the Castlegate, gave off what they were doing and joined, fleet-footed, in the chase.

It cannot have taken much more than five minutes to get from William's backland to Shiprow and the top of Shore Brae, from where I could get a good view of the harbour and the troop ship anchored further out in the river mouth beyond. Relief flooded through me at the sight of it there. The waves were choppy enough off Torry already and the sky was turning from a deep grey to almost black. A storm was coming from the north, as if all Lord Reay's grief and rage had taken hold of the skies and were hurling the worst that they had against the town of Aberdeen. I knew that no ship's captain, supposing a dozen lieutenants should hold their pistols to his head, would take his vessel out into the open sea in such weather.

William came up behind me and saw too what I did. He put an arm on my shoulder and leant on me to get his breath back. 'Thank God. He'll be safe on the ship till the storm passes, and by then we'll have boats on both sides ready to go out and stop them getting out to sea. Get you down to the harbour master, and I'll go and warn the sheriff. I'll have messengers sent round by the Brig O' Dee to Torry that they might prepare themselves. All will be well with the boy, Alexander. And then,' he said, before he turned towards the tolbooth and the Castlegate where town's officers and messengers would be found, 'you will tell me all you have not told me these last few days, and I will decide if I will ever speak to you again.'

'It has been a madness,' I said, never taking my eyes from the ship, 'but it is one that will never be repeated.'

William nodded to me, and I could see the hurt and the uncertainty still in his face, but he asked no more and set off at pace for the Castlegate.

And so I watched the ship where the man I had thought my closest friend had taken my nine-year-old son. For whatever Katharine Hay might say or believe, Zander was my son, and he was more to me than all the Hays and all I had once felt for them ever could be. The knowledge of what I had risked for the sake of an old fantasy, a vision of myself long gone, made me sick now to the stomach, and I bent over, retching. I put out a hand to support myself against a wall and was still standing like that when Sarah and Elizabeth appeared behind me.

Sarah's face was flooded with tears, and Elizabeth's a mixture of anger and confusion.

'What in God's name is going on, Alexander? Where is

Zander, and who is this Sergeant Nimmo you have let have him?'

I opened my mouth to begin answering her, but a huge crash from the quayside took my attention – a stack of pallets had been blown over and had clattered into barrels of salt herring awaiting loading onto a ship bound for the north of Spain. As I looked on in horror, I saw that the ship would never see Biscay, for a terrific gust of wind had sent it veering sideways, and its mainmast had caught the top of that of a ketch berthed alongside it. A splintering sound was followed by a dreadful creak as one mast tipped over into the water and the other came smashing down on the quayside, narrowly missing the dockworkers who had been struggling to salvage more cargo waiting there.

The sea was angry now, even in the river mouth, and the recruiting ship rocked dangerously on the waves. Sarah was gripping my arm. 'He will be terrified, Alexander.'

'I know.' I could hardly speak, hardly breathe. The storm had rampaged furiously from the open sea down into the Dee and was hurling everything in it around with undisguised contempt. Smaller vessels crashed in to the quayside and splintered there like flimsy crates. Before our very eyes, a ship's mate who had jumped from his vessel, a three-masted barque loaded with timber from Norway, was swept into the sea by a wave twenty feet high.

Sarah was howling in the wind, shouting at me. 'Do something, Alexander, for the love of God, bring him back!'

All round us, people were running, up from the shore

or down to it – to rescue their goods, find husbands, sons, seek shelter from the violence of the storm as it flung slates from roofs and rolled stacked timbers like marbles down the brae. Elizabeth had gone running to get William – to what end I suspect even she did not know. The wind had lashed Sarah's hair across her face. I pulled it back so I could look into her eyes, so that she could see into mine. 'I will. I promise you. I will get him back. I will make it up to you – all of it.' She looked at me, uncomprehending, then her gaze went across my shoulder and a scream of horror issued from her throat. I whipped round in time to see Ormiston's ship break its moorings, the anchor cable snap against the irresistible current and the ship begin to toss on the sea like the discarded toy of a wilful child.

The wind had careered around and was taking the boat from the south-east now, driving it away from its Torry mooring towards the inch in the river mouth. It would go aground, surely. But a desperate effort, some madman's gamble, had raised a sail in a doomed attempt to harness the wind. The gust that followed almost lifted the five-hundred-ton vessel from the waves. It rocked violently from side to side, but by some miracle of God or man was carried past the inch and towards our shore. I realised now that Sarah had left me, and was running down the brae, shouting Zander's name. William, with some other men too, appeared at my shoulder. 'It's going to smash against the bulwark. They will all be drowned. We're going to get the ferry boats out.' It was insanity, and we both knew it, but there was no other chance. I was already running down the brae, after my wife. I had looked in her eyes and seen, if I could ever have doubted it, that there was nothing she would not do to save her son.

The upper ferry, at Clayhills, was too far away and not so able for the open sea, but the lower boat, the Torry ferry, was already being taken from its shelter at the top of the slipway to prepare for launch should the ship come to grief. I glanced behind me and saw people beginning to gather on the Castle Hill and St Katharine's Hill, readying themselves to witness what must come.

Four of MacKay's men were already at the boat by the time I got there. Amongst them was Ossian, Lord Reay's own physician. 'You cannot risk yourself,' I said.

'Risk nothing,' shouted the man taking an oar to his left. 'He is the best oarsman in Sutherland, worth four oars to another man's two, and can hook a man from the sea easier than you would lift a herring in a net.'

I nodded my thanks to the physician and grabbing the oar that was thrust my way, set my shoulder to the boat as it was launched down the slipway. William was beside me, Louis Rolland and another three men from the town in front of him. The ferryman, pole at the ready, shouted his instructions into the wind, and it was only as we hauled ourselves over the second huge wave to assault us that I saw Sarah, almost obscured by Ossian's bulk, drenched and clinging to a bench at the back of the boat.

'Get back!' I roared at her, but it was already too late.

We were out from the slipway now and could not turn around had we wanted to.

She shouted back, over the sound of the storm. 'I can swim as well as you can, Alexander, and I am not going ashore again without him.'

We rowed, uselessly at times it seemed, against the waves that were driving the recruitment ship ever faster towards the bulwark of the quayside wall. Every so often, I had to lift a hand from the oar to scoop water out of the boat with the buckets habitually kept there, but I did not see how we could keep afloat ourselves, never mind pull anyone safely from the water and back ashore.

For all we struggled against the tempest, I knew there could be no hope that Ormiston's ship would not come to grief on the bulwark, and it soon became clear that those aboard the vessel knew it too. All struggle and ingenuity with sail would avail the captain nothing: he must know his ship lost. We could see, when the spray did not blind us, men up on deck give up their efforts to bring the vessel under their control and lash themselves instead to masts, to wood, to railing – anything that might save them from being swept overboard into the implacable rage of the sea. More figures began to appear on deck then, not the sailors now but, I realised, the recruits, boys and men, desperate and with no idea how they might save themselves. I scanned their number hopelessly for some sign of Zander, or of Archie or even of Ormiston, but I found none. I managed to look round for a moment at Sarah, but her face was frozen in disbelief as she watched the living horror that was unfolding before us.

After what seemed like hours but can only have been a few minutes, I saw the mariners begin the work of untying the lifeboats from the side of the ship. There was no possibility that the three small boats that hung there could accommodate even a third of the desperate men aboard. And then, at last, I saw them, getting into the smallest of the boats as it was lowered, swinging dreadfully in the wind and clattering into the side of the ship. Sarah saw it too, and tried to stand up, almost toppling herself into the raging water as she did so.

'Get down,' I shouted to her, 'Tie yourself to that loop under the gunwale . . .'

Given some hope now, she did as I bid her. We had got as close to the ship as it was safe for us to be, and the ferryman barked out instructions in an effort to keep us from getting any nearer. I could hardly hear him, for all my attention was taken up in struggling with my oar as I watched the small lifeboat crash at last from the side of the ship into the sea. The ferryman had seen it now too, and had us work our craft around and in pursuit of the lifeboat. In it were four men – Archie and Ormiston, I was certain of it, and another two officers that I had often seen about the lieutenant. Unlike the other men, Archie rowed with one arm only – the other was clasped tightly around the figure of a small and frightened boy. Sarah was screaming his name, but Zander could not hear her over the sound of the storm and the men everywhere, shouting instructions at each other or crying out to God for their lives. For my part, it was Archie's name I called, called it until I was hoarse. And at last, just once, he seemed to hear me, looked around, looked right in my face. There was no dissembling there, no lie. It was the face of my friend and in it was his final sorry, his final goodbye.

I could not believe that they would make for the open sea, rather than for the other side of the river mouth. It was not impossible that they might win to Torry, and from there flee south. And that was what I prayed for, for they would not take Zander with them then. Their small boat made less progress against the wind and currents than our own, and time and again was pushed back towards the ship, but at last they seemed to master it, and drive it forward. I could not believe what I saw then, for the shouting between Archie and the lieutenant took on a different tone. I could not see Archie's face, but in Ormiston's there was a flash of anger, a refusal of something, and then from beneath the cloak which he had wrapped round Zander, Archie drew a pistol which he aimed at Ormiston's head. The lieutenant, after the briefest, stunned, hesitation, gave up his argument and bent again to the oars. And now it was that I saw where Archie was taking them, neither out to sea nor to the distant southern shore.

'The inch!' I shouted. 'They're making for the inch.'

The ferryman had taken in in a moment what was happening, and so drove us forward to the island of land that was covered by sea in the spring tides, but exposed at this time of year. I could not see how they could land on it and ever expect to get away again. Archie was giving himself up, giving all of them up, for the sake of my son. Such was our progress, with the extra men at the oars, that we looked set to gain the inch before them. Shouts of alarm from the quayside and the Castle Hill were rising over the sounds of the storm, but all my strength now was set on getting to the inch and returning Zander safe to his mother's arms. My life from now on would take its beginnings from that point. But then even I heard it, what all had dreaded: the tremendous crash as the recruiting ship was thrust at last against the harbour bulwark. Screams of men could be heard above the smashing and splintering of wood and then the supernatural creak as the ship seemed to hesitate a moment before slowly keeling over on to its side and disappearing beneath the foam.

There had been so little time. Those who had not jumped from the ship went down with it, those who had could not be seen in the boiling mash of wave, wood and debris. Then, miraculously, one or two figures began to emerge from the waves to grab on to a passing barrel, a broken plank. Frantic activity on the quayside saw ropes, rafts, buoys thrown out to the water, the urgent need to save even one human life overtaking all who watched.

One human life. The life of the child on the boat fighting its way towards the inch. We should have been there before it, ready to haul them in, take Zander, leave the rest to the

Devil they had given themselves to if need be, but the sudden submerging of the ship sent a huge wave slapping against, then careering back from, the quayside wall. By the time we realised what was happening, it was on us. The wall of water hit us full to port, tossing us in the air with the contempt of an angry bull. I tried desperately to hold on, but found myself flung into the freezing waters as the vessel came back down, its hull upwards, and was carried away from me on the choppy sea. I looked round frantically for Sarah but there was no sign of her. I tried to call out her name, but another wave overwhelmed me and I found myself desperately struggling to keep from being forced under by it.

The same thing happened three times before I could get my head up far enough to open my eyes and see what was happening around me. All was chaos – lost oars being borne away in the wake of the overturned ferryboat, the heads of men I knew emerging, then disappearing again beneath the stinging spray. The shock of the cold had almost deprived me of the power to breathe, but I had mastered it again now and tried to summon the strength to keep myself afloat. Another wave was survived and another, and between them I called out my wife's name, but of her I could see nothing. A few feet to the left of me, I briefly saw the head of William Cargill. I shouted to him and somehow managed to force my way towards him. Another wave threatened to pull us both down, but then a voice called my name and I saw through the crashing sea that the recruiting ship's lifeboat was still afloat. The voice calling to me was Archie's, and at the risk of capsizing his own craft he had reached an oar out towards where William and I were trying to keep each other from being swept away.

'Take it!' he shouted.

'Zander!'

'The oar, damn you, Alexander! Take the oar.'

And so I did, and with William Cargill clinging fast to my waist, Archie, Ormiston and their two officers towed us to the safety of the inch. The moment we felt sand beneath our feet, William let go the oar and began to drag himself up on to the shore, but I held fast.

'Give me Zander,' I shouted.

The boat had come as close as possible to the inch without running aground and Ormiston was already pulling away.

'Give me my son,' I yelled, plunging back into the water after them.

It was only the briefest hesitation that I saw in Archie. He turned to Zander and I heard him shout, 'Can you swim, boy?'

I saw Zander nod and then heard Archie say, 'Then swim, swim for your life,' before heaving him up and throwing him as far towards me into the water as he could.

My world disappeared for a moment as I saw him go under, but then his head came up three feet from me and I had him under the arms before he could go down again. William was back in the water too, and between us we dragged him, terrified and choking, to the shore.

I held Zander briefly to me, then yelled at William to take him higher up, to a place of greater safety.

'But what about you?' William shouted.

'I must find Sarah.'

'No, Alexander, you cannot.'

I was already back in the water, desperately scanning the tossing black sea, and still William was shouting. He was behind me. He had left Zander alone and he was holding me, pulling me back.

I summoned what strength I had left to try to throw him off.

'Let me go, William!'

But he held fast and he would not.

'You cannot go back, Alexander. You cannot.'

His grip gave way and he was weeping, and at last I saw what he had already seen.

'No!' I yelled. A howl greater than that of the wind, more destructive than the storm. He let me go at last and I stumbled into the water, to take from the arms of Ossian, Lord Reay's physician, the limp and lifeless body of my wife.

24

'Madness, and Blindness, and Astonishment of Heart'

All around me was darkness, and the voices that spoke were in whispers. I could not lift my head because of the stone on my chest. There was a presence in the room that comforted me somehow. I reached my hand towards it and felt the firm, familiar grasp.

'Jaffray.' Who else?

'Aye, my boy, it is me.'

'You cannot mend me this time.'

His voice was heavy and something broken. 'I know it.'

Two nights and a day had passed, while I lay insensible and body after body was washed up on the shore of Aberdeen. Young boys who had hoped for adventure, older men seeking a purpose, running from failure, from mistakes. They would never see the German wars – the wrath of Scotland's jealous God had kept them all. No sign had been found of Archie or the lieutenant, and in spite of all, I hoped that they might have got away safe, and somehow be a means towards ending the war that had so ruined them.

The children had been taken to George Jamesone's house,

and William and Elizabeth had sat day and night with me. They had brought Zander to see me, for he would not believe that I was not dead too. In my dreams of Hell I had called out for him, again and again, and they had had to take him away again.

Before darkness set in on the second night, Jaffray had arrived. Sixty years old, he had ridden from Banff without stopping save to change his horse. The man who had delivered me, who had tended my every childhood illness, who had saved me from the very edge of oblivion and talked me out of folly more than once, had come to try to heal what the ministrations of Dr Dun, Ossian, and all the other learned physicians in the town could not put right.

'She is gone, James,' I said, when I finally managed to open my eyes.

'She is lying in St Mary's Chapel. We will take you to her later.'

I tried to get up, but couldn't. 'There is a stone on me, Doctor. A great weight on my chest.'

He held his fist to his own chest. 'It will get lighter. As time goes on, it will get a little lighter.'

At some point they opened the shutters to let the light in, a low, bright, winter light. Fresh, and clean, and empty. They brought me decoctions to swallow, covered my head with poultices, rubbed ointments on my chest. The stone did not go away; as the light grew, it became all the heavier.

In the early afternoon they took me downstairs and tried to feed me some broth. I could not swallow it.

'You must take it, Alexander,' Elizabeth said.

'I cannot.'

'You must. For the children. You are all they have now.'

So I swallowed it and the day went on. There were visitors, so many at the door, taking time for Sarah's sake in a town already leaden with mourning. Some were allowed in, for a few minutes. Dr Forbes, my mentor from the King's College, who understood grief and suffering and prayed with me; John Innes, my dear kind friend from King's; Peter Williamson, who had come from the Marischal College to comfort me, and who sat before me and wept. And George Jamesone came, with flowers from his garden, a posy of yellow flowers.

'They are like Sarah,' I said. 'They were her favourites, and I cannot even remember their name.'

'Primroses,' he said. 'Autumn primroses. In the midst of decay they come to life and brighten the desolate garden.'

'You told me I must learn to know the difference between what is dormant and what is dead. Do you remember?'

He nodded. 'I remember.'

'Well I have learned it now. Too late.'

After George, they persuaded me to sleep a while. There was more food in front of me when I woke, darkness encroaching on the town. I managed to eat a little. And William, whose eyes were dark hollows and who looked as if he had not slept in two days, and probably had not, at last went home.

It was an hour or so later – I may have been dozing, for

Jaffray seemed to ply me with nameless concoctions every time I opened my eyes — that there was a quiet tap at the door. The doctor gave a sigh of mild impatience and muttered that it was over late for visitors, but he went to the door all the same. The voice I heard was something familiar to me, although I could not quite place it. After admonishing him to stay no more than ten minutes, Jaffray stepped aside to allow the caller in. If I had taken a moment to recognise his voice it would have taken me longer to know the man himself. Fresh-shaven and clear-eyed, his hair cut and his sober suit of dark clothing clean and pressed, John Leslie stepped into the kitchen something like the image of the new young minister I remembered from eight years ago, and some distance from the husk of a man William and I had found at St Fittick's Kirk only a week earlier. He walked straighter, and he had begun to lose the look of a man haunted.

I got up to take his offered hand. 'The world has turned with us, John,' I said.

'And I grieve with you for it.'

I felt unsteady and sat down again. 'But I am glad to see you well, again.'

He nodded. 'I feel God's forgiveness, Alexander. What our brethren on the presbytery will say, I have yet to learn. But I have my Father's forgiveness and that is enough.'

He sat, awkward a moment, and I began to think he had not just come here to console with me. 'What is it, John?' I asked eventually.

He glanced at Jaffray, who was busy at the table, writing, but who I knew would be following every word.

'You may speak freely in front of the doctor,' I said.

'Indeed,' agreed Jaffray, 'for I am as deaf as a post.'

John Leslie smiled hesitantly, and then began. 'I would not have disturbed you, Alexander. I would never have intruded. I wanted to see William Cargill, but he has been called up to the tolbooth – there is much legal business to be set in hand with the shipwreck.'

'The boy should be at home in his bed,' muttered Jaffray.

'That was his wife's opinion too. I went up to the tolbooth, but I couldn't get near the advocates, there is such a press of people. And so, I've come to you.'

I had hardly the energy to listen to him, but I waited while he sought the best means of continuing. 'You see, I think you believed me, did you not? You and William Cargill – you knew it wasn't drink or witchcraft, what I saw.'

'Yes, we believed you. Although you said many foolish things before your session.'

'I know it, I know. That's why I cannot go to any of them.'

I leaned forward a little, as if being closer I might understand him better.

'You see, a body was washed up at Nigg Bay.'

I sank back in my chair. 'John, there are bodies lying all along the coast, they tell me. There will be bodies washed up for days to come.'

'No, but you see, there should not be any at Nigg. The tides – the tides were wrong. There is only one. This one, and . . .'

Just then, there was a rap on the door, louder and more confident than that of the minister had been.

'For the love of God!' fumed Jaffray, stomping over to the door and pulling it back with little ceremony. Words were spoken and Jaffray's frustration grew. 'I cannot understand you, man.' He opened the door wider. 'Alexander, do you know this boy? I cannot make out a word he says.' Standing there, in the darkened yard, was Hugh Gunn, one of MacKay's men at his side.

'Uisdean,' I said, speaking to him in Gaelic now out of habit. He was even more the Highland soldier now than he had been when I had last seen him at his vigil in St Ninian's Chapel four days ago. The colour had returned to his cheeks and the terrible gauntness was gone. He stood more upright and no longer looked like one in need of the support of others. All trace of the young scholar was gone, and it was difficult now to picture him in the cap and gown of our college. He was again the favoured foster son of a Highland chief, and he was ready for war.

'You are leaving us,' I said.

'Aye,' he replied. 'Tomorrow I march south with the others for Dundee. We take ship for Sir John Hepburn's regiment in France.'

'May God go with you.'

I was turning to introduce him to Jaffray and John Leslie,

and to explain the matter of his speech, when I saw the minister of St Fittick's rise from his seat with an expression of dawning horror on his face. Hugh saw it too and took an involuntary step backwards.

'I . . . I am sorry,' he said, 'I didn't mean to disturb you.'

'It's all right,' I said, still looking at John Leslie. 'It is no disturbance.'

But John Leslie's balance had gone and he was stumbling back down into his chair. 'The tongues,' he said, staring at Hugh. 'You speak in the tongues.'

And then I knew. I heard again what he had said to us in that day of ranting and delusion in the kirkyard by Nigg Bay.

'Dear God,' I said, also staring at Hugh. 'It was not a woman at all.'

25

The Spoil of War

Jaffray had ranted and raved, but when he saw that I would not settle otherwise, he had at last consented to it, on condition that a horse would be made ready to take me from the ferry landing to the kirk. The crossing was made at first light, Lord Reay's men rowing in silence across water as still as a mirror, that only three days ago had been a monster of unanswerable fury.

The church was cold and still, the sea outside coming so quietly to shore, as if it feared to wake him. But there would be no waking Seoras MacKay now. They had laid him on a trestle before the altar, and covered him with the best mortcloth they could find. The session clerk nodded respectfully to his minister as John Leslie led us slowly up the aisle of St Fittick's Kirk. The clerk made as if to lift the cloth, but with the merest nod Ossian stayed him and, gently, did the job himself. There was no drawing in of breath, no shock: we had all known it would be him – there was no need to turn to Lord Reay and look for confirmation that it was his son who lay there dead before us.

Ossian folded back the rest of the cloth and placed it aside, to reveal to us what the sea had washed clean.

The low sun of the winter morning found its way through the thick glass of the kirk window and lighted on the dead boy's face. Lord Reay put out his hand and stroked his son's cheek. 'You are cold, my boy, so cold.' I saw the desolation in the old soldier's eye and I looked away. I could not face the grief of another. A groan, more than a groan, a great sob wrenched from somewhere deep within him came from Hugh Gunn's throat and he went down on his knees beside the body of his friend. 'Seoras, I never meant to leave you.'

MacKay took hold of the boy's shoulder and held it firm. 'You never would have done. Do not blame yourself for what you could not help.' His face was grim. 'And I was the fool that trailed round that ship after Ormiston, Seoras hidden there all that time.'

I knew he must be wrong, but it was Ossian who said it. 'I don't think he was ever on that boat, your Lordship.'

'What do you mean?'

Ossian murmured something to Jaffray and Jaffray nodded. 'I have seen many men drowned and Seoras did not drown.'

I looked down at the face of the boy I had last seen two weeks since; there could be no doubt of it, and Lord Reay must have known it too, for the body was not bloated, neither eyes nor flesh harvested by creatures of the sea.

They had found him on rocks at the foot of the Girdle

Ness, at the extreme north edge of the bay, where the waves rarely reached.

Jaffray spoke gently. 'I think he must have lain dead there some time, his body preserved in the frost, before the storm of Friday night brought the sea crashing up onto the land. He had been beaten, and soaked and frozen, but he did not drown.'

To my surprise, John Leslie leaned forward and carefully pulled the hair back from Seoras' neck. 'No, he did not drown,' he said, his voice dull. 'He was hanged.' And indeed the marks of the rope by which Seoras MacKay had been hanged from the tree in St Fittick's kirkyard were still there plain for us all to see. Leslie let the hair fall back and touched for a moment the sodden and torn plaid that covered Seoras' thighs. He almost whispered to himself, 'And I thought it was a woman in her skirts.' He turned suddenly to Hugh, who was staring now at him, his face contorted in an effort to understand. 'Don't you remember, boy? You must remember.'

Hugh started to mouth something, but stopped, the words still eluding him.

Leslie was determined, the old, half-mad look back in his eye. 'You *must* remember. Come, see.' He put a hand round Hugh's arm and pulled him up from the floor. Ossian made to stop him, but Lord Reay held him back. 'Wait,' he said, as Leslie took the stumbling Hugh down the aisle with him towards the church door. Jaffray and I went after them, and as soon as I saw what Leslie was pointing at, I began to understand.

'The branks, boy, the branks,' he kept repeating, desperate almost. 'Don't you remember?'

And as Hugh looked at the iron head-piece, chained to the wall by the kirk door, I saw that he too began to understand, or at least to remember. He reached out a hand towards the contraption, but pulled the hand back without touching, as if fearful of being burned or bitten. Then he brought his hand up to his own face, worked his own jaw until he got to the mouth. He swallowed uncomfortably, tested his tongue with his teeth, as if there were no place for it to settle in his mouth.

The branks. They had chained Hugh to the wall, fitted the iron guard over his head and clamped his tongue with the iron gag used to punish scolds and gossips, to punish those who talked when they should not. To silence him. When John Leslie, in his drink, had heard Seoras MacKay call out in terror in his native tongue as Ormiston's men set a noose around his neck, when he had heard Seoras' strangled cries as the horse to whom the rope, slung round the branch of the tree, was tied, had been whipped and goaded into a panicked canter, Hugh Gunn had been forced to watch all in helpless silence.

Hugh looked from the branks, to John Leslie, to the tree. He spoke in Scots for the first time in two weeks. 'It was you. You came from the church.'

John Leslie nodded. 'May God forgive me, for I did not know what it was I saw.'

'What happened when the minister came from the church?' I asked Hugh.

He narrowed his eyes, remembering more now. 'He was screaming. I'd seen him and they had not, but then they heard him. He turned and ran back into the church, and before they went in after him, they began to shout amongst themselves about what they should do. Eventually, they cut Seoras down and they carried his body somewhere over there.' He pointed in the direction of Jessie Goudie's grave. 'Some ran into the church after the minister but they couldn't find him. They argued a minute about what to do with me: some were for killing me too, but another said no, that it had only been Seoras the lieutenant had wanted dead – I was to be freed. And then they broke open that thing,' he indicated the branks, 'and dragged me away with them. I remember nothing else until I was found back in the town.'

Lord Reay was at an utter loss. 'But Seoras? Why in God's name did Ormiston want Seoras dead?'

The words of Isabella Irvine came back to me. 'His wounds will not heal until he has avenged his brother's death.' I spoke to Lord Reay, but could not lift my eyes to look at him. 'Because he was your son, and I had told him that very night that he was your son.'

If I could have returned to that night two weeks ago, and been put in the branks myself, lost the use of my tongue before I could have told the lieutenant that, I would have thanked God for it. I remembered now, and I could have ripped my own tongue out. I remembered how ready Ormiston had been to have the signature of Hugh Gunn, until I had warned the boy what Seoras's father in Strathnaver might do.

'What difference should it make, that Seoras was my son?'

I was not yet fit to stand so long, and Jaffray insisted we go back inside the church, that I might sit. Our breath in the cold air was in front of our faces. It seemed a long way, a different world, from the heat and the filth and the smell of that inn, and yet the simple trestle table in this ancient church was where Seoras MacKay's evening there had led him to.

And Lady Rothiemay, who must have heard the true tale of Ormiston's brother's death from Isabella, had suspected it, because she, unlike the rest of us, could truly understand it. 'Vengeance,' I said. 'Since Stralsund, the lieutenant had lived and fought for only one thing: vengeance.'

MacKay did not understand. 'But I was not at Stralsund. I should have been, but I was held up with the raising of new recruits in Scotland. Good God, we spoke about it at dinner, aboard Ormiston's ship, that things would have been managed differently had I been there. I told him so myself.'

'And that is it, exactly. If you had been at Stralsund, his brother would not have died.'

Still MacKay did not follow. 'Men die in battle. Ormiston is a soldier. He knows that.'

'He also knows that not all men are condemned to be

hanged by their own commander for asking for a roof over their heads.'

And then at last I saw the truth begin to dawn on Lord Reay. 'Oh, dear God . . . do not tell me Ormiston's brother was one of those . . .'

I nodded my head in affirmation. 'Duncan Ormiston was eighteen years old when he was hanged with two of his comrades, on the instructions of the Dane who held command in your stead, for asking a bed for the night from the burgermeister of the city of Stralsund. The lieutenant has never forgiven it, and has dedicated his life since to avenging his brother's death.' I looked to the boy lying cold and motionless in front of us. 'Seoras is his vengeance.'

We travelled with Seoras's body slowly, back across the mouth of the Dee. Hugh Gunn, Scots speech only slowly returning to him, sat on the bench beside me, shivering in the shock of what we had all just seen, and what he now remembered. 'Once we were out of the inn, there was nothing for it but Seoras would cut through the garden. I should have stopped him, but I was fed up and wanted nothing but my bed, so I gave in and went in after him. We weren't in there two minutes when we were set upon. I knew straight away they were soldiers – the way they were armed, the way they spoke. They asked which one of us was Lord Reay's son. I warned Seoras to shut up, but of course he was having none of it and would stand on his dignity: he was and what of it? That was when they went to lay hands on him. They told me to keep out of it and I would not be harmed but well . . .' He did not need to explain. His whole life he had watched out for Seoras – he would not walk away then, in the face of a pack of armed men in the night. 'We gave a good reckoning for a while, but they were too much for us in the end. I remember nothing else until I saw them hauling him up on that tree, and I could not move or speak, because of the thing they had on my head. I don't even know how we got there.'

'Nor I,' said Lord Reay, 'for there is a watch at the harbour, with a special regard to that ship, every night.'

'I don't think they were taken there by boat,' I said, 'but overland, round by the Brig o'Dee and Tullos.'

'But how?' said Hugh. 'We were neither of us fit to walk.'

'You didn't have to walk. I think they had you strung over the back of a horse.' The horse that had been stolen from Davy Durno at Woolmanhill that night, and found wandering and terrified out of its wits, with a cut rope round its neck, near Nigg Bay the next day. 'The watch at the port of the Brig o' Dee would have thought nothing of a packman leaving that town with an old horse heavy-burdened. Especially if he was given a handful of coins for his trouble. They must have rowed you back to the town much later, further up the river out of sight of the watch and brought you in somewhere near the Putachie Burn, where you were found.'

'But why did they not just kill me too?'

I could not say it in front of Lord Reay, but then he said it himself, Seoras' father said it. 'Because Ormiston has a kind of honour, boy. My son for his brother. An eye for an eye. No less, no more.'

There had been too much death in our town of late, and few watched as the bier bearing the body of the missing student Seoras MacKay was brought ashore and carried up to the college, to lie in the Grayfriars' kirk, where Dr Dun, Peter Williamson and all the other black-robed teachers of the college, along with Seoras' classmates, waited to receive it. Jaffray, who had railed against me taking part in this expedition in the first place, urged me to go home and rest, but I wished to join my colleagues in the church for a while. 'And perhaps,' I said, 'I will be able to reflect on God's purposes with us.'

After prayers had been said, and psalms sung, the college began to troop out of the kirk, their respects paid to the memory of a boy who would soon be forgotten by them. And yet still I could not make myself come away. There was something not right, something that kept me there, watching, with Ossian and Lord MacKay and Hugh, and John Leslie too. It was Ossian who finally voiced the question that must have been on all our minds.

'What I do not understand,' he said, ' is why, if Ormiston's men cut Seoras down and set him behind that grave, his body was found so far away, amongst the rocks on the shore.'

I raised my head slowly to look at John Leslie. The minister, understanding it all at last, mouthed a silent 'Yes'.

Seoras had not been dead when they had cut him from that tree, nor dead when they dumped him down the steps of an old well behind the grave. I saw again, I almost smelled, the animal lair William Cargill and I had come upon that day down the steps of the Lady Well. Whenever he had come too, he must have drawn sustenance from the water. Five days, until, half-starved and delirious, he had managed to haul himself back up those steps in search of help, nourishment, the way home. It was Seoras' misfortune that in his ragged and desperate, scarcely human state, he had come upon a man whose mind was only beginning to piece itself together after the madness and ravages of drink. John Leslie had seen not a fellow creature in need of help, but a diabolic vision from the mouth of Hell. He had run back into his church, his mind again deranged, and Seoras MacKay, helpless, had staggered to the shore, to die alone with seaweed in his mouth.

Epilogue

Aberdeen, November 1635

William sat in his old steward's chair by the fire, his head in his hands. Elizabeth stood at the kitchen table, her palms pressed hard on its smooth pine surface, as if she might go through it otherwise.

'Alexander, I am begging you, *begging you*, not to do this thing.'

'Elizabeth,' I began.

'What? Will I go down on my hands and knees? Is that what you want?'

'No, Elizabeth, please, I . . .'

But she would not listen. She rounded on her husband. 'Have you nothing to say? Nothing?'

He lifted his head wearily. 'I have tried. 'Till I'm hoarse. And Jaffray too. He will have none of it. There's nothing more we can do.'

Her face was a picture of disbelief. 'What? Is there no recourse to law?'

In spite of himself, William laughed. 'Law? What do you think he is doing, woman? There is no law of this land that says a man, a teacher, a minister of the kirk, for God's sake, cannot take his own children and live where he wishes, if that town will have him.'

'Town? Is it even a town? What manner of town is it? He will take Sarah's children to live amongst savages? And Zander, that I have known since the moment he first drew breath . . .'

She crumpled at last to the bench, the tears that she had been trying to deny beginning to roll down her cheeks.

I went over to her and put my arm around her. 'I cannot stay here. I cannot live in this place without her, see her shadow everywhere and not be able to touch it. I will go mad, Elizabeth, if I stay here.'

Mad with grief, mad with anger, mad with guilt. I could not tell her that last, that it was that above all that drove me from this place.

She looked up at me, the anger gone, her eyes red and swimming. 'But the children . . .'

'I cannot leave them. They are my all, and I must take them with me.'

William cleared his throat and raised a subject I had known must come since I had told him two days ago of my decision to accept Lord Reay's offer.

For a man much used to making speeches, arguing his case, the words would hardly come out. 'But surely,' he said eventually, 'would you not think of leaving Zander here with us?'

'William . . .'

He rushed on, refusing to let me have my objection. 'He is James's brother in all but blood and name, and this has been near as much his home as your own.' His eyes beseeched me. 'We would love him as much as any parents could, and your names would be on our tongues every day. He would still be your son . . .'

'I know that, my dear, good friend. But Zander was the beat of her heart, and since I first felt him move in her belly I have been bound to him as to my own blood. More.' I took a breath. 'I will not part from him.'

Ever since Sarah's death, words spoken to me in St Ninian's Chapel in the Gaelic tongue by Hugh Gunn had repeated themselves over and over in my head. *Cha buin me an seo*. 'I don't belong here.' This was no longer my place, and I could not see that it ever would be again. 'I have not the fight for it,' I said. I could not live like Katharine Forbes, Lady Rothiemay, a prisoner now in Edinburgh, or William Ormiston, forever a fugitive from his own land, living only on their dreams of a just vengeance. I could not walk the streets of this town, where I had had to denounce Matthew Lumsden, one of my oldest friends, for the murder of a young girl, listening for the echo of my wife's dead footsteps. I was thirty-five years old. I might die in forty years' time, or be called to my maker before dawn, but whatever life I had left to me could not be lived in the mausoleum to my past life that this town had become.

I would go north, far to the north of this web of intrigues and old resentments. I would go further even than the mountains and straths where Guilluame Charpentier still roamed free, as was thought, spreading the doctrine of his priesthood, and winning succour from strangers for a son in Spain I would not see.

'Run from us, run from your memories if you must, Alexander,' Jaffray had said to me before he had heaved himself on his horse and set off wearily back to the town of Banff, 'but you cannot run from He who knows all.'

'I will take that burden with me,' I had said, 'and seek a better way that I might carry it.'

And so it was that little more than a week after Lord MacKay, Hugh Gunn with him, had begun their voyage home, taking Seoras to his rest, that I, with my three children, and all our worldly goods, boarded the ship that would take us to those far northlands of our country and the old collegiate church of Tain, on the edge of the Dornoch Firth, where we might begin again.

Endnote

The foregoing story is a work of fiction, but many of the events, locations and characters are based on fact. As indicated at the beginning, Scots fought in the Thirty Years' War in their tens of thousands. One of the largest recruitment drives was that undertaken in 1626, and built upon in subsequent years, by Sir Donald MacKay of Strathnaver, Lord Reay (d.1649). The first consignment of troops in his 'Scots Brigade' sailed from Cromarty on the Black Isle for Gluckstadt on the Elbe in 1626. They served first in the armies of Christian IV of Denmark, and from 1629 in the armies of Gustav Adolph of Sweden (d.1632) and his daughter, Queen Christina. Lord Reay, on a recruitment drive for troops to serve Sweden under the Marquis of Hamilton in 1631, was imprisoned in the Tower of London for having passed on to the king rumours of treasonable activity on Hamilton's part. The details of this episode have never been fully explained, but the experience ruined MacKay financially, and he never returned to the wars. Following heavy defeats for the Swedish forces in 1634 and the Peace of Prague in 1635, the remnants of MacKay's Scots brigade joined Sir John Hepburn's 'Hebron' regiment in French service, again against the Habsburgs. While MacKay is a real historical character, his 'son' Seoras and the events in Aberdeen involving him in this book, are entirely a work of fiction.

While Lieutenant Ormiston is a fictional character, he was of a type who could make his fortune in foreign service, and recruiting parties were a familiar feature of Scottish life. Parents of students in Edinburgh complained to the Privy Council about their sons being enticed away from college to the wars, and in 1637, during a storm in the night, four ships anchored on the Dee off Aberdeen broke their moorings and many new recruits bound for Sweden were drowned, their bodies subsequently being washed up along the coast.

Some of the episodes recalled by Archie Hay in this book are based on the experiences of Colonel Robert Monro of Obsdale in Easter Ross in his 1637 work, *Monro, his Expedition with the Worthy Scots Regiment called Mac-Keys*. Specifically, the fall of Bredenberg Castle in 1627, the details of the siege of Stralsund in 1628, and the 'making merry' together of Scots officers from opposing armies at Freistadt in 1632, are all adapted from Monro's account. The story of Ormiston's brother is based on Monro's account of an incident at Stralsund. Three soldiers, forced to sleep out on the streets of the besieged town for four nights, were condemned by the Danish commander Holck, on the drawing of lots, to hang as a punishment for some of their company having gone to the home of the town's mayor and demanded quarters from him. Of the three, one was a Dane and two were Scots. On the intercession of their officers, Holck conceded that only one should hang. As Monro notes with a certain grim satisfaction, it was the Dane who eventually drew the paper marked with a gallows.

There is a vast literature on the Thirty Years' War. The best starting point for anyone interested in Scottish involvement in these wars is Steve Murdoch's *Scotland and the Thirty Years' War* (2001). The involvement of Scots in the military, diplomatic and religious interests of the Habsburgs is dealt with in David Worthington's *Scots in Habsburg Service, 1618-1648* (2004).

Aside from those related to the war, other characters and events in the story are also based in fact. Katharine Forbes, Lady Rothiemay (c.1583–1653), was a kinswoman of Sir Donald MacKay of Strathnaver, and did found a girls' school in Aberdeen (although not until 1642). Lady Rothiemay was a truly remarkable and formidable woman. Married to William Gordon of Rothiemay, with whose family her own was periodically at feud, she was widowed in 1630 when her husband, a former Justice of the Peace, was killed by one of his family's Crichton enemies while resisting arrest by the Sheriff of Banff. A few months later, her eldest son, along with a son of the Marquis of Huntly and other young kinsmen, was killed in a fire in a tower house belonging to the Crichtons while their hosts looked on. Her castle and lands were plundered by relatives and her younger son removed from her care, but Lady Rothiemay was unbowed and relentless in her quest for vengeance. In 1635, the Privy Council of Scotland declared that 'in all the disorders and troubles quhilks hes of lait fallin out in the north pairtes of this kingdome Katherine Forbes, Ladie Rothiemay, hes had a speciall hand', and ordered her arrest. Only in February of 1637 did the king ordain she should be released from her imprisonment in Edinburgh. Despite her vicissitudes, she remained staunchly royalist throughout the Covenanting Wars, and her daughter married a son of Robert Gordon of Straloch. After the wars she appears to have lived relatively quietly, strongly suspected of being Catholic and staunchly ignoring the censures of the local presbytery.

Lady Rothiemay's host in my story, Baillie Lumsden, is also a real historical character. I have avoided using his Christian name – Matthew – to avoid confusion with his fictional nephew whom I thoughtlessly named Matthew Lumsden in the first book in this series. The real Matthew Lumsden (d.1644) was a much more respectable character, a successful burgess, baillie of Aberdeen and parliamentary representative of the burgh. Despite suspicions of crypto-Catholicism, Lumsden actually supported the Covenanting cause in the town. His home on the Guest Row, now known as 'Provost Skene's House' after a subsequent owner, was one of the few sixteenth-century buildings in New Aberdeen to escape the civic vandalism of the 1960s. It is now in the care of Aberdeen Art Galleries and Museums, and it, and its mysteriously painted Long Gallery, are open to the public, free of charge.

While photographs of his home on the Schoolhill survive, George Jamesone's house and garden are both now sadly gone, but it is a matter of record that in 1635 the painter was granted the use of a former public playfield (open-air theatre and recreation ground), fallen into misuse and neglect, for his own use as a private garden during his lifetime, on condition that he repaired walls and drainage and made the place secure. The events I have portrayed as taking place in these gardens are entirely fictional.

The name of the French master of Aberdeen in 1635 was not Louis but Alexander Rolland. I changed his Christian name to avoid confusion with my main character. The character of Christiane Rolland is purely fictional. Patrick Dun (1584–1652) was principal of Marischal College from 1621–1649.

The Hays of Delgatie as I have portrayed them in this series are not the historical Hays of Delgatie, but very largely a figment of my imagination. The more fascinating, and true history of the Hays can be read in their castle, restored by the late Captain John Hay of Delgatie, open to the public and run as a charitable trust.

Translations – I would like to thank my niece, Ellen MacPhee, for the Gaelic translations in this book.

Shona MacLean,
February 2012.